Harmony

in

Flesh

and

Black

Harmony
in
Flesh
and
Black

Nicholas
Kilmer

Henry Holt and Company
New York

Henry Holt and Company, Inc.
Publishers since 1866
115 West 18th Street
New York, New York 10011

Henry Holt® is a registered
trademark of Henry Holt and Company, Inc.

Library of Congress Cataloging-in-Publication Data
Kilmer, Nicholas.
Harmony in flesh and black/Nicholas Kilmer.—1st ed.
p.   cm.
1. Art—Collectors and collecting—Massachusetts—Boston—Fiction.
2. Veterans—Massachusetts—Boston—Fiction.
3. Boston (Mass.)—Fiction.   I. Title.
PS3561.I39H37   1995   94-21896
813'.54—dc20   CIP
ISBN 0-8050-3663-6

Henry Holt books are available for special
promotions and premiums. For details contact:
Director, Special Markets.

First Edition—1995

Designed by Paula R. Szafranski

Printed in the United States of America
All first editions are printed on acid-free paper. ∞

1   3   5   7   9   10   8   6   4   2

Blame Bill Guthrie

Harmony

in

Flesh

and

Black

1

The dark-haired woman reaches into the pond to gather lilies, frozen amid slashes of yellow blooming flags, the captured light struggling against cloth, the paint laid out to stretch and dry. That's violence, Fred was thinking. There's nothing innocent about it, nothing safe anywhere in the operation. He looked across the downstairs room he worked in, at the painting he had pulled out of the bins to think about while keeping his mind clear.

Art is violent from its inception. As long as he had worked for the man, Fred had not been able to make Clayton Reed recognize this. It's dangerous, Fred was thinking, not to understand the nature of your opponent, to believe it simply lazy, languid, beautiful, and harmless. It's dangerous to collect and keep it around you, not knowing what it is.

Fred loved pictures, but not the same way Clayton Reed did. Clay acquired them with the enthusiasm of those who collect stamps or rocks or money, as objects they believe have risen above the dirty tug of living in the world. For Fred a picture was alive, an animal, something whose design and color had a feral purpose.

This made Fred the hunter, the guide, the beater, out front—with Clayton often hanging back, rising above, perched on his elephant, his rifle ready. These days they were both edgy on account of the big project they were working on, which something, they both knew, could blow out of the water any minute.

Fred had his jacket on and his keys out, ready to leave Boston to the likes of Clayton Reed and head for Arlington and Molly, when the outside door opened onto old brick and springtime and Clayton stepped from the street into Fred's office, downstairs from what Clay called his flat, on Mountjoy Street on Beacon Hill. Clay owned the whole building, a brick row house, like himself tall and thin, but with an apron of ivy out front. Fred's office and Clayton's storage were downstairs, on the ground floor.

Fred Taylor's space was filled with books, in cases and stacked, and with the storage racks for Clayton's paintings. Fred had a desk, file cabinets, and an uncomfortable chair to keep him awake when he wasn't out and moving. Clay's flat occupied the three next floors.

"The perfect peace of a pure summer day," Clay said, looking at Curran's painting of women in summer dresses harvesting floating lilies from a green rowboat, which Fred had propped against the racks. "It's better than Terra's," Clay said. "Curran is thinking in mine. In Terra's he's half asleep."

Clay sat on the edge of Fred's desk, tense and trying to look unflappable. He was excited about something.

"I'm glad I'm in time to catch you, Fred," Clay said. "Would you pick something up for me on your way?"

Clayton Reed didn't pick things up. He might suffer a crease. He rubbed his hands, his lanky limbs almost dancing. Though he didn't smoke, he looked like someone who might pull out a cigarette holder at any moment, with his lean features, prominent nose, and shock of hair prematurely white, which he maintained à la Stokowski. If you needed a character to look like the aesthete for a movie you were doing about the 1920s, Fred's friend Molly said once, you could ask Clay.

The back of Fred's neck itched. Obviously Clayton had got up to something on his own, which could mean trouble. The genes for practicality had not been braided into Clayton Reed's makeup, and he sometimes exacerbated that deficiency by acting with unmerited self-confidence. Clay had enough money so he could make mistakes, but Fred couldn't stand to let them happen.

Clay, coming in, was happy with himself, wanting Fred to see he'd landed something good alone and unaided. If Clayton, on a secret project, had done anything to cost them the Heade, Fred wouldn't forgive him. That was the big thing now.

"Here's the address, Fred," Clayton said, handing over one of his neat three-by-five index cards. "Third floor rear. I've just come from there. I'm going to get clean. Don't mention my name, which he does not know. Arthurian is the flag of convenience I elected to sail under in this transaction." Clay made that expression of his that fell halfway between distaste and exultation.

Fred couldn't make Clay understand the principle of the ambush: Don't move. Do not call attention to yourself. Unless you've tried it, you can't know the experience of lying all night and half a day in swamp, waiting for something to come down the trail looking to kill you. You don't want them to see the water shake.

"You're playing games, Clay," Fred muttered. "You're going to cute yourself right out of the Heade. Keep your eye on the main objective. Otherwise you start losing your people."

"One of the good things about the art business, Fred," Clay said, "—and perhaps an improvement over a previous occupa-

3

tion of your own—is that in the art business losing is not normally measured in terms of numbers killed."

"As we're going for the Heade I don't want anything else to muddy the water," Fred said. "If you're using a fake name, you're out of your depth."

"I was inspired by the moment. I must wash. I acquired a painting," Clay said. "A virgin. The conditions in which I found it are obscene. I want it out of there, Fred. You'll understand why I was moved to represent myself under a nom de plume. I don't want anything I own to remain in that hideous place. I'd appreciate your retrieving the picture on your way home."

Clay looked down at his gray suit and rubbed invisible stains from it with the inside of his wrist. He shuddered. "You are receiving it from a Mr. Henry Smykal. The name's on the card. He expects you. It is not out of your way, Fred. Bring the painting Monday. Find a safe place to keep it till then, if you would."

"I wish you'd stay clear of the secret-agent stuff," Fred said.

But there was no correcting the fact that a natural hazard of Fred's current occupation was the quirk of absolute bullheaded secretiveness in his employer. Clay's business was Clay's business, unless he made it yours.

"It's a slight detour—nothing that will intrude on our main objective, as you call it," Clay said. "But it's been an unsettling experience for me," he added, mounting the spiral staircase toward his living quarters. "I am shaken."

"You want to tell me what the picture is?" Fred suggested. "So I know what I'm picking up?"

"Smykal's a fool," Clay said. "But he knows what I bought. I'm upset, Fred. I must wash. I can't stand my picture to be in his hands any longer. You'll understand. Please don't dillydally. Think of it as a rescue mission."

Traffic this Friday evening, after Fred left the office, was slow and heavy out of Boston. He drove with the window open, enjoying the cool air. The Charles River was steel gray, like the sky. The city and land showed hints of spring—strokes of green, splurges of incipient blossom. Fred took the River Street bridge and cut through Central Square. The middle of Cambridge was not on his way home unless he made this detour.

Driving, Fred told himself that Clay was right to keep him guessing. Clay knew he was a sucker for a new painting. There was nothing like it. A good painting is filled with unique intricacy, and intimate with ferocious purpose. It is something and it does something. It is like reading a hermit's mind—a hermit with no inhibitions. A good painting is as much a revelation as looking out over acres of Iowa farmland, knowing that's good dirt eight feet down. That's wheat in there. That's corn. And it'll hold a tractor up. Not like the fucking swamps with thin green hairs of rice growing, flat gleam of floodwater, and under it the spikes, the mines, the bones—well, but that had been filled with beauty, too, hadn't it? Fred had left beauty behind him there as well as terror.

It was amazing that Clay did not know, surrounded by his collection, how a painting could have both love and terror in it. It is a sunny pasture where children run and scream in birthday games. A painting is what you see when looking from shadowed jungle into a burned-out village in the rain.

At this point, however, Fred's instinct told him that almost anything could spoil their concentration on the prime objective, the object of their present stalk, "The Heade"—the big project he and Clayton had been working on for months. It was scheduled to come to a climax in a week, at Doolan's, the Boston area's main auction house for works of art.

Whatever Fred was making this detour into Cambridge for, it couldn't be worth what they would stand to lose if Clay, with his alias, had made the water shake.

The current status of the project was delicate and tense. Some months before, Fred had been doing research in the

5

microfilm collection at the Archives of American Art, whose Boston office was a few blocks from Clayton's place on Beacon Hill. He was skimming the journals of Fanny Apthorp, a nineteenth-century resident of Newburyport who had gathered paintings as well as Dutch china and chinoiserie.

Fred was grinding the crank of the microfilm reading machine, seasick, finding Fanny Apthorp drowsy work. She had much to say about the weather, none of it original. Her most interesting observations—spiteful commentaries on servants, friends, and relatives—did not advance the cause.

Fred's object was to see if Fanny had ever mentioned Fitz Hugh Lane, who had painted a ship portrait that Clayton owned of the *Hester A. Prynne*, a schooner that went down in a Pacific storm along with Captain Apthorp and a cargo of dried sea slugs loaded in Fiji and bound for China.

Lane wasn't showing up on the gray film, but suddenly Fred's hunting instincts sparked. "July seven," Fanny Apthorp wrote. "Damp. Martin H. for tea. Entranced by an effect on the marshes back of the house. Said he must paint it. Could I give him a surface? I let him have the lovers dear Dickie gave me, which I never could abide. It served admirably. The little man has given me the picture for a keepsake. Put it to dry in the attic. Catherine in a pet. May clear."

Martin H., Fred reckoned, had to be Heade.

Martin Johnson Heade had painted haystacks, magnolias, and sunsets in the late 1800s. He had painted the best sunsets in St. Augustine, Florida, the best magnolias in the world, and the best haystacks in Newburyport, Massachusetts.

When Fred mentioned the reference, Clayton's eyes lit up and he began pacing the area they kept clear, in Fred's office, for that very purpose.

"The lovers," Clay said. "By golly, it makes sense. North Shore, China Trade; and Fanny Apthorp wouldn't know a Sèvres vase from a chamber pot. Here they are, the devils. Hidden in a haystack all this time. It has to be my Vermeer."

Occasionally, as now, the combined forces of luck and intelligence produced strokes of brilliance between them. It allowed them to withstand each other.

Fanny's "lovers," Clay reasoned, had to be the lost painting by Vermeer that, unbeknownst to Fred, he had been trying to get a line on for years. Clay knew the picture had once been in Boston because it had been exhibited at the Mechanics Hall in the mid-1800s. He had a description of the painting and a rough drawing of it but no name for its owner.

"It makes perfect sense," Clay said. "Why not let Heade paint over it if she didn't like it? A Vermeer, in those days, was worthless costume drama. It was ballast, like Ming china—and perfect from Heade's point of view, too, since it would present a smooth surface to work on. You wouldn't waste a week sanding down the lumps, the way you'd have to if you wanted to paint over a van Gogh."

Fred said, "Coincidence or not, this seems a stretch. There was plenty of junk around to be painted over. Why aren't we talking about some bad Victorian—okay, *pre*-Victorian—parlor schmaltz with doves in it? Unless there's something you're not telling me, this Vermeer seems a blue-sky proposition to me, Clay."

"I do have other evidence," Clay said. He pursed his lips. "I may or may not share it with you. It will depend upon your need to know. It is of a delicate nature. Suffice it to say I have been hunting many trails that lead in this direction."

What Clay did not say was that he simply hated to share a research triumph. It was bad enough he had to share coincidence when it was visited upon them by an act of God or serendipity.

In a coincidence by no means rare with such operations—once the broth is stirred, everything from the depths starts visiting the surface—Doolan's, a few weeks later, announced that it would sell at auction, for the (partial) benefit of a couple of hospitals, the residue of the old Apthorp estate. Sure enough, there in the flier, illustrated alongside the blue and white Ming spittoons, was a small, square, indifferent Heade representing haystacks at teatime.

The value of the Heade was well under a hundred thousand dollars. But the Vermeer that might lurk beneath it could be worth eight figures, the high eight figures—miles beyond Clayton's range. Because it was to be offered at auction, the whole thing was a gamble whose outcome couldn't be predicted. Clay couldn't buy the object except by participating in the auction, where wrestling bulls might drive the price up too far for a Heade and hence beyond what Clayton wanted to hazard; because of course there might be no Vermeer under the Heade after all. There was no way to find out beforehand without ruining their chances, for if they even hinted at the wrong question, the tide of excited speculation that would result would blow the painting out of the sale and beyond reach forever.

Clay had to become the owner of the Heade, as cheaply as possible, and then find out.

A project of this magnitude was worth keeping your concentration fixed on. It made Fred uneasy to have Clayton Reed wandering alone into Cambridge, with his codes and secret spy rings, playing games, with so much at stake and so near the goal.

"He's going to screw it up," Fred said through his teeth, turning his car from Massachusetts Avenue onto Turbridge Street.

2

Turbridge Street was not far from Harvard Square, on the seedy side where rent control kept dwelling units in a condition illustrating the triumph of disappointed private enterprise over democracy. It was a one-way street lined with apartment buildings: three-deckers, some of them wood, some brick. Henry Smykal's was wood, painted yellow long ago.

This being the end of April, vegetable blooms were venturing out even on this side of the square. Magnolias made fat canopies over the daffodils. It was a chilly evening. The chill would make the blossoms hold.

Fred's car fitted into a space reserved for residents of Cambridge. Next to mailboxes with permanently sprung doors, the buzzer alongside "Smykal, Henry" got him a damp snarl and a click that opened the door, and he found his way up two flights of dark stairs to a landing where he was met by the odor of drowned cigar.

Fred told himself he should have noticed the ragged shadows

circling the building. It smelled as if Smykal were keeping large birds in his place, buzzards that hunched back out of sight when he opened his door at the sound of Fred's step on the landing.

Smykal was about Fred's height but noticeably older, maybe the same weight. Fred's weight was muscle, though, in back and shoulders. Smykal was thin on top and heavy below, a pear past its time and settling. His color was waxy gray, with a blue cast reflected from the suit he had been wearing day and night for years, since he found it at the back door of a funeral home. Smykal had taken special pains to trim the native hair on the face of a head and body that otherwise were redolent of intimate personal neglect. He sported a nasty ingrown off-white goatee and a sparse mustache curled upward at the ends and stained with tobacco. He put a twisted mini black cigar into the middle of it, stared at Fred, and puffed.

"I've come for the painting," Fred said.

Smykal flinched. People often flinched the first time they saw Fred. He was large and had a face that made people remember things they wanted to forget.

"Arthurian sent me."

"Come in," Smykal said, leading the way and sniffing—an act Fred would avoid if he could, here. Inside, the smell was worse: Smykal's cigars and what Fred thought was male cat, though he didn't see the cat.

The room Smykal led Fred into, a sitting room, was overstuffed with Victoriana: furniture and bookcases filled with magazines, books, and whatnot. Heaps of magazines and papers lay on the floor. Dust was thick over all. But what you noticed were the walls, which blared with black-and-white photographs lovingly framed. Apparently abstract, they quickly resolved into close-ups of selected portions of human female bodies. They looked hung out to dry: something to feed the buzzards. The pubic region especially seemed to command Smykal's attention.

The feel and odor of the air alone were enough to account for Clayton's unease; it was not, overall, his kind of place.

"Please," Smykal said, motioning toward a chair. "Make yourself at home. I was about to indulge my taste for sherry. You will join me?"

Fred shook his head, standing. He didn't want to put anything in his mouth here. "I can't stay. I'd like to take the painting. I'm pressed for time."

"I assured Mr. Arthurian that with an eye such as his, he must have talent." He sniffed. It wasn't just the dust, and fungus, and filth, and cigar smoke. It was nose candy working, eating into the septum. "I thought he might return himself. I teach, as well as being a creative person in my own right," Smykal said, gesturing toward the walls.

The photos of female crotches were Smykal's own work, then, which he justified as art. A pile of it cackled on the floor when Fred brushed against it by accident, as if the man's buzzards were sharing a private joke in poor taste.

The cigar trembled in Smykal's face.

"I offered him my standard arrangement," Smykal said. "I provide camera, studio time, instruction, models, everything. Everything is in-house, even my darkroom. Total, total privacy. Such a good eye he has, I was impressed. Amid all this he spotted the painting right away. I sensed his native talent. Like many, he is shy of his indwelling potential. I'll telephone him. I mislaid his number."

Fred thought to himself, Clay, I forgive you, if the painting's any good. The man, the place, the circumstances were so appalling, anyone could allow intrigue to replace good sense.

"He'll be in touch himself," Fred said. "When he is ready."

Smykal sniffed. The blue suit was almost shiny enough to reflect his pitted face.

Fred said, "I'm in a hurry."

"Another time, then," Smykal said. "For the sherry. Sit down. Make yourself comfortable. I'm wrapping it in the studio. Would you care to visit my studio? What may I call you, sir?" He opened a closed door off the sitting room, revealing a brief and surprising expanse of white clarity. Fred shook his head.

"I'll wait," Fred said.

Smykal closed himself into his studio.

You don't need to wrap a painting to carry it, but Smykal wouldn't understand that. Half the people who own them don't know about paintings. They have them, but it's like a gorilla trying to take care of a baby bird. Let the man wrap his painting if he wanted. If the person's leaning in your direction anyway, don't push.

Fred sat in an armchair of abused velour. He listened to Smykal grunting and wrapping in the next room. He'd be later getting to Molly's, that was all.

On the gray wall opposite Fred's chair, over a bookcase crammed with magazines and bottles, was a horizontal stain of absence on faded wallpaper that, between the gynecological displays, was dotted with crimson roses anyone's granny would enjoy. The disembodied crotches looked wise and solemn, omniscient, indifferent, like visitors from outer space. The velour on his armchair began crawling.

If that stain was the size of what Clay had bought, the canvas Smykal was wrapping was roughly two by three feet. Fred saw a handy toolbox in red plastic on the floor under the vacancy, and picture hooks lying ready, and several of Smykal's framed prints waiting to take advantage of the opening.

"I trust I made the right decision," Smykal called from the studio. "We artists are not suited to the marketplace. I could undoubtedly have sold it for much more if I had held out. I am an innocent. We artists are. God must care for us."

Fred stared at his knees. They were nicer than anything else here: hard knobs in brown twill.

Smykal stuck his head out of the studio, his mouth, between the hair, making words and pursing between them for emphasis. "Arthurian's interest in fine art could be so easily extended to the film."

Smykal said "the film" the same way some people say "the dance."

Fred stood up, looking at his Timex.

The package, when Smykal brought it out of the uneasy starkness of the back room, was, as Fred had guessed, about two by three feet, bulky at the edges on account of a paste frame that Fred could feel crumbling behind the newspaper. It was bound like a mummy in string and tape. Fred took hold as soon as he could because Smykal was having trouble with it, sliding it along the floor and making tracks in the greasy dust of a rug whose generic color Fred classified as Barbizon, or Blakelock.

Smykal wagged the stump of his cigar. "Mr. Arthurian must call me. I found him an interesting person. So cultured. But a man of the world. He was taken with my work. We are soul mates. I felt him responding."

He leered. The cigar had gone out between his lips. Anything would. "Perhaps you yourself, even," he suggested. "You won't believe how easy and releasing it is. I am arranged for total privacy. . . ."

"For God's sake, give it up," Fred said. "Arthurian knows how to reach you if he wants to make prints from your hired vaginas."

Smykal gulped and blushed, spluttered, looked from side to side, said, "For goodness' sake, we don't think of it like that . . . ," and saw it was no use, Fred was moving. Smykal waved forlornly. "Farewell, then, little one," he said. Fred gave a start. Then he understood that Smykal was talking to the package, the painting, telling it good-bye.

As Smykal opened the door to the landing, he looked as if

he might try to snatch the package back. "Why should we even think of money? God must take care of us," he said. "Like the birds of the field, or the lilies of, the lilies of—" He hesitated.

Fred said, "I'm off."

He reached the sidewalk and breathed in again, but the smell followed. It was embedded in the package Smykal had made, a crumpled oblong wrapped in newspaper that smelled of bacon grease and old dust, crotches and cigars.

Fred, being a lapsed bachelor right now, was living outside Boston, in Arlington, with his friend Molly Riley and two children. The house and children were Molly's. Fred was liking being there, despite it being a big change for him, and they seemed to be glad to have him around. Molly, alert and protective of her children and her turf, was fond of him, and Fred thought he was getting somewhere with the eight-year-old girl, Terry. Terry would take his hand, even, sometimes, without thinking. The boy, Sam, twelve, was harder.

Fred hadn't thought to be attached to anyone, to anything, again. If he looked at it, he couldn't understand it, nor could he trace how this had come about from the first pleasure he had found, more than a year ago, joking with the nice woman behind the reference desk at the Cambridge Public Library before going back to sleep on the mat in Charlestown in the bare room in the house he had bought—was still buying—with the other guys.

Fred saw the guys still. He occasionally played chess there in the evening. And he paid his share of the mortgage though he wasn't using his room now and he knew someone else was sleeping there regularly. All he needed the place for now, it seemed, was for somewhere to keep a locked box of things he didn't want at Molly's. And it made a home base to return to if it came to that in the future. He paid more than his share since he was making money and others could not. The guys could use the help, and there wasn't much coming from anywhere else, whether out of the Veterans Administration or from the alumni association of unmentionable clandestine activities.

He was late, and he was getting to like the feeling of being expected by a woman and two children. Fred had his own primary objective, and he wasn't going to let Clay's business crowd in front of anything as fragile as what he was working on with Molly and the kids. It was going to be tough to find a safe corner at Molly's to keep a picture, what with bicycles, hair dryers, fishing rods, the portable TV, and the rest of it; and he didn't really like mixing Clay's business into that part of his life. But Clayton would have to take his chances.

Fred turned right at the river and then headed west on Route 2.

He'd thought for a long time that he was destined always to be a loner. He was changing. His prime objective now was not being a loner. He didn't have men to watch out for anymore; so let it be Molly and the kids, if they would let him.

He was eager to see Molly. Molly was a very pretty woman. Fred told her that she could be found in paintings from the school of Fontainebleau, and that she'd been prefigured by Italians working for French royal taste—though she was pinker, on the whole.

Molly said that didn't keep her, with her short brown curls— and especially when she was wearing an apron—from looking like the kid sister of the rosy farmer's wife in children's books from the thirties. If she didn't watch it, she'd get fat.

Traffic was slow and heavy. The green and pink dresses of spring were ruffled across the trees along his route, making him think with extra pleasure of Molly waiting for him.

The thought of Clayton Reed in Smykal's place was amazing, interesting, and most spectacularly odd. What devious twist of fate or research had brought him there? Whatever it was, Clayton had been seduced by the package now in the trunk of Fred's car. Out in the air, with the close reek of Smykal's nest of slime receding, Fred's appetite began emerging cautiously. He was anxious to see the painting Clay had discovered in such unpleasant surroundings.

But he had to wait. Molly had invited her sister, Ophelia, for dinner. It was to be the year's first backyard barbecue. Molly flagged him down as he turned into the driveway, and leaned into his car window to give him a kiss and warn him about what was impending in the backyard. Molly had been doing something with mint, whose crushed scent greeted Fred with her kiss.

She was dressed in a blue skirt and cardigan over a white blouse, and her skin was flushed with a Dutch color, rose: the color Renoir had goosed up and made monumental in those late nudes. Her green eyes glowed.

"I'm just home from the library," Molly said. "Ophelia's back there trying to start the picnic by herself. Don't let her come into the kitchen and help, you ugly man."

Fred left Clayton's package in the car, locked the car in the garage, and headed around the house to Molly's backyard, where the pear tree bloomed against the house and sea gulls, if there was no competition, liked to walk on the twenty-foot square of lawn next to the brick patio where Ophelia was prepared to receive.

"You make the yard smaller," Ophelia said when Fred appeared. "We have been waiting for you. Where have you been, great hunter?"

"Bagging a virgin for Clayton Reed," Fred said. "Where's the kids?"

Ophelia shrugged, gesturing toward the house. She was in an aluminum chair, wrapped in a pink blanket, drinking gin and tonic from a tall glass. Although the sun was almost gone, she had on the shades with the bangled corners. She was the perfect blond; she looked as if someone had reached into a Hockney painting and jerked her across the country from Hollywood. She should have palm trees around her, and a blue pool—not Molly's tiny yard, which, as Ophelia said, Fred made smaller.

Fred was never sure if Ophelia was making a play for him, or was making fun of Molly, or liked him, or was pretending to like him on Molly's account, or was pretending not to like him (also on Molly's account), or had something else on her mind. Molly's sister, Ophelia Finger, had kept her first husband's last name, a rock of stability as she blew from the reef of one marriage to the storm of another. Married three times, Ophelia was presently between marriages. She operated in the world at a success level that amounted to a public nuisance. Ophelia's achievement was based on the fashion of faith healing that disregarded any system requiring either more or fewer than twelve steps. She sold people what already belonged to them: the American Dream.

Her best-selling book, a pamphlet fleshed out with photographs, *Learning to Love the Body You Have*, was the offshoot of seminars she had done around the country before large audiences. The lectures led to a TV series that featured Molly's sister, pert and chic and fit in a skintight golden gown, addressing the limps, bulges, and goiters of a crowd of persons of both sexes whom she had persuaded into white leotards. They were learning to love, under Ophelia's direction and amid the lights and cameras, those parts of themselves and each other that all the other seminars told them they should get rid of with exercise or starvation.

"Tell me about the virgin," Ophelia said, licking her lips and making her eyes bright for the cameras.

Fred looked around for Sam to see if he wanted to light the fire, but Sam was lying low, as was Terry. They had a program on TV that they depended on about this time, Fred knew, and it drew them as urgently as their aunt repelled them.

"I can't imagine Clayton Reed's knowing what to do with a virgin even if she were completely bagged," Ophelia said.

Molly had insisted on introducing Ophelia to Clay, and it hadn't worked.

" 'Virgin' is a figure of speech," Fred said, brushing dust and charred grease from the grill. "It's what the collector likes best, a painting no one's seen for ages. Everyone wants to find and buy a picture before it's offered. Anything that's marked For Sale, already tagged with chalk marks and price stickers, has lost value in the collector's eye.

"Eliminate the middleman. The collector, if he relies on his own judgment, as Clayton does, loves to take the first fruit straight from the tree. You should have seen the tree this one was on."

"The virgin you're talking about is a painting," Ophelia said. "I get it. How interesting." She yawned and took a long, elaborate sip from her glass. It seemed to Fred that Molly was taking her time cutting carrot and celery sticks inside.

"I want your opinion, Fred," Ophelia said as he began shaking charcoal into the grill.

Ophelia never wanted anyone's opinion. It was her opening gambit when she had something to brag about, such as a fabulous honor or a large sum of money.

"It's a new series I'm starting, and I can see the book in it already, though I don't want to crowd my first best-seller prematurely. What do you think of the title *Finding the Me in You?*"

Fred could see it right away. Another winner, guaranteed. Molly's sister, the genius.

3

After dinner Ophelia drove off toward her home in Lincoln in her Mercedes of subdued maroon. Molly and Fred washed up together in the kitchen while Sam and Terry, enjoying freedom from homework at the kitchen table since it was Friday, rode their bikes outside in the dusk with friends from down the street.

They played Hearts together after that, before Molly sent the kids up to pretend to sleep, as they were permitted to do on Friday and Saturday nights—they could read or do whatever they wanted that sounded like sleeping.

In the evenings the phone at Molly's house rang frequently and was for Molly or Sam or Terry. Fred was surprised when Sam called down at around 10:45.

"It's for you, Fred. It's Clayton. Mr. Reed."

Fred picked up the kitchen extension.

"That creature cheated me," Clay said.

"What are you talking about?"

"You have my painting?" Clay asked.

"I guess so," Fred told him. "I haven't had a chance to look at it. He wrapped it. Smykal did."

He had clean forgotten the painting. That was one of the problems with Clay's having kept him out of the foreplay. It hadn't been Fred's business, and he'd not had the scent of the quarry in his nostrils. But he recalled the stink of Smykal's place now and regretted it.

Clay said, "Unwrap it. I'll call back."

Fred said, "What do you mean, he cheated you?"

"Hurry, Fred, would you?" Clay urged. "Open the package, look at the painting, see if a letter's in with it, and call me back? I'm at the Ritz bar."

"What's that about?" Molly asked, drying her hands after washing the coffee cups she and Fred had been using.

"What that's about," Fred told her, "is what made me late getting back: a picture I picked up for Clayton that sounds like a problem. A virgin, Clay said. Let's take a look. Rare bird where it came from, if true."

They went through the kitchen into the garage, turning lights on. Fred got the package out of the car, and they worked on Smykal's string and tape together, using scissors, going carefully.

"It stinks," Molly said, her nose wrinkling at the greasy package.

"Clay sounds like he's been conned," Fred said. "Which is what happens to your average paranoid. He digs his own trap, playing games, then tiptoes in."

"If that's a virgin," Molly said, standing back and looking at the picture with her hands on her hips, "if that's a virgin, no wonder it's an endangered breed."

Fred was behind the unwrapped picture, looking without success for anything resembling a letter, perhaps taped to the back of the frame, or caught in the wrapping. But Molly's tone brought him around front.

"Don't she make the Rokeby Venus look like a sick pig?" Molly went on. Molly was a direct, no-nonsense critic.

It was a nude of shocking elegance: a female figure reclining, her back toward you, her rotundities fully realized. The figure made a startling white diagonal of flesh against black draperies with red and gold accents in luscious, loaded slabs of paint: a fan, the carved gilt edge of the couch she lay on. A mirror in front of the figure, reflecting head and breasts, held painted gestures that suggested the striding legs—in black trousers—of a man entering the room in back of the viewer. The subject looked at you out of the mirror, surprised but pleased that you had found her. It did a strange thing with space, even in Molly's garage, because the viewer was eliminated. Molly and Fred couldn't exist if the reflected entrant was as present as they felt him to be. The garage, the bicycles, the lawnmower, Fred's car couldn't exist since they didn't reflect.

It was a painting of alarming intimacy.

"You're right," Fred said. "The Velázquez is an image that stays with you. Whoever did this young lady spent an awed afternoon beforehand standing with his mouth open at Rokeby Hall—unless Agnew's had it already, off H. E. Morritt. The National Gallery in London didn't get it until after nineteen hundred, and this painting's earlier."

It shook Fred to think of the pathetic vulgarity of the den from which he'd brought so arrogant a testament of beauty.

"Who's the lucky painter?" Molly asked.

Fred looked. It was usually the first thing he would do, but the command of the painting had distracted him. They both looked. They shone a flashlight at likely spots for a signature, examined the back for clues, and tried spitting on a thumb and rubbing to remove the layer of surface dust to expose—no signature.

Fred could guess a lot from a quick look at the painting's

style and at its architecture front and back. He told Molly what he was thinking while he looked.

"It's by an American, done in the eighteen eighties. He's done the Grand Tour. Given the modeling and the celebration of grays, the painter was trained in Munich and then finished in Paris, where the painting was made, since you see here, on the back of the canvas, the inked stamp of Durand's shop on the Avenue des Ternes. The artist was a craftsman who knew his business, someone of Sargent's polish."

"That's no Sargent," Molly said. "Sargent was too mean with the female nude, never wanted to get any on him. He couldn't show affection or appreciation for the subject. No, Sargent was a drapery man, in my opinion." Molly stood back, studying the image of the naked woman, pinching her face between the fingers of her right hand.

"Jeezus Heezus," Sam said from the doorway to the kitchen, still in his jeans and the green Champion sweatshirt Fred had given him. "Is this what you two do after you think we're in bed?"

Fred turned.

"It's Mr. Reed again. Didn't you hear it ring?"

Fred went back to the kitchen for the phone. Sam stayed with his mother, looking at Clayton's picture.

"No letter," Fred told Clayton. "Nothing."

"The painting's all right? A female nude, late nineteenth century . . . ?"

"The painting's a stunner," Fred said. "Whose is it?"

"Mine," Clayton said briefly, gloating. He knew Fred meant, who painted it? "So there's a limit to Smykal's perfidy. I can scarcely bring myself to speak his name. You're certain there's no letter? Wrapped with the painting?"

"Molly and I both looked," Fred said.

"The villain's playing games," Clay said. "He gave me an envelope that he said contained the letter—which I saw myself,

22

I'm no fool, Fred—and switched it. It's a blank paper. He's holding out. What does that creature want?"

Fred answered, "He mentioned your appreciation for his photographs, which he calls art. You show promise, he told me. He is eager to receive you into his bosom as an apprentice."

"I improvised and gave the man the impression that I abetted his perversions," Clayton said. "The situation was complex. I would like this never to be mentioned between us again, Fred. I still reek of it."

Clay, trying to be cute, had been screwed. It was going to cost Fred time and Clayton money.

"Let me think," Clay said.

Fred could hear fragments of refined hilarity from the Ritz bar.

"I should have checked the letter before I left the man's apartment, Fred. Go back and get it," Clay said.

"It's late, Mr. Arthurian," Fred said.

Fred did not say—since there was no point, it was indeed late, and he had designs on Molly—The mistake was yours, Clay, keeping me in the dark, putting down money, and walking away without what you paid for.

"Stop the check," he suggested, knowing there had been no check. "I'll go first thing in the morning."

"He's got his money in a form I can't retract," Clay said. "Being so shaken by the circumstances, I made an error. I should have thought of this possibility and told you to take precautions. There's no alternative. I regret that you must go back, Fred."

"Call him."

"He does not answer the phone," Clay said. "I have tried every half hour since I opened the envelope and saw how I was taken in."

Sam went through the kitchen, heading upstairs, calling back to his mother, "I'll take a shower tomorrow, promise. It's only been a week."

"Who's the painter?" Fred asked again.

"Without that letter, no one," Clay said. He was upset with himself, so he would take it out on Fred by stretching out the coy. But Fred was not about to play that game with him, not over the phone at close to midnight, for all that the painting proposed an interesting puzzle.

"We'll talk in the morning," Fred said. "I agree with you, by the way."

"You do?"

"You made an error," Fred said. "Meantime, I'll go lean on the guy. What am I looking for?"

"You'll understand it," Clay said. "The letter is an essential part of the transaction. It is an autograph, from the painter to the original owner, who happens also to be the subject of the painting. The whole thing will come clear to you, Fred. You know paintings."

"You won't say who wrote the letter?"

"No need. You'll know it when you see it."

Fred knew Clay well enough to feel him twisting on the point of what he might be losing—whose full extent he did not want Fred to understand unless Fred saved him from the loss.

"What does the letter look like?"

"White stationery, no heading, folded, about four by five inches. The paper is foxed. Six lines of writing. It includes a drawing you will recognize. It is signed," Clayton said. "Nickname only, but it will make immediate sense."

"Nickname, eh?" Fred said. "Some of these fellows had distinctive nicknames. Like Twatty."

"Twachtman, I suppose," Clay said. "No, Fred. It isn't Twachtman. I don't know what put that into your head."

Fred hung up, furious. Clay's penchant for unresolved romance had made trouble, and Fred hated the idea that he'd have to see Smykal, or Smykal's place, ever again. Between the

24

pornographer and Clay, at that moment, it was hard to decide who he would rather hang up by the ears.

Fred went back into the garage, where Molly was still looking at the painting.

"I know a Duveneck of similar quality in a collection in Chicago," Fred said. "Same slather, all black and rich and opulent in this fin-de-siècle way. But the Duveneck's too hard for close comparison: it's beautifully, even tenderly painted, but the tenderness is all for the paint, not for the model."

And you could feel a glowing warmth of sentiment in the picture Molly now carried into the kitchen, saying, "She can't spend the night in the garage. She doesn't look as if she's used to it. Does Clay say what she's worth?"

"Clayton won't tell me anything. You know Clay."

"You know where she comes from, at least," Molly said.

"You don't want to know. You don't have the stomach for it," Fred said. "I certainly don't, knowing I'm going back. I can tell you it's a scumbag. And that's just an unconsidered off-the-top-of-my-head hint of Henry Smykal's lovely home on Turbridge Street," he added. "I'll give you the whole miserable picture later if you want. I have to go, since the guy's playing games with Clay."

Molly objected strenuously when she understood that Fred was going out again, but there was no help for it, and they both knew it.

"I'd like to horsewhip that Clayton Reed," Molly said. "If I had a horse."

They put the painting in Molly's bedroom closet.

"Poor kid," Molly said, patting the model's rump gently before they closed her in. "Whoever you are, you're in for a lonesome stretch, honey."

4

Fred parked on Turbridge Street and gritted his teeth against the coming stench, preparing to beard Smykal in his den. In the darkness after midnight, the prospect was not pleasant. But this should not take long. Fred was in no mood to be gentle with him.

Fred rang the outside buzzer and was clicked in without ceremony. So Smykal was home now.

His door opened a crack to Fred's knock. The scent, exacerbated by bright, hot light, rushed out from behind Smykal's surprised face. Fred heard his telephone ringing.

"You're not him," Smykal said, trying to force the door closed.

Fred told him, "I'm him enough for me. I want that letter."

"I'm filming," Smykal said. His telephone continued ringing. "What letter?" Smykal looked down at Fred's foot in the opening of the door. The telephone rang again and stopped.

"The letter Arthurian bought."

The door was on a chain. Smykal kept pushing it against Fred's foot.

"You can't come in," he said. "It's art film. I guarantee privacy." Smykal sniffed, the unconscious, habitual sniff of the user.

Fred heard a muted voice in the background. He saw the bright vertical segment of Smykal's chamber of art, flooded with stinking light that shone through the studio door, which was ajar.

"You can't come in, not now," Smykal repeated.

"I'm happy not to," Fred said. "Pass me the letter, and I'll be on my way."

"I gave it to him."

"Empty," Fred said. "As you know."

The phone began ringing again.

"Just get out," Smykal snarled.

"With the letter," Fred said.

The telephone stopped. A female voice whined.

"It's not here," Smykal whispered. He sniffed. Blotches of red were developing in his gray face. His concave beard bristled with exertion.

"Look, to tell you the truth," he went on, "I decided that for my own protection I wanted a copy. Why should I trust anyone? I'm having my own copy made. At Kinko's." Smykal looked at his watch. "I pay my models by the hour. I'm expecting—"

"I'll wait," Fred said. He pushed against the door. Smykal tottered. They could both feel how fragile the door's chain was, each knowing Fred could splinter his way in.

"Smykal," Fred said, "don't screw around."

"Sorry about the mix-up. I'll call him and explain."

The man was as devious and hopeful and stupid as he was pathetic. Hard man to discourage. He was holding out in order

27

to force Arthurian to receive, once more, his slimy invitation to make photos of normally secret flesh in utter privacy.

"I'll call this minute," Smykal said. "Give me the number."

"Arthurian is not listed," Fred said.

He turned and left, clothed, descending the staircase.

Fred left his car where it was. The night was clear and cold, and the town quieted down in these streets off Harvard Square. Before he forced the issue by breaking in, he had decided while palavering with Smykal on his landing that he might as well check out the old boy's story.

Kinko's was an all-night copy place on the other side of Harvard Square. Fred was there in about fifteen minutes. The man behind the counter, as young and plump as he was harassed, talked on the phone with, apparently, an irate Iranian couple who were in the process of organizing their divorce while they gave him directions. The machines thumped and banged and bent paper behind him, and he turned to respond to alarm signals. Now and again he yelled into the back room, "Billy! We got people here lined up."

He turned toward the counter and his waiting customers, shrugging, spreading out his hands to indicate, What can I do? My partner's back there with the trots.

Two seedy academics of the male persuasion, burning their own midnight oil, were already waiting, and Fred was behind them. Each was burdened with extraordinary complexity in his approach to the copying experience.

"Lost his slip," Fred said, presenting himself with a sheepish grin when his turn finally came. "I'm supposed to pick an order up for first name Henry. Henry Smykal."

The plump boy rubbed his hand through his short black hair, picking up glints of light from the street on his earring. He yawned.

"How big an order?" he asked. He turned and yelled toward

the back, "Billy! A lot of people don't get paid by the hour to do what you're doing in there."

"It sounds like the order's pretty small," Fred said. "Tell you the truth, I forgot to ask Henry. I can tell you what Smykal looks like, if that helps." He described Smykal, using the clenching in his gut to guide him as to the accuracy of his report. The boy shook his head.

"He's not familiar to me," the boy said. "But I try not to look at the customers. Anyway, I just came on an hour ago. I'll look. What was that name again?"

Fred watched the boy turn to the shelves of work completed and waiting projects, reading the names on the order forms.

"You spell that S-M-Y-X-A-L?" he asked, picking a package up.

"You got it."

"Three fifty," the boy said, taking Fred's money and giving him change. "We're not supposed to do this," he confided, handing over the package, a bag about a half-inch thick showing pink, "if you don't have your claim thing, you know?"

Fred turned to go, saying, "I appreciate it."

"Hold it," the boy said.

Fred turned back.

The boy stared at him with a lewd gaze, as pink as the paper showing through the bag he'd given Fred. He licked his lips. "You want your original?"

Fred gave him a big grin and reached out for the sheet: one page, 8½ × 11, suitable for use as a poster on light poles and store windows. He took it into the lighted street and looked at it.

LIGHTS °° CAMERAS °° ACTION, it said, most visibly, in bold letters. It was an ad for Smykal's little hobby. The large words, meant to catch the eye, were followed by a short paragraph of almost random junk—small fee; equipment provided; work with °° LIVE °° MODELS °° in perfect privacy; release the hidden talent that resides in you—and a telephone number.

Smykal was a geek, absurd and absolute, and he'd told Fred the grudging, automatic half-lie that's always the one most likely to succeed because it carries a fragmentary ring of truth. Smykal did indeed have an order at Kinko's—but not what he owed Clayton.

He'd lost a good deal of time waiting for Billy's peristalsis and the march of democracy at Kinko's. Good. Smykal should be more responsive if he had to be awakened.

Fred headed back for Turbridge Street, checking his watch when he reached Smykal's building. It was 3:35 A.M., with early random tulips in front of the three-decker sucking at the chill damp of the dark. He tossed Smykal's posters into a rubbish barrel next to the building before he went to the entrance door again.

Fred held the door for a young man dressed in formfitting rubber, coming out into the world alone and wheeling a bicycle. He received his smile of thanks and slipped into the building. The smell in the stairwell eased gratefully into his reluctant nostrils. Immediately his nerves jumped with the wrong current bristling in the air as his feet hit the stairs, moving quickly and as silently as his bulk and the old wood allowed. The air in Smykal's building had gone wrong.

Amid the dust and the brown painted plaster walls, nothing was remarkable or changed in the stairway to the third floor (above which would be only the standard flat tar roof), other than the increase of stench that Fred knew was normal to it. But Smykal's door was ajar and, where earlier hot lights had shone, dim. He stood a few moments listening outside the apartment door, letting his instincts work.

The stench had turned worse. It was no longer Essence of Jersey City but rather Old Calcutta, with the addition of fresh blood and feces. Old Man Death was in there. Old friend. Fred knew it well.

"Beautiful," Fred said, enveloped again in the persuasive reek of mortal danger.

He listened until the silence was convincing. Nothing lived in there, not even the man's buzzards.

Fred edged into the room, using his shoulder to open and then close the door behind him, checking to see that it locked so he could be alone with whatever he was going to find. The front room was dark and empty except for the clutter he had seen earlier today, even more kicked and broken now. The red toolbox was overturned, the space on the wall still waiting. Fred pushed open the door to the studio that he had earlier declined to visit. Henry Smykal lay on the floor, grinning up at a dim overhead light and staring.

Smykal's teeth were stained. The gash in his face where his teeth were, amid the trimmed hair around his mouth, looked like something in one of his art photos. He had bled a good deal from the crushed place on the right side of his head. Fred saw where a hammer had been tossed across the room and now lay against the wall. The simple story winked with eloquence: a man and his hammer. The hammer's claw had got into the act also; the blow to the skull had been the last in an organized series.

Smykal's blue suit stank and shone, so maculate with blood that nobody was going to use it again, not even to burn him in. Aside from the body, the room was surprisingly empty after the hectic, tawdry flea-market-and-whorehouse ambience of the sitting room. Its floor was carpeted in fabric as cheaply fake as it was white: a big remnant spread across the room for Smykal to bleed into. The red stains had gone brown already, in big, deep, caked puddles. It was a great deal of blood, as if he'd danced before he dropped. It spread to splashes and stains on walls and furniture as well.

The windows were boarded with painted plywood. In addition to the overhead socket, where a dim bulb burned, large photographic lights were placed on stands around the walls. They had been turned off but still cast vestigial warmth to a hand held near them. Along one wall of the room, a shelf held three or four Nikons. We supply the equipment. The furniture consisted of one double-bed mattress covered with once-white sheets and a loveseat in pink plush. One wall sported a large mirror.

Roses on the dirty wallpaper in the stricken room—the same wallpaper as in the front room—carried the color of Smykal's blood onto the wall, where their cousins, splotches of actual blood, joined them. Cardboard coffee cups stood or lay on the floor, some used as ashtrays. Pot was among the smells, its rancid reek striving against that of Smykal's emptied bowels. Although the man had apparently been filming when Fred was here earlier, there was no immediate sign of his work, nor of who had been here with him.

Decisions must be made, Fred knew. The important thing was to keep himself and Clayton out of this. With the man dead and Fred caught unexpectedly with his cooling meat and listening for company, the first thing he did was to remind himself of the large horizontal stain of comparative cleanliness on the wall in the front room, where the newly exposed roses were pinker and more hopeful, marking the place from which Clayton's purchase had come the afternoon before. In Molly's house, at this minute, was a painting Fred had brought from here. Anyone with half an eye would see that something was missing.

"Beautiful," Fred said.

Unless more fruitful lines of inquiry opened, the cops were going to put together the beaten corpse and the absence on Smykal's wall, which would match a painting on Clayton's, in case unhappy future accident should tie Clay to his alias, and lead a team of inquiry to his doorstep. Fred rearranged some of the larger crotch-art photos so that the painting's former home was covered by Smykal's crasser, more direct, more vulgar predilection.

Cambridge is a city. People go in and out of buildings all the time. Nobody notices, maybe. But Fred had been at or near Smykal's apartment three times in less than twelve hours, and he'd just not ten minutes ago held the downstairs door open for a smiling young man and his bicycle. He'd asked for Smykal's stuff, using his name, at Kinko's—and Smykal's name was about to be a household word. For all the normal inattention of the human witness, Fred tended to stand out. He looked like something Max Beckman had painted, Molly said, walking into a Glackens picnic: a large, hard-looking, crew-cut man whom someone must have seen, more than once, entering the building—most recently at about the time Smykal passed over.

Fred looked at the terrain and listened. The body had been dead for over an hour, in his judgment; if sirens had been alerted, they would have been here already.

He'd come for a letter, and he might as well take a look, since there was not going to be another opportunity.

I'll give it seven minutes, Fred thought. After that, Clay's on his own.

Fred moved with practiced silence, touching nothing with his skin, using his handkerchief to shift anything he had to move. The pockets of Smykal's clothing were explored first, since Smykal lay on his back and his coat had fallen open. The limbs moved easily, not yet acknowledging the diligent messengers of death that tell you, Stiffen up. The meat sighed involuntarily when moved, as new-made bodies do. Smykal had nothing Fred wanted in his suit coat or in his other pockets, except for the Kinko's receipt in his wallet, which Fred took in order to deep-six it. It was just as well that Clay's letter wasn't on the body: soaked with Smykal's fluids, it would complicate the painting's provenance more than it would help it.

Aside from studio and sitting room, the apartment had kitchen, bathroom, and bedroom, everything thick with greasy dust. The bathroom doubled as a darkroom. Tub and sink were full of trays, which had been knocked about, as if the discussion that Smykal had ultimately lost in the studio had started here. The room was fixed with red light and festooned with strings and clips for drying prints.

Smykal's bedroom was so filled with offal it was difficult to get into. The papers on and in the desk were in disarray, tending to be bills. Fred went through them, finding nothing—neither the letter he wanted nor any sign of Clay's payment. The single bed was unmade. A green blind on the room's only window was nailed down so it could not be lifted to let light in, or air. Dirty clothes bulged in a bag on the painted brown wood floor. Other dirty clothes hung in the closet.

Fred checked the bureau. The open top drawer held a busted gold watch and chain, collar tabs, stamps, cuff links, a class ring from Boston College, odd things there wouldn't be names for, knickknacks, and a tin box whose cover showed lavender lozenges. It shook like lozenges. The rest of the drawers held only clothes. Soiled garments were in the upper drawers, clean in the lower. Smykal had a migratory system to eliminate the need for washing machines. Fred realized, looking up from his search, that only the cool glass over the dresser, a mirror that one could tip, was almost clean.

Smykal's phone sat on a bedside table. The man evidently had not read in bed but had used a good deal of Kleenex, which he scattered around the room in stiff wads. Smykal had favored khaki blankets and sheets of a compromised gray. There ought to be papers. If the man had been as obsessive-compulsive as

all photographers—or pornographers—must be to be successful, he should have kept files of annotated prints and negatives,
records in general. On the room's apparently Oriental rug, next
to the dresser, Fred found corner indentations and an oblong
shape delineated by a lesser degree of ground filth, suggesting
the shape of an absent file cabinet.

Whoever took the old man out, Fred thought, took out a box
also.

It was the likely place for Clayton's letter.

Fred studied the situation. "All this sex," he muttered. "That
and the dope and the smell—everything about him—the guy
had a million chances to rub someone the wrong way.

"It's not your business, Fred," he told himself. "At least, so
far. Let's keep it that way."

With each moment the possibility of his being discovered
increased, and that would complicate things. He must get outside
and signal Clayton Reed to maintain that neither of them had
been here, until and unless it became impossible to deny.

Fred looked down once again at Smykal's grotesque corpse:
seedy, shabby, sliding into full decomposition.

"Farewell, then, little one," he said.

To get out by the back door, Fred had to pass through the
kitchen, whose smell was more intense but different, going
colder, heavier. It had settled to waist level, like a fog. Unwashed
dishes leered in the sink. Almost-empty cans and jars bulged in
crammed garbage bags under the sink: offensive heaps of semi-
abstraction without conviction or purpose.

Fred checked the fridge (sour milk and unused film), the
stove, and a bookshelf that served as pantry for cornflakes, mustard, canned peas and corn, and boxed puddings you mix yourself. Bottles of port and sherry lurched on the bottom shelf,
jostling against nasty special gilded glasses. No letter, and no
sign of Smykal's supply of sweet white powder, either. Like as

not, what Smykal had decided to do with Clayton's money was stick it up his nose; the absence of a stash was suggestive, like the absence of the money itself.

"They'll find cocaine in him. If we're lucky, the story's going to be cocaine," Fred said. "A drug buy or bust or rip-off. It's how they'll have to read it."

Even if the man had had not a friend in the world, and even if his neighbors had hated him, his body and its immediate circumstances were going to be, very soon, in the public domain. The cops soon would know too much about Smykal.

Fred had done what he could without making things worse. The letter was a lost cause.

He took the back way out and watched the street, sitting in his car in the dusk before dawn, before he drove away.

5

To Molly's question, mumbled sleepily as she made a place for him in the bed, Fred answered only, "No, I didn't get it." He had showered and slipped in beside her, not wanting to alarm her. He did not want to lay his worry on her unless events made it unavoidable, mostly because he was reluctant to bring an ugly murder to her bed. He'd seen worse things than Smykal, living or dead. Having done what he could, he put it away until he had to take it on again.

Clayton he'd called right away, from a pay phone after he left Smykal's, waking him up to tell him, Do not mention Smykal to anyone, for any reason, until we talk. Don't telephone his number. We've got trouble. He had not decided how much he could say to Clayton, but he was determined to get the painting out of Molly's house this morning. That would mean driving into town.

So Fred was drinking coffee in Molly's kitchen when she

came in, and looking at the painting Clay had got them into, which was propped against the oven.

"Sorry," Fred said. "My Saturday is screwed. I've got to spend time with that little lady."

"It's hard to imagine what that poor girl will find to do in Clayton's house, hanging around in her birthday suit," Molly said.

This was not really fair. Clay had been a widower since long before Fred first met him and they started working together; and he remained a devoted husband to his wife's memory. She, a Stillton, from one of the Boston families whose names and wealth are coextensive with the towns on the North Shore, still gazed in moist rapture from a silver frame in Clayton's study. But nothing in Clayton's manner, nor his social interests, now distinguished him as one for whom an intimate relationship with another human, female or male, was possible. That was a closed chapter for him, something he had done and finished with.

On the rare occasions when he made a reference to his past history—speaking with Fred perhaps on a late evening when both were tired from some project—Clay would suggest the vestiges of a truly bewildered confusion, as if, in marriage, he had awakened in bed one morning surrounded by large, damp clockwork.

But when Clayton ran his hands with tenderness along the contour of a frame or laughed over the juxtapositions of forms and colors in a painted image, Fred thought he saw the man who had had the capacity to court, and marry, and stand by a young wife while the cruel surprise of a wasting illness carried her off.

You had to work at it to see it now, though, and you couldn't always summon the patience. Molly, perhaps on Fred's behalf, had far less patience with Clay's foibles and mannerisms. But Fred suspected that Molly, being a direct sort, was imagining herself in the position of this naked, unnamed model, hanging around in Clayton's house while he failed to remember that manners are a flimsy substitute for conversation and the rough give-and-take of affection.

Fred had been staring at Clay's new picture for a half hour. Looking at it now, he figured there might be fifteen Americans who could have painted in that manner, at that time, that well. The drawing was well schooled. There was no fudging at joints or appendages. The paint was handled with confidence but without that bravura or show-offishness that could be so tiresome in work from the period. The painter had considered, and rejected, the daubery of the impressionists, but you could see that he was familiar with them because of the way color found its own shapes in the reflected image in the mirror. The painter could be direct and subtle, too, both in the same picture.

Because he had made what could be a big mistake, Clay was going to be reticent about the unsigned painting in order to save face and seem somewhat intelligent. He'd keep his knowledge to himself. Clay's task would be proving what he knew, making it stick. The missing letter had to do with this aspect of the matter. The letter must provide the equivalent of a clear title.

An unsigned painting of whatever quality is trouble. If you don't know who did it, you have to start by figuring out the author. Even once you yourself are satisfied that you know what the painting is and who it is by, you still have to demonstrate those things in a way that will satisfy the scholar who knows that painter best.

When you go to "the guy" (also called the expert) who is the authority on a particular painter, it helps if you can give the history of the picture, where it's been, who owned it before, where it was exhibited, how it got from there to here. It's like a title search. If the object is of special purported value, and there's a big hole in the record, it can be as much of a problem for a picture as it is for a house. And a picture is harder to follow into the past than a house, being more portable.

Fred left Molly's at about eight, with the painting in a green garbage bag to protect it from the cold drizzle that had elected to fall on Arlington. He tuned the radio to programs divulging local news, but there was no report about the body ticking on Turbridge Street, preparing to make a most unseemly noise. Fred listened for it but kept it otherwise out of his thoughts. He'd done what he could.

The road was wet and empty, the trees dripping with rain and pink and white blossoms. What he regretted most was Sam. He'd had to tell the boy last night, before he left for Cambridge, that he likely couldn't come to his game this morning. Sam had stared at him, disappointed and suspicious, not mollified when Fred told him that Clayton Reed had messed up something that he now had to go out and try to fix. Sam had said only, "Would you turn off the light, Fred, so I can sleep?" Fred had suspected that under the covers Sam was wearing all his clothes.

His route took him past the damp lawns of Arlington, obediently edged with daffodils and tulips, then down Fresh Pond Parkway and along and across the Charles. Beacon Hill was almost deserted this early on a Saturday morning. It looked like what it wished to be, a piece of London, but steeper.

Fred parked in the spot Clayton owned beside the row of houses and let himself in. Clay heard him arrive and came spiraling down into the office. Fred was taking the picture out of the green bag. Clay looked at it, gloating. It burned into the room and made Clay smaller.

"She's not a bad little painting, is she?" Clayton said. "But what did you mean this morning on the phone? What did Smykal say? What's happening? What do you mean, there's trouble?"

Clayton Reed was wearing the red satin bathrobe he called a dressing gown, which signaled that he was in a state of leisure. He wore it on top of, not instead of, his clothes, omitting only the suit jacket. Fred kept a chair empty next to his desk for

Clayton's visits, but Clay wouldn't sit this morning. Fred had picked up a large Dunkin' Donuts coffee to keep warm on the hot plate and was having some of it, but he didn't offer Clay any since Clay did not approve of stimulants. It was barely nine o'clock.

Clay tapped his fingers on Fred's desk, waiting for Fred to rise to the challenge in his questions. "Whatever the trouble that man claims, I must have that letter."

Fred did not normally lie to Clay without good reason. But given that there'd been nothing on the radio concerning Turbridge Street, he couldn't count on Clay to act the part of innocence unless he was kept ignorant.

"Forget that either of us has ever heard of Smykal. It's important, Clay. Smykal did not answer his door," Fred said. "I sat out front in my car, watching the street for his return. Suspicious activity began around his building, which I thought might generate a crowd and involve me and therefore us and our business. Smykal's dangerous, and you are going to be hurt if we get caught near him. We must keep a low profile. So I left. The main thing is the Heade. Let's not compromise that."

"Speaking of trouble, I might as well tell you," Clayton Reed said. "It's all I can concentrate on in any case. We are in trouble. Serious trouble. We are about to lose the main objective. I cannot think about that horrible man, not now. As far as the Heade is concerned, the sharks are gathering."

Fred took a drink of his coffee and waited. Things were going to keep getting worse now, as he had feared.

"Albert Finn is in town," Clay said.

"Shit," Fred said. "Sir Albert."

Finn's presence so close to their quarry could represent disaster.

"I ran into him at the Ritz bar after you and I talked by telephone," Clay said. "I called you from the Ritz, if you remember? I was obliged to drink with the man, at his expense. I am certain Finn is onto something. He wouldn't come up just for the affair at the Gardner."

"Did Finn mention the Heade?" Fred asked.

"Of course he didn't mention the Heade," Clayton said, exasperated. "Any more than I would signal interest in it myself. Finn says he's here for the Gardner benefit, to help console them for their carelessness in having all those paintings stolen. You know his cheery laugh."

March 18, 1990, had been a black day in Boston's cultural history, when thieves in uniform, after gaining access to the museum by appealing to the humane sympathies of its guards, had made off with a select group of paintings, including a Manet—the best piece in the collection—two of the three Rembrandts, and Vermeer's *The Concert*. There wasn't a Vermeer left in town now, other than the one Clayton suspected lay waiting for him, asleep in the hay.

"Makes sense that he'd come for the benefit," Fred said. "He loves an admiring crowd of the unknighted."

"Then he said that if I was going to the preview at Doolan's this afternoon, he had nothing important to do, and if I wouldn't drive on the wrong side of the road, he'd ride with me and keep me company."

"Whoops," said Fred.

"I couldn't say I didn't care what was at Doolan's," Clay said. "That would tip him off. So I must take him with me and trust he'll get so mired in admirers that I can look surreptitiously at the Heade. I'm not happy about this. I don't know how one of Finn's hangers-on could miss the reference you discovered, Fred, in the archives, which any fool could find—that is, I mean to say, the archives' microfilms exist in duplicate in all the major cities in the country. It's not as if we have exclusive access.

"The man's no scholar. He's a showman," Clay continued.

Whereas Clayton Reed studiously cultivated the art of the

low profile, Sir Albert Finn accomplished his ends through a mastery of self-promotion. Clay twitched and fretted and started the speech he frequently rehearsed in preparation for the day that would never come, when he would be called on to give the keynote address in the roast of Albert Finn, his nemesis.

"His books litter the world's coffee tables. His students and former students fan out across the globe disguised as curators, critics, researchers, and gallery personnel. Major collectors buy nothing without his nod. The sticky strands in the web of favors, alliances, and enmities in the art world, both academic and commercial, invariably lead in his direction. He is the Moriarty of art history."

This man, Albert Finn, recently knighted in honor of his contribution to the march of British aesthetics, had thrown his lot in with the Americans, accepting control of the Department of Art History at Newark University, minutes from the largest art market in the world. He was presently working with a large government grant, a network of aides, students, and researchers, and a central bank of computers. His stated project, rather open-ended, was to compile the *World Encyclopedia of Western Painting After 1400*. His real goal was to add riches to honor. With Kenneth Clark out of the way, and nestled among the rubes in the New World, he did not anticipate or brook serious opposition.

Any scrap of information about any painting in private hands that showed a corner anywhere in the world eventually got into Finn's computers. Then, in a transaction quick as a frog's breakfast, the painting (if it was the *right* painting) would disappear into another private collection without trace, or into a gallery with great fanfare—all the time gathering money and shaking it off like a dog coming out of a pond.

And Finn would lean back and smile. He was short, rotund, and rubicund, protected by the armor of academic purity that appears to repudiate all interest in cash. He wore shabby suits and shoes that had given up all attempts at reflection many years before. He kept a poor man's wife.

"You know his cheery laugh," Clayton had said. Indeed Fred did. And he knew how it raised Clayton's back hairs. Clayton, through patient research, had once discovered the estate of an interesting Boston painter, an impressionist who had died in Geneva leaving one child, a daughter, who had married and moved to Antwerp. Clay found her and arranged to visit her.

But Clay made a mistake, unusual for one so naturally secretive that he hardly informed himself what he was eating for breakfast. He brought his quarry up in conversation with a friend of his, the curator of graphic arts at the Boston Public Library. He mentioned only the painter's name. The next day—no more than twenty-four hours later—Clayton received a call from Alexander Newboldt in London, one of the big dealers and a friend of his.

"As a matter of professional courtesy," Newboldt said, "I want to let you know that I have an agent in Antwerp who is on the point of making a telephone call for me to the daughter of an American painter who I understand may be of interest to you. It is an estate I wish to buy."

They went back and forth. How did Newboldt know of Clayton's interest? Through "a scholar" who occasionally gave him advice.

Clayton learned later, too late, that his librarian friend was a former student of Finn's at Cambridge.

Clay had never challenged Finn concerning his role in the hijack. There was no point in it. Their relations remained cordial, infrequent, and careful.

The affair at the Gardner, scheduled for this evening, was a benefit cocktail party entitled "In the Pre-Raphaelite Mode," to which Boston's Best had been invited to come wearing formal dress or appropriate costume, dropping three hundred bucks a head for the privilege. Clayton wouldn't miss it. He worked that kind of thing well, even enjoyed it. Fred had let his own invitation lapse.

Clayton and Fred worked together but were like occupants of a rain forest who traveled in different layers. Clay kept to the canopy, while Fred did his best work closer to the ground. And Clay knew his leafy canopy. He was smart and had money. If outrageous, opinionated, and exasperating, he was hardly original or unique in those departments. Fred, for his part, understood the rustlings in the underbrush and brought size and physical skill to the operation, and a direct style that sometimes made people flinch. And he knew something about tactics.

A person with a serious interest in collecting, like Clayton, must, as a practical consideration, keep track of what happens in the social circles where things are owned—which means, in Boston, where they are inherited. Clay had a natural knack for this activity, as well as having married into the network of Stillton aunts, uncles, and cousins, which resembled the road map of the North Shore in its illogical complexity and gave him access to what was otherwise marked, discreetly, Private Property.

"You'll have to keep your eye on Finn at the Gardner," Clay said. "He'll be doing his bit to make up for Berenson's absence."

"I hadn't planned to go tonight," Fred said.

"It should be a nice party," Clay said. "And since Finn's in town, it's important to keep alert, see how the game is moving if we can."

"Not to change the subject to the nude you bought, but why don't you tell me how much the painting cost?" Fred said. "So I can get a feel for what the stakes are."

Clayton would normally tell you nothing you didn't have to know, especially when the subject concerned his money. If Fred was going to an auction to bid on a painting for him, Clay even hesitated to reveal how high he wanted him to go. Fred told

Molly it was like having a partner at bridge who was so pleased with his cards that he wanted to keep even his partner in the dark and wouldn't bid his best suit.

"Art is a function of the spirit," Clay said in his most infuriating manner.

Fred looked at the painting. Its cheerful subject looked back from the far side of her langorous naked hip, an innocent mocking the horrors in the house she'd left barely in time.

"All right," Fred said, "if you want to keep me guessing. I'll do what I can for the young lady. We'd best not show her, Clayton. Not even to Roberto. In fact, let's hide the picture. If Albert Finn should drop in, or some such—not that it's likely—I'd as soon not have to defend the young lady's honor, even if she's La Belle Conchita."

Out of the blue, without premeditation, blurting it out without thinking, Fred had hit the nail on the head. Clay jumped as if he'd been goosed—an infrequent occurrence in his social circle. Fred had guessed the model's identity without intending to. He gave a big and lazy smile.

"Naturally," Clay said, miffed but pretending Fred's accidental brilliance was the obvious. "Who else could she be? I discovered La Belle Conchita, and I have set her free." He went all formal, his disappointment plain at losing, this fast, half of his secret.

"Spare me the details. I shall rely on you, Fred, to do what you can to get that letter when you think it prudent, and to let me know when you succeed. By all means put her in the racks. I can't enjoy the painting now. I am too tense. God help me, I must spend the afternoon with that ass Finn."

He went corkscrewing up the stairs to his quarters, leaving the painting of La Belle Conchita, as nature had intended her, for Fred to put away. She wouldn't be allowed upstairs until she had been cleaned and a new frame chosen for her.

6

Fred hit the road. He turned the radio on and listened for news amid the chatter. Nothing. Smykal's body, armed and triggered, lay as unremarked behind his locked apartment door on Turbridge Street as a Vermeer might, lurking beneath a Martin Johnson Heade.

Traffic in Cambridge was picking up as it got closer to noon, and rain fell into the world in a hesitant way, slowing pedestrians. Fred drove slowly along Mass. Avenue and looked up Turbridge Street for the activity that would give away the presence of concerned authority. Nothing stirred. It looked as if a person could go up to Smykal's door, ring, be admitted, and find the leering fellow hale and vertical. The past twenty-four hours had not happened.

Fred parked several blocks away and sat in the car thinking, looking into the spring air at a Saturday he was not spending with Molly's kids.

He did not want this to be his business. Was it conceivable

that someone had come back with a barrel and cleared the thing away, carpet and all?

Since he could think of nothing to defuse the problem or even signal how large a problem it might be, Fred put it out of his mind. That left the Heade, and Albert Finn.

Finn's presence on the scene was a hazard about which, at the moment, nothing could be done. Fred put that out of his mind, therefore, as well, and enjoyed feeling smug about his lucky guess concerning the identity of the subject of Clayton's painting—La Belle Conchita.

An intelligent subconscious had accomplished its mission. Let Clay think Fred had done it through good fieldwork.

Aside from lucky guesses, there are two ways to find things out. One is through research; the other is by standing people in a corner and asking them questions. The fact that Fred had in the past shown talent for the latter method did not negate his capacity and preference for the former, and indeed he was as good working from the printed page as Clayton was; it was just that he had the ability, also, to do research under fire, while he was losing blood and friends of his were screaming not far off.

It wasn't anything he talked about with Clay, except once, tangentially, when he had first explained to him how Clay needed help he could provide. That was three years ago now? Four?

Clay had needed a bodyguard, and that was how they had met. Fred had not mentioned at the time—because what Fred craved wasn't what Clay cared about—that he also needed something: to touch things that were beautiful and not designed or intended to harm people. The paintings he handled for Clayton were objects in which Fred found a passion of intelligence, even where that passion (as he felt it to be in many paintings) was shaped by creative energy beginning in the artist's hatred, frustration, or despair.

If nothing was beautiful, nothing could be funny, either, and it was hard to be alive. Fred had needed a reason not to finish a brief life curled on a grate, a parasite and predator. He wanted beauty other than the functional perfection of a killing tool, and a quest whose object was not extinction or betrayal.

As time went on, Fred's instincts, his education and life experience, and his talents proved to complement Clay's, and his role shifted accordingly, though it was never defined. When he could, he enjoyed losing himself in research. The fact that he worked with paper and images, and that the people involved tended to be long gone, added a spice of history to the work.

The chase after La Belle Conchita had been fun. Fred, working hard, had followed her into a dark alley and left her there after fruitless attempts to find where she had gone next. He'd lost her trail in Baltimore, in 1895.

La Belle Conchita, known to her less intimate acquaintances as Conchita Hill, had caught their eyes first as one of the few American women painters whose work was accepted for exhibition at the annual Salon in Paris.

They had been amused and intrigued by her name. Clayton was further interested by the titles of her pictures, which suggested that she had been painting in Giverny at around the same time Monet was doing his haystacks.

Conchita Hill had been born on a ship off the coast of Brazil in 1865, the daughter of an American sea captain whose wife lived on board, as was not uncommon in those days. Hill's name appeared on the roster of the Art Students League in New York in the early 1880s. By the time she arrived in Paris, she was traveling with her mother, like three quarters of the Americans then studying art in that city.

Conchita seemed, from the brief references available in the writings of her colleagues, not to have distinguished herself for demureness. Fred was convinced that this was the very girl he discovered dancing at the Moulin de la Galette, in randy dishabille, in an 1893 lithograph by Toulouse-Lautrec entitled *La Belle Conchita*.

Whether or not this was she, they believed that the subject of their search had had extensive acquaintance among artists who were of interest to them. Practically every painter of consequence, American or European, had been in Paris at some point during the 1880s, and the papers of several referred to Miss Hill or to Conchita. Often the references suggested that she was having a very good time. There couldn't have been many Conchitas.

Clayton was determined to discover what had become of her paintings; nothing by her had ever surfaced on the market. To find her paintings, they first had to discover what had become of her. There was no record of a permanent alliance: no marriage; no later exhibition of paintings by a Conchita anything, née Hill; no siblings; no city, even, that either parent might have come from and she might have returned to. She sailed from Le Havre on a ship bound for Baltimore that docked in October of 1895, and there she disappeared.

Fred had worked hard on her story and recalled it easily while looking out at Cambridge. He'd seen her now; that was flesh to attach to her story, and to another, Smykal's.

The city was moving slowly as the rain lifted. Buses geared up and droned. Dogs walked their masters and mistresses. Children dressed for soccer converged on the parks. At this moment Sam was playing baseball in Arlington, and Fred was missing the game.

Who was the author of the picture Clay had bought? Fred's lucky hit of the morning made him itch to establish the painter's identity. And thinking about it would distract him from the loud noise he was waiting for on Turbridge Street.

Fred found a meter open in front of a place on the other side of the square from Turbridge Street, and he went in and drank coffee, running through his mind the names of artists who could have been close enough to Conchita to record her in her skin.

Such things were not the same in 1890 as they are now, not even in gay Paree. There was as much of a social gulf between artists and models as there was between artists and peasants or, for that matter, between peasants and professional models. The peasants would not take off their clothes except for two or three occasions in their lifetimes: birth, marriage, death. In Paris, models who undressed, either for students or for artists, were inclined to be not French but Italian immigrants. Some French city girls who had no expectations were also willing to work hard and preferred modeling to the more dangerous other option available.

Students and friends did not then, as they do now, model for each other, unless clothed. For all that the human nude was exhibited as frankly and commonly as cows and chickens, only the rare American young lady would have had the presence and aplomb to serve as the original for the painting Clayton had purchased. But from the little they'd been able to learn about her, it seemed Conchita had been a jolly, open-minded girl, quite willing to test social frontiers.

Seven or eight names roved in Fred's mind as he finished the coffee and tossed the crumpled cup in the basket next to the door as he walked out. He realized while he was thinking that he had been lowering his head unconsciously to look into the mirror he remembered behind the reflected hip of Conchita Hill, trying to see the rest of the man whose legs showed in the glass.

They had, those legs, the look of Robert Louis Stevenson's, skinny, in their dark trousers, striding, in Sargent's Calcot paintings. No, Calcot was 1887—the Stevenson portraits were 1885, at Broadway. But Molly was right: the painting was too tender for Sargent.

Fred took himself through Harvard Yard, the campus busy now with students, and to the Fogg Museum's new addition on

Prescott Street, where Harvard University keeps its fine-arts library. He had a bone between his teeth, time to kill, and an itch in the back of his mind to keep at bay. It was time to do some searching in the stacks.

Harvard, encouraged by its development office, counts as alumni all those who have ever been enrolled, however briefly or disastrously. So Fred had an alumnus card for the library. The stacks are underground, at the foot of a perilous staircase. This being the end of the school year, Fred expected to find students gnashing their teeth over lost footnotes, but the place was almost deserted.

The stacks are concentrated in a single room around whose sides hunch the desks, or carrels, that graduate students are assigned. Only three or four of these were occupied. A florid young woman in a blue print dress was leaning back in her chair, her feet up on her desk, a large volume on ancient Near Eastern pottery on her lap, and she herself as fast asleep as if she were enjoying a curse brought down upon her as a result of breaking into the wrong tomb.

A few of her fellows searched the stacks. Way down at the far end, near the cage where sales catalogs and precious and/ or dirty art books are kept locked, a young man in jeans, white shirt, and bow tie sat at his desk in a puddle of lamp light, looking down at a book and then up, as if he were a bird swallowing water, then down again, to scribble on a yellow pad. He had a suitably frantic air for this time of year. He seemed almost to tear at his long blond hair.

American painting is in the middle of the stacks. Fred's plan was, if he could, to deliver himself to the same random forces that had worked so well already that morning, another form of research, sometimes the most successful, being serendipity.

He walked along the stacks, smelling the slow decay of leather, paper, glue, and cloth and looking for the trunk and head, and the fine hand, that would complete the male legs in the canvas mirror: the artist striding toward Conchita Hill, whose smile was greeting him. Paul Wayland Bartlett? Not too exciting. Frederick Arthur Bridgeman might have done it, but he would have stuck in something Moorish—perhaps a harem motif to give him an excuse for the nudity. Chase? There wasn't much on him in the stacks. There was Frank Duveneck (who would have wished to keep such a liaison secret from poor, ailing Elizabeth Boott), but Fred had dismissed him the night before. Lucy Lee-Robbins, now. Suppose the artist was also a woman. Lee-Robbins had a murky story and a body of paintings that was well hidden. She had painted well-realized—even fon-dled—female nudes who looked as if they were about to have tea. Lucy became the mistress of her teacher Emile-Auguste Carolus-Duran, who was also Sargent's teacher. The American manner of Clay's painting, after all, had its origin in French fashion well established by Carolus-Duran, which Sargent, being trickier than anyone, could rub French noses in, going them one better.

How about Charles Sprague Pearce? If the picture was by Pearce, it would be better off anonymous. Nobody wanted a Pearce. Sargent Fred had already written off. Molly was right about Sargent. He was a drapery man. Whistler?

Well, what about Whistler? Fred's heart did a little thump. The fan was right. The colors. Whistler could have executed such an image and called it *Harmony in Flesh and Black*. Lord knew Whistler could draw a woman when he wanted to.

But Whistler liked in his finished paintings to brag, Anyone else, to accomplish all I have done, would have been obliged to invest five times as much paint. The picture of La Belle Conchita, by contrast, had been done with delicious abandon, luxuriance, almost profligacy, in the use of material.

Still, it made a tempting story to go beside the one about Whistler's mistress Jo, whom Whistler, in a gesture of fraternal comradeship, had delivered over to Courbet as a model. Also,

Fred loved the title *Harmony in Flesh and Black*, so nearly right for a Whistler.

But no, it wouldn't work with Whistler as the painter. The props were right, but not the manner. Fred had come to the end of the alphabet. He looked at his watch. He had been over two hours. The young lady with the interest in pottery was still sleeping soundly. The little fellow with the bow tie had disappeared.

Who, during the time in question, the 1880s, was exhibiting nudes that looked like the one Clayton had bought?

That question took Fred to the illustrated catalogs of Salon exhibitions.

Fred called Clayton from the pay phone upstairs. Clay was on the point of leaving for Doolan's, intending to collect Albert Finn on the way.

"Amusing," Clay said, "to think how we will tiptoe past each other, conversing and exchanging wisdom while I attempt to look at the Heade without showing interest and he tries not to be noticed noticing my pointed lack of interest.

"Then there's the Gardner. Finn must be watched there. You don't think you and Molly could do me a tremendous favor and come after all? Your lady Molly can get anything she wants out of anybody, so we could aim her at Albert Finn."

Fred told Clay to forget it.

"I suppose there are limits," Clay said.

Fred left the library and walked past Turbridge Street, along Harvard, looking down at its usual quiet.

Not reporting the ugly fact of Smykal's murdered body had been a crime. But reporting the thing on the floor was not going to make Smykal any less dead. Fred could go in again now, have a more careful look, and then report the body—take some initiative to shake things loose.

But no. Turbridge Street was a trap, nothing to mess with. He'd let that work according to its own logic. It took discipline to put the scent of murder, and its retinal impact, firmly enough to the side to determine the best course to follow. He had a life to lead with Molly and her children, and he would give a great deal to keep it free from the random, searching stain of death by violence.

Fred drove back to Arlington. Some of Saturday was left. Despite the pitfall waiting on Turbridge Street, the afternoon had cleared enough for baseball. Fred caught Terry as she was leaving for her Little League game. She looked pretty, with her thin brown hair matted and raspberry jam on the shirt of her orange uniform. On the days when she worked, Molly had to rely on the kids to fend for themselves and remember what their appointments were.

"Wait a minute. Put your bike away, and I'll go with you," Fred said.

An afternoon of idyllic, nonessential conflict would be a good thing. He could watch Terry pitch—she was really quite good—and at the same time be well away from anywhere he was expected. They put Terry's bike in the garage, and Fred drove her to the park and sat among the moms and dads watching the game get started.

Fred would lie low this afternoon and tonight, while Clay was hobnobbing with his cohorts at the Gardner. Depending on how soon Smykal rose to the surface, he might even wait until Monday to talk with Clay again.

Why shouldn't Fred enjoy some aspect of a simple life? Why shouldn't he quietly watch Terry play baseball? Afterward he would drive her home and take the family out for Chinese. Later he and Molly might see what developed.

Sitting in the chilly sunlight, enjoying the children's struggle with the game, Fred was amazed, almost alarmed, at what his life, at this moment, looked like. He resembled someone with a wife and kids.

As he watched the game, he felt anger blossoming that he knew had been seeded as soon as he looked down on that sordid, murdered thing on Turbridge Street. It had no right to spoil his chances. It had no right to threaten to cast its cloud—Fred's cloud—over the little family where he was finding a civilian purpose.

He wouldn't stand for it. And why should Molly?

In Molly's company things could be funny. Unless Fred ruined it.

That was a kind of beauty, funny. Like the children.

Fred saw Terry's team suffer a beautiful and ignominious defeat. He bought her an ice cream and comforted her for her skill and heroism, and they arrived home as the cold rain of evening started again. Molly met them at the door, dressed in a damp towel, moving fast.

"You shit," she told Fred. "You didn't leave a message where you were. I've been on the phone to Clayton. You never told me he gave us tickets to the party at the Gardner. I had to stop on my way home to have my hair cut. I ordered pizza for the children. Can you pick it up while I dress? I don't know what you're going to wear."

7

The style of the Gardner Museum was what Molly's mother called Italianette. The building squats on Boston's Fenway, a stucco cube embracing a covered garden courtyard that Mrs. Gardner built to segregate a segment of nature for the enjoyment of herself and her collection, including her husband, Jack. She bequeathed it in trust, to be maintained for posterity as she had left it, with nothing to be added or taken down.

Molly and Fred were ushered in, ditched their raincoats at the door, and became beautiful.

Molly's routine did not normally lead her to spend time with the glitterati. She looked with interested pleasure across the ebb and flow.

"Of course they're only doing what they can to get into one another's pants," Molly observed. "Robbing each other, telling tales, backbiting, setting each other up as fools and criminals, stealing from each other, wrecking each other's jobs and marriages, generally making hell for each other—but don't they look lovely doing it!"

Musicians played instruments in the courtyard: strings and reeds. It was a mob scene. Each paying guest was one of the elect. There was barely room in the corridors, staircases, exhibition rooms, and balconies for the happy few. Old Isabella's collection was hard to see except for what was suspended above crowd level: the tapestries and Oriental screens. Isabella had led an extended rape of Europe's churches, burdening ships with cargoes of rood screens, altarpieces, baptismal fonts, and fossilized saints. "It's as if I'd kept Terry's room just as she left it this morning," Molly said. They'd gone to a third-floor room to make a first survey of the place. Above the crowd, Titian's bull carried Europa off, the bull being headed toward them across painted water like a duck while attendants worried in the background, on the shore. Europa managed in spite of everything to keep her nightgown from riding all the way up, "maintaining a nice sense of priorities," as Molly said.

When Molly had met him at the kitchen door, so mad at him and so eager to go to the ball, Fred had objected. Clayton had pulled a fast one, stacking the deck by sneaking her the invitation. They'd almost had a fight, but not quite, and Molly was prepared to have a good time and be friends, if Fred would only "cheer up and be a good loser."

As long as Smykal's undiscovered body festered in secret, surrounded by the trophies of his hobby—correction: his *art*— it was probably just as well for Fred to be visible, looking his normal self.

"Golly, Fred," Molly had said, driving with all deliberate speed through the dark, wet streets of Arlington. "You look better than an eight-dollar salad in your costume, and for goodness' sake, it's only a party."

Fred had angrily thrown together something resembling a

camouflage outfit for jungle warfare as conceived by Bill Mauldin in 1944.

"Remind me," Molly said, "what they mean by their theme of the evening, 'In the Pre-Raphaelite Mode.'"

Fred wrenched his mind away from where it was and toward the companion he had chosen. "I will instruct you, dear young lady," he said, "if you will forgive a man for having been infected by a brief time of youth misspent among the undergraduates at Harvard, a university in the American Northeast."

"Lay on," Molly said.

Fred harrumphed and commenced. "The Pre-Raphaelites are to painting what 'Italianette' is to architecture. Invented in the late eighteen hundreds by exhausted English Puritans who had not given up romance, the style works like an omelet made with boiled eggs. They—William Morris, Burne-Jones, Lord Leighton, and so on—undertook to imitate the style and ideals of fifteenth-century Italian painters who were in turn imitating the style and ideals of Roman painting, which had entirely disappeared before they started imitating it but which they guessed must have looked like the Greek statues the Romans had stolen. The nineteenth-century version, of course, was improved by Christian and Victorian ideals.

"The Pre-Raphaelites eschewed representing such common and depressing contemporary themes as coal mines, hangings, or the profession of collecting night soil, and instead chose imagined ancient scenes to elevate the spirit and demonstrate morality. The subjects are often nude except for their suppressed genitals—Burne-Jones used the airbrush long before it was invented—or they wear Roman dress, or medieval dress based on the Roman. Except for Rossetti, all of these painters depict the traditional British stiff upper lip, though other exposed parts remain flaccid. William Morris had an extraordinary thing for feet."

"Ah," Molly said. "The perfect choice for a theme party in Boston. You have been most helpful, Fred."

Once surrounded by the party, Molly complained, "Apart from the serving wonks and wenches, the Pre-Raphaelite theme eludes me."

"Bostonians are shy," Fred told her. "Unlike myself."

Few of the elect had chosen to come in costume, something that, at the last moment, had been Fred's only option. Most of the men wore black tie, the more adventuresome showing a dab of color at the waist. The women wore their standard evening things, which this year looked like outfits designed, and then rejected as too silly, in the late fifties: short skirts, with large spots, checks, and bows serving no structural function.

The Gardner's board of trustees had wisely voted to compel youths and maidens, hired to take coats and serve champagne, to dress according to the theme. They were all young and comely. The youths wore tights and velvet doublets from a costumer; the tights and doublets were of different colors. The maidens wore diaphanous pleated tunics, some long, some quite short, in a variety of pastels.

"You see," Fred told Molly, "you could have been a bacchante. You would be perfect in a belted sheet."

She'd chosen to wear her basic black, which made her look delicious and suited her to most occasions.

"And you could have worn my yellow Easter panty hose," Molly countered, accepting champagne from a maiden.

They went back down to the courtyard, lush with palms and potted blue flowers that looked to Fred like a cross between pansies and linoleum. Clayton Reed, in black tie (he was born in black tie), appeared, kissed Molly's hand, and asked Fred more loudly than necessary, "What do you represent?"

Having been trapped into attending the party, Fred was prepared to be belligerent concerning the costume he had cobbled together. He wore a white shirt, open at the neck, and on his head a wreath woven of ivy and spring flowers torn out of Molly's garden. To this he had added pants, his darkest available pants.

"I'm surprised you don't recognize the allusion," Fred answered. "You are familiar with John Reinhard Weguelin's *Toilet of Taunus*, also known as *Adoring the Herm*? Oil on canvas, forty by twenty-three inches, signed and dated 1887, in which a young bacchante is crowning, with a wreath, the herm of Bacchus? Offered at Sotheby's in New York on May 24, 1988? You don't remember? Lot ninety-six. I'm being the herm."

"That explains the wreath," Clay muttered. "The John Reinhard Weguelin allusion eludes me. Is it necessary?"

"You can check with the John Reinhard Weguelin guy," Fred said. "That's Vern G. Swanson of Springville, Utah, director of the Museum of Art there. It's probably necessary at least to Vern."

"I understand, Fred. This is blather. You are joking, yes? Meanwhile, Finn's here," Clay said grimly. He pointed upward. "I saw him presiding over that balcony, from which he may yet bless this multitude should the divine afflatus move him. The man's a miracle of heated air. All afternoon I had him. And at Doolan's—he stood for fifteen minutes with that haystack in his hands, talking about how grand he is, and how modest a thing is Heade in comparison. Dismissing it. Yes. Yes, indeed. But I saw him on that balcony. He was talking, nay, whispering, with Higginson."

Higginson was an intern, a temporary assistant to the world's expert on Martin Johnson Heade. The expert himself was traveling this year, which made Higginson, in Higginson's opinion, world expert by default pro tem.

"Right," Fred said. "He'd have to be. Admitted it's a small world, but it is unfortunate that the Heade guy should be a local boy. Why couldn't it have been he, and not Swanson, who took the job in Springville, Utah?"

"Let me have your ear, Molly," Clayton said, leading her toward a table groaning with little things to eat. Clayton was not over six feet, but he was so thin and graceful that he gave the appearance of being very tall. His full mane of white hair made him seem older than he was; also, he looked distinguished. In fact, Fred thought, considering the scene from under the sticky shadows of his wreath, Molly and Clay made a distinguished-looking couple.

Fred had warned Molly, driving in, that Clayton's motives in procuring entrance for them were not pure.

"Poor herm. Even this party is almost like work for you, isn't it?" She grinned.

The main work Fred was doing consisted in his appearing within this gathering as someone totally unburdened by guilty knowledge. It was why he had chosen the wreath's conspicuous disguise.

Fred watched Molly disappear into the throng on Clayton's arm. Clay was looking smooth, concerned about nothing, happily exploiting his canopy. Molly was as good as Clayton at working a crowd: affable, personable, and able to converse without ruffling feathers. These were skills Fred did not have and could not make up for with directness and candor. It was a mark of the creative working relationship between them, not to mention also of Molly's willing versatility, that even when tricked into attending this function against his better judgment, Fred, without prior planning, could slide Molly onto Clayton's arm and send her off to help him.

Meanwhile, there were people whom Fred could watch and talk to and, as both he and Clay acknowledged without having to spell it out, get somewhere with, whom Clay himself would only make bristle.

For one thing, there is a line between the collector and the dealer, though for many that line is blurred. Clay was pure collector, while Fred kept nothing. This gave Fred a fellowship with those who lived by their wits, many of whom, dealers, turned out for such occasions as tonight's, and for the same reason Clay had dragooned Fred into attending: to see what was rustling in the underbrush. Many of the revelers were Clay's relations by marriage. Fred had come to know some of them. Those who did not use Stillton as a last name tended to exhibit it prominently in the middle of their other names: thus if you had to be a mere Lowell, you could at least be a Something Stillton Lowell.

Fred knew most of the players in Boston's art scene by now. Some had become friends. The fact that business matters occasionally led to moments of confrontation over a piece of merchandise or information was seldom a serious problem, and there was even a camaraderie among some that resulted in a system of mutual aid. But none of them forgot they were in competition, and their business prospered best by being strictly guarded. In the art business you learned quickly who could be trusted and who not; whose word was good; who couldn't tell the truth; who bragged; who manufactured secrets; who was spiteful; who trafficked in facts and who in innuendo; who was attached to substance and who floated free. All this was important to know among people who bought and sold objects to which society attached great financial value, in a business absurdly free of regulation.

In such a gathering as this evening's there were people whom Fred would like to see anywhere and would enjoy talking to. Other people he'd as soon never see but might have reason to talk to. Still others he'd talk to only if he had to, such as—Fred saw him now across the courtyard, ostentatiously drinking beer from a bottle—Buddy Mangan, the current enfant terrible, wild card, and cause célèbre of the art business in these parts.

Mangan was attending the benefit in his normal uniform: baggy Farmer Jones–style blue jeans with straps and bib, a checked work shirt, and a hanging, untied bow tie. His curly hair was blond and short, his awkward grin infectious, his laugh loud. A man in his early forties, he had begun to appear, coming from nowhere, in the auction houses of Boston and New York two years previously. He had with ruthless speed blasted a place for himself in the Boston world of art dealers—or at least in the auction end of things. Because when he set his sights on something, he normally continued bidding until he bought it, and he paid cash.

Fred, when he spotted Buddy Mangan, was talking with Oona, who had an antique shop resembling an old-fashioned general store on Boston's Charles Street. They felt they had a lot in common since Fred had come out of farmland in the Midwest and Oona was from Hungary. She said she was old enough to be Fred's mother, looked as if she had been strung together from dumplings and melons, and flirted outrageously. Oona this evening had already consumed more than her share of Italianette champagne—Asti Spumante—and was so complimentary about the wreath he wore that Fred feared she was about to follow the bacchante's example and commence to adore the herm. Oona tutted, looking crossly at Buddy Mangan.

"He does stick out, doesn't he?" Fred said. "Like a sore thumb, as we say in America."

"Like a sore, a ham . . . a hem . . . what is it you Americans have that sticks out and gets sore?" Oona asked. "That's what he sticks out like. He should be ashamed. I am going all the way up to the third floor now to look at that old woman's snuff boxes again."

Fred wandered, greeted friends, tried some of the minute things to eat, had a glass of wine, and enjoyed the music. The waitpeople did a good job of circulating. It was a pleasure watching the maidens in their diaphanous garments and their Pre-Raphaelite lack of underpinnings. Some pictures in the museum he liked seeing again, though on the whole he would have

advised Isabella differently, starting by suggesting that she ditch
Berenson and steer clear of the more flagrant fakes. But you
had to forgive the near misses given the one remaining Rem-
brandt; the ghost of Vermeer's *Concert*; the Titian; the Velázquez *Philip IV*.

Fred passed Mangan near the drinks table. Mangan was
telling a joke, evidently, surrounded by an attentive coterie of
South Shore dealers. Mangan's own spread, down near Cohasset,
was reputed to have pastures, docks, swans, and outbuildings—
a Mount Vernon of its kind, Fred had heard said. Mangan, like
any large predator, gathered around him lesser dealers who
watched for bloody crumbs too small for him to snap after a
second time. He never joined their pools at auctions, preferring
to sneer with pleasure when it became known that he wanted
something and the bidding faltered in dismay.

Mangan, being a bully, would be a bigger problem for Clay
than Finn if he set his sights on the Heade. If he was going to
be witnessed losing a picture at auction, he'd make the price
rise to where it punished the opposition. He played the under-
bidder's role as smartly as he did that of the "successful" com-
petitor, even finding ways to slide right under a rival's top left
bid. The thing was, though, behind the loud vulgarity of his
presence, Mangan concealed a good eye, and Fred believed the
Heade was simply not a good enough picture for him.

His joke finished, Mangan erupted with a paean of gurgling
laughter that caused a ripple effect. He raised his bottle. "Here's
to crime. Keep the stuff circulating," he roared. The crowd
cringed outward from him in rings, like punch into which a
noisome object had been dropped. The old Bostonians moved
austerely, their money so ancient it wouldn't crackle. The gentlemen floated, frozen as if caught forever by Ignatz Gaugengigl.
The ladies swished away like Sargents, even the ones wearing
the silliest dresses.

The trick with Mangan and his action, and what made him

most bitterly resented as a wild card, was that the cash he spent was based on a different value system from the currency anyone else could bring to bear. (No one doubted that it was money Mangan might have trouble accounting for; people muttered about his large spread's access to the waters of the bay.) Nobody could compete on a level field since Mangan's dollar was worth five times anyone else's.

Fred went up to find Albert Finn. As if Mangan's laugh were causing an echo, Fred heard Finn's booming chuckle before he saw the man. Finn was still holding forth on the balcony, looking down onto the crowd in the courtyard. He was a blimp of benevolence. He blossomed in used black tie, sporting but one decoration, a modest Legion of Honor citation in his lapel. Finn was engaged in impressing a small group of the particularly elect. One of them, a bald man shiny with rings and watches and wearing a plaid cummerbund and a pink jacket that might pass in Dallas, was gaping in delight at his place next to the great man's side. He was probably a new collector on Finn's string.

A blond youth attended them, offering a tray filled with glasses. Finn whispered a special blessing in the waiter's ear. The youth, in lilac tights and lime doublet, looked nervous and broke away, but not before Fred relieved him of part of his burden: one glass for himself and one for Molly, if he found her in time.

Finn knew Fred, even in the wreath, but did not choose to recognize him to speak to. Fred had hoped he might overhear him talking with Higginson, but Higginson was not in Finn's group. Fred stood on the balcony looking down and spotted Higginson hobnobbing in the courtyard. Descending the staircase again, he passed Molly, still on Clay's arm, on her way up. "I don't expect miracles," Clay was saying to her. "But anything you find out, I'd love to hear. Some flavor."

Fred gave Molly her wine and kept going.

8

A direct assault on Higginson made the most sense. Fred encountered him as if by accident, but they fell to talking together naturally.

Fred had to be careful. William Wadsworth Higginson represented the biggest potential obstacle to their success. As a matter of protocol, in the absence of the expert, Higginson would have been asked by Doolan's to look the Heade over. He had access to all the space-age equipment at the Museum of Fine Arts; if it had been a dull day he might, for the hell of it, run the picture under their X-ray machine, and spot anything funny, like a Vermeer, under it.

If the Vermeer was there.

The expert's own research on Heade could already have brought the Apthorp story to his attention. It was not exactly hidden—no more than a piece of hay is hidden in a haystack. It was there for the finding, but looked like the other hay. Their best hope was that only Clay had taken note of the reference to the Mechanics Hall exhibition, and that he alone had correlated it with the Apthorp possibility.

Higginson liked a fruity academic joke, and they made conversation concerning the themes of lilies and haystacks in late-nineteenth-century painting, Fred keeping things more or less focused on Heade, hoping to catch vibrations or see if Higginson tried to steer attention away from the Apthorp picture. Fred gathered that Higginson accepted the Heade as genuine but dismissed it as not of museum quality.

"I really don't think they care," Fred said later, brushing into Clayton near a tub of flowers behind which one of the flautists was sneaking a smoke.

"Something's gotten to Finn," Clay said. "He's not himself. If anything, he's worse."

"You left Molly with him?"

"Yes. And her sister," Clayton said, shuddering. Clay would not forget his and Ophelia's meeting and might never forgive Molly for having engineered it.

"Ophelia can make anyone nervous," Fred reminded Clay.

Fred hadn't known that Ophelia was coming. She had not mentioned it last night, and she didn't usually fool with the art crowd. Normally Fred's and Ophelia's professional paths did not cross. But Ophelia was an eager beaver, and everything, as Molly's mother put it, could become grist to her mule.

"Why don't you stop by Turbridge Street on your way home?" Clay asked Fred, whispering. "It's on the way."

"We'll leave it till Monday," Fred said. "I'm serious. Forget it. I promise you, Clay, that's the best plan."

Clayton circulated. Fred went looking for Molly.

The crowd was starting to thin out. Late dinners were planned in Boston and the suburbs to capitalize on and prolong the festivities. In growing numbers people moved into the rainy darkness. That made it easier to see long distances inside.

Fred spotted Ophelia, dressed in leopard skin, her long blond hair loose around her shoulders. She was hanging on to the arm of Albert Finn, looking up at him as they descended the stairs to the great hall. As Fred approached them, he heard her say, "I love your books. They're marvelous. So, like yourself, approachable. You keep the common touch." She blushed. Molly had told Fred that as a child, Ophelia could also fart on purpose.

"Ah, well," said Finn. His hearty laugh made Titians shake. "You know what they say about King Kong."

Finn pronounced his English in the manner of one constantly tormented by peanut butter on the palate. Fred knew Ophelia would give Finn what he wanted. She paused, a master of timing.

"No," said Ophelia. "What do they say about King Kong?"

"The bigger you are, the nicer you are." Finn's chuckle of delight occupied them both while Fred edged past. Ophelia, noticing Fred, said, "We're going to dinner at the governor's. Will I see you there? I need a date, and Sir Albert has obliged."

"Please, call me Al," Finn said to Ophelia.

"I promised Molly something else," Fred told her.

Finn was edging closer to the exit, but Ophelia held back, her eyes sparkling, to ask Fred, "What is it you're supposed to be?"

"I am glad you asked," Fred said. "The antique Greeks had a practice of placing, at crossroads, where travelers could rub them for luck, tremendous stone monuments representing the male generative organ in full display. They were called herms— after Hermes, the god whose organ was being celebrated. Such a monument presented a special problem in artistic license for the Pre-Raphaelite painter. John Reinhard Weguelin, in his picture *Adoring the Herm*, as Al Finn knows, did nothing to dismay the sensibilities of the time. He represented a marble bust of a bearded male, wearing drapery, on a pedestal, and simply *called* it a herm. Except for the beard, I am his vision of the herm."

"Ha, ha," Finn said.

"Art is a favorite of mine," Ophelia said, turning to join Finn's hasty trundle toward the door.

Fred watched the pair of them waft away. Sheep that pass in the night, as Molly's mother would say. He found Molly, and they collected raincoats and made themselves scarce.

"I couldn't learn much," Molly said in the car as they maneuvered through the evening traffic toward Arlington. "Except for this: Albert Finn was upset, said he's expected in Paris Monday but something has come up that forces him to stay in Boston. For the moment his travel plans are on hold, he says."

"That's ominous. How did you get the great man to tell you?"

"I was saying how boring it is to be emotionally involved with a man in the art business—that's you, Fred—who's always running around the world without notice. Finn had to top it. You learn things when you get a man to complain, which he can't do without bragging."

"He took off with Ophelia," Fred said.

"So he did," Molly said, and she commenced singing, under her breath, "Herm, herm on the range."

Molly wanted to find a hamburger in Cambridge and follow it with coffee in Harvard Square. Fred let his route take them along Massachusetts Avenue so he could get a sense of whether Henry Smykal had continued to maintain a low profile.

Turbridge Street, when they passed it, was choked with police cars, fire engines, and ambulances. Policemen forced people back behind yellow plastic tape and sawhorses, and the traffic was so slowed by the festivities that Fred was able to stare up the street toward the focus of activity, Smykal's building. The cat was out of its bag.

"Something's going on there," Molly said.

Fred nodded, feeling a traitor on account of the silence he was maintaining. But if there was anything he wanted to provide for Molly, it was what former employers of his had called denia-

70

bility. He'd wait, like other civilians, to let information reach her through normal channels.

They stopped at a Cambridge restaurant they liked. Fred left his wreath in the car. They sat over supper for a long time, then went for coffee at Pamplona, no more than seven blocks from where the functionaries of law and death were dealing with Smykal's body.

"I enjoyed Clayton Reed's asking me to help him maneuver," Molly said, stirring sugar into an iced cappuccino. "And his taking me into his confidence. He hasn't done that before, which shows how much respect he has for you, Fred. I understand it's a crucial and exciting moment in the game."

"Molly," Fred said. "I guess I talk about it like a game, and it plays like a game. If we win, we'll feel like the smartest kids on the block. In town.

"There may be forty Vermeer paintings known to exist in the world. Five are among the most wonderful paintings ever made. If a Vermeer were offered for sale anywhere in the world now, there is no way I could have it in my hands. No way Clay could get near it. Clayton can spend at most one or two hundred thousand at a time; a Vermeer could bring fifty million.

"So this is the only way Clayton can get a Vermeer. And I'll tell you something true about that fellow. He wouldn't care if it was worth eighty million. He'd keep it. It would never turn into money. He'd laugh with joy because he'd got a Vermeer, and under hundreds of very intelligent noses."

"A Vermeer that he hasn't seen," said Molly. "Don't forget."

"But if it's there, we know what it looks like," Fred said. "It's of two lovers standing by a table that's covered in carpet. He's in uniform, a cavalier. She, on the left of the painting, is in a window—you know the window Vermeer does, moves back in a diagonal, lets in a shaft of silvery golden light. The couple is looking toward a velvet cushion with a pearl necklace on it.

She's in a long dress, her hair bound up, looking down, in profile, her neck bare, accepting the gift."

Fred put his hand on the back of Molly's neck, stroked it. "The part of a woman the Japanese say is the sexiest part to expose, the base of the neck at the back. . . ."

"Never mind," Molly said. "I follow you perfectly."

Fred had no trouble seeing the colors of the painting, though he could be wrong. All he and Clayton had to work from was the drawing made at the Massachusetts Mechanics Hall over a hundred years before. In the painting as Fred envisioned it, the woman wore dusky yellow. The cavalier was in blue with a red sash. The Turkish rug was so dark you would have to study it to find the pattern. The wall was cream plaster, with that map pinned on it. There would have to be green somewhere—a subtle green, probably, in the meanderings on the map, and the velvet cushion maybe a deep green to show off the pearls and to prove that the color of the meanderings was green as well.

The downstairs café was filled with people, and the open door to the street let in cold springtime air. Fred kept his eye open in case he should spot, by some hideous accident, the face of the young man with the bike who had seen him last night, late, entering Smykal's building.

Fred said, "There are as many man-hours of labor in a Vermeer as there are in the Brooklyn Bridge. And as much engineering."

"If it's there."

"Well, yes. It's why Clay's willing to buy the picture like an expensive Heade. At least he'll have the Heade, then, which he says isn't that bad, though I don't agree."

"What I really don't understand is," Molly said, "suppose he gets the Heade, then what?"

Fred stretched his legs, his big feet extending toward a neighboring table where three old ladies sat with a single man around a table made for two. A few cars passed outside.

"Suppose we get the Heade," Fred said. "I do the bidding, obviously. Clayton doesn't bid. Clay won't even go to the auction. I bring it back to your place. We stash it in the bedroom closet."

"Jesus! Fifty million?"

"Just a picture. Then when it's convenient I drive it to Clayton's and we look it over together, Clay and I. Clay picks it up, looks at it from every angle, holding it out in front of him and tipping it to get the raking light.

"You know how aerial photographs taken when the sun is low, in the morning, will show old earthworks in farmland?

"So we'll look to see if there's any sign of the underpainting. But there isn't. Clay would have seen that this afternoon, when he went to the preview with Albert Finn, and he didn't mention it. The lack of visible underpainting doesn't mean anything, though, since Vermeer painted very smooth, and the Heade is done with unusually heavy impasto. Heade would have known that oil paint gets more transparent with time and allows underpainting to show through. He wouldn't want lines from the Vermeer to bounce out later and spoil his haystacks."

"Gotcha," said Molly, and she started tickling at the ice in the bottom of her glass. "Get to the part I don't know."

"Anyway, then Clayton calls Higginson and says, 'Guess what, I bought the Heade,' and Higginson says either 'I'll tell the boss when he calls; he's in Japan,' or 'Why would you want that?' The conversation results in Clayton's being invited over to look at the thing with Higginson under the museum's machines."

"And little Fred comes along," said Molly. "Because Clayton doesn't pick things up. Go on."

"If there is an older painting under there, you can adjust your levels of penetration to find it. An X ray will pick out the metals in the whites, and that gives you a starting outline of the picture underneath."

"So," said Molly. "Say you don't draw a blank at that point, and there's the Vermeer. First Higginson has a fit. Then what?"

"We take it to Roberto, and Roberto tests a corner. It will be tricky because the Heade is old. Oil paint gets harder over time, and the harder it is, the more resistant it'll be to solvents. But that makes the Vermeer, in theory, two centuries harder than the Heade. What amazes us both, incidentally, if anyone did examine the painting seriously, is that nobody noticed the age of the canvas. You can see the fabric when you look at the back, and it is entirely different from what Heade should have worked on. One thing Clay said—we had about three minutes to talk behind Isabella's big arras, the one covered with ducks near the punch—if it isn't a Vermeer under there, it's something else. Something old and Flemish. It's like a Victorian church built on Roman foundations."

"So," Molly said, her green eyes burning. She was excited now because it sounded as if there had to be something there.

"After that it gets technical, and you'd have to talk to Roberto. But if there's another painting underneath, Roberto will find it. And let's hope it wasn't abused before Heade covered it up. We'll hope also that a good layer of dirty varnish gave it a cushion to protect it from Heade's brush. That would make it easier to separate, too. For all I know, Roberto can slip a solvent between layers and float the Heade right off so we'll have them both. What will dissolve the varnish in its layer might not get through to the paint on either side if there's enough of a buildup of greasy candle smoke and dirt to insulate it.

"A painting works in layers, like a cake. If you cut it in half and looked at the layers, you'd start at the bottom, with the canvas. Then there's the ground to make the cloth stable—that should be rabbit-skin glue on a Vermeer. Then maybe a layer of color. Then the underpainting, drawn with paint. Vermeer, though—you get this in Chris Norgren's book, an obscure one, but Clay swears by it; I think it sold about five copies, and Clay bought one of them, *Jan van der Meer van Delft*—Vermeer didn't draw on his canvases. His forms are seen in color, not in line. Then the painting itself, done in stages, glazes, over a long period of time. Months. Then a layer of varnish. Then dirt. Then two hundred years of new layers of dirt and varnish, and possibly somebody now and again painted on improvements. Films of smoke. And then the Heade, the icing, covered with a lot of Apthorp dust. Thank God they're selling it in estate condition and haven't cleaned it. That could have given away the whole show right there. And thank God Higginson's boss is in Japan. He'd look at the painting, into it, and not just see himself in it, as Higginson likely did—everything in the world being his mirror.

"Whatever happens, if what we suspect turns out to be likely, after we do the tests, there'll be a committee of conservators sitting around this picture for a year just thinking about it, like diamond cutters around the Hope diamond before a single blow is struck."

They tiptoed into the house late. The kids were watching *Saturday Night Live*.

"Come on, herm," Molly whispered in Fred's ear, and leered. "Help peel me out of my basic black."

9

The blossoms of Molly's pear tree tapped at the window. That side of the house got the sun early, so you woke to the sound of bees.

Molly was shaking Fred, alarmed.

"That man's dead," she said.

"What man?"

"The one you told me about, where the nude came from—the one who still owes Clayton Reed a letter—Smykal. Henry Smykal."

Fred woke up.

"It sounds awful," Molly said. "God, Fred. We saw it. That was the fuss on Turbridge Street."

Her yellow robe flapped. She was holding the front page of the newspaper. Fred smelled bacon.

He smelled Smykal's apartment, the old bacon-fat smell, the dust and cigar smoke; saw the hot lights behind Smykal's head; felt the pressure of Smykal's door against his toes. Saw the caked blood around Smykal and the depressed slack in the side of his head.

"I know," Fred said. "Sorry about this, Molly."

"You *know*?" Molly stared at him, stunned, going white, trembling.

"Let me get Clay on the phone," Fred said, reaching across Molly's bed toward the table on her side where the phone was. He looked up into her staring face.

"What do you mean, 'I know'?" Molly yelled, flushing and then going gray. Fred could see some of the awful thoughts that were pressing against her.

"When I went back to get that letter," Fred said, "he was dead. It's more complex than that, though, since I went twice, talked to him the first time and found him dead the second. I elected to leave the body, saying nothing. I didn't tell you because I didn't want you either to take my part or not to. Still, I'm sorry to bring this with me to your bed."

Molly dropped the newspaper and left the room.

Fred rushed through the article. One of the tenants in the building had Smykal's key, had been asked to come in sometimes and feed the cat (what cat?), had entered Saturday night and seen the body lying in its large, pooled scabs, and had called 911. The police weren't giving out information, but the reporter had found a willing bystander who'd seen the bloody mess. Smykal would have been happy about one thing: he was described as a "Cambridge artist."

Fred smelled the bacon cooking downstairs. With great reluctance, he dialed Clay and got no answer.

"My God," Molly said when Fred came into the kitchen. "What did you think I was going to do, tattle-tale on you?"

She was angry, and crying, as well as burning the bacon, standing in the middle of her kitchen and wringing her hands. "What am I, Fred? Someone to play with, for God's sake? The bacon's burning." She went to tend to it.

77

"Molly, I'm not going to invite you to join me in a crime."

"All the time, over coffee at Pamplona, talking about Heade and Vermeer—and after—the whole time, you were hiding what you knew. That filthy thing. Horrible thing."

"That's true," Fred said. Molly had coffee on the stove. He put some in a mug.

"Again the bold hunter stands between his little woman and the world," Molly said. "It's why so many little women think the world looks like a man's back."

Fred said, "You tell me I have a nice back."

Molly turned on him furiously. "Yes. And I can read the scars on it as well, which we seem to agree never to speak about. Another of your secrets. For God's sake, whatever your wonderful mysterious past is, I know you, Fred. You'll do the decent thing. You used the word *elected*? Listen, Fred. I 'elected' to accept you as a companion. That's a risk I freely take. It's faith. It's risk.

"So have some faith in me. Take a risk yourself."

Molly opened the kitchen door to the backyard. The air was refreshed by last night's rain, which the bees disturbed among the pear blossoms. It was eight-thirty. The backyard glowed with spring promise. There was still ivy under Molly's maple tree; Fred hadn't used it all making his wreath. You could feel Spy Pond not far away, though you couldn't see it. Sea gulls wheeled overhead, and crows. It was cold, with bright sun twisting fronds of vapor through the damp yard. Fred followed Molly out, and they stood drinking coffee while Fred recounted what had happened Friday night.

"You'll have to tell them," Molly said. "You were there. Someone saw you. You did nothing wrong, but they'll think you did if you don't report it, if you don't talk to them."

"Clayton was there, too, earlier," Fred said. "That makes the situation more complex."

Molly said, "People will see—people who knew him—that the picture's missing. They'll assume you killed him and stole the painting."

Fred said, "Maybe. But the killing wasn't about the painting. That's coincidence."

"I didn't see how he died," Molly said. "The paper said 'by violence.'"

"They don't tell you," Fred said. "Until they can get the official word. He was pounded to death. With a hammer."

"How horrible," Molly said.

Fred nodded. The man had been horrible also, but maybe not as horrible as his death. "He was pathetic," Fred said. "His place smelled bad. He looked like one of those losers who can't keep a friend, can't finish anything, be anybody. He was doing pornography. As well as cocaine. I hate bringing you this, Molly, but there you are. Probably it's a simple thing; maybe someone discovered that he had Clay's money. Then it wouldn't matter who he was or what he was doing."

Molly said, "You didn't tell me about the pornography."

"Sorry," Fred said. "I'm taking first things first."

Molly said, "If he was involved in pornography, it's another story. Pornography can mean organized crime. The people involved in that stuff could have any number of reasons to kill someone."

"I don't know," Fred said. "When we were little boys and girls, maybe, but now? It's common as popcorn."

"I hate your being seen there, Fred," Molly said. "You're no picnic to look at. People remember you." She began tidying the place under the maple tree where Fred had gathered ivy the night before.

"He had other people in there when I first tried to get in," Fred said. "At least one voice, a woman's. Smykal was 'filming.' But there was no sign of that activity when I found him. That's nagging me."

"So," Molly said, straightening up and brushing crumbs of dirt off her hands. "What do you plan to do with the situation?"

"Nothing until I talk to Clay, who doesn't answer his phone."

Clayton appeared at the side gate. He was wearing a blue suit for this Sunday morning, with a white shirt and a sedate necktie. An orange blossom flourished in his buttonhole. He was ready for a wedding. Fred opened the gate for him.

"Yes," said Clay, looking at both of them. "I have seen the newspaper. The matter of Henry Smykal has lost its simplicity. You did not kill him, Fred?"

Clayton was just asking.

This was only the second time Clay had come to Molly's house. The first was when Molly had made Fred invite him to a Christmas party a year back. It had not been a success. Ophelia had been there—part of Molly's plan. She and Clayton had not got along, but only Clay had realized it, Ophelia being more of an optimist.

"No coffee," Clay said, spurning the cup Molly offered automatically. "I do not require stimulants. The garden's beautiful."

Clayton was a gentleman. He apologized for coming around back. He hadn't wanted to wake anyone by knocking. He thanked Molly for her efforts the previous night and asked after the children.

"They'll sleep till noon if we let 'em," Molly said. "Today we'll let 'em."

10

Fred said, "You paid Smykal cash?"

Clayton and Fred sat in the yard in folding chairs while Molly stood in her kitchen doorway in the yellow terry wrapper Fred had given her, holding her coffee mug, from which the steam had long since stopped rising.

Clay made an expression of distaste. "The man said cash was the only form of payment he would consider. He could find someone else if I was not interested. He gave me three hours. Bluff, of course. But I didn't want him to try. I immediately cashed a check, came back, gave him cash, took the letter, as I thought, and arranged that you would pick up the painting an hour later."

"Did Smykal understand what he was selling you?"

"He did and he didn't. I told him enough to make my interest reasonable. Of course not. He knew basically what it was. He knew what he wanted for it."

Clay was stalling.

"Look," Fred said. "I have to know, is there anything to show you were in that apartment?"

"If Smykal made notes, he didn't have my name. It's obvious he wanted to keep our transaction secret. Let them look all they want for Arthur Arthurian."

"How did you find the man?" Fred asked. "What's the connection? How did you locate the painting of Conchita Hill there? From the mark on the wall, he'd had it a long time. It's dangerous to keep secrets now, Clay. Can someone follow this project back to us?"

"There is a remote chance."

Molly's hiss of indrawn breath was clear as a kettle reaching the boil.

"I think not. I think it is remote enough," Clayton said. He didn't want Fred to learn his methods.

"Clay, there are times to play games, and games to be played, and games I don't need and won't play. I'm in this, too. Come off it."

"Sarah Chatterjee at the Genealogical Society. She did the research under my guidance," Clay said, smirking until he recalled the corpse. "Conchita Hill married Simon Goodson. In Baltimore. They had a daughter, Sarah, who married Franklin Arbuthnot. In Cleveland. Their daughter Annie married Henry Smykal. Senior. Of Somerville, Mass.," Clayton recited from memory. He would have it all down on file cards as well, translated from Miss Chatterjee's report. She'd have told him where everyone had gone to school, the names and numbers of offspring, and the rest.

At least Clay hadn't discovered it himself, Fred thought.

"And Miss Chatterjee is . . . ?" Molly asked.

"In Bengal for six months, visiting her mother," Clay said. "That is our good fortune, I imagine."

"Therefore the woman in the painting," Molly said, counting

on her fingers, "was Smykal's great-grandma. In that nasty place."

"I should probably tell you," Fred said, "that I found Smykal's body and concealed the fact."

Clay looked at Fred, thinking. He stroked the Unitarian stripes on his necktie, settling them down. "I'm glad to hear that, Fred," he said. "Therefore you had a chance to search for the letter."

His look turned expectant.

Fred saw Molly start and open her mouth to say something, and then close it again, tight, saying it to herself through clenched teeth instead.

"It wasn't to be found," Fred said. "Not in the time I had."

"A shame," Clay said, still solicitous of number one. "I want that letter. It has to be somewhere. Between the time I saw it in his hand and when I brought the money to him, on Friday, he had three hours. Where did he put it? You don't suppose you could go back now . . ." His voice trailed off in response to Fred's snort of incredulity. "No, I suppose they have the apartment sealed or whatever it is they do."

"If you gentlemen will excuse me," Molly said, "I'll get dressed."

She slammed into the house.

Clayton was badly spooked. Fred had been right to tell him nothing. A murder happening near enough to the both of them for them to feel the wind of it—that was alarming. "A rude reminder of mortality," Clay called it. They were sitting in the aluminum chairs, which Clay also found, it seemed, a rude reminder of mortality, to judge from the way he crossed his grasshopper legs and fidgeted.

They looked the situation over. In the course of twenty-four hours, it appeared, they might well have lost, simultaneously on two separate fronts, their advantage on the Heade and the hope of completing the provenance on the recumbent Conchita Hill.

As far as Smykal's murder was concerned, what was their exposure? If either Clayton or Fred had been seen at Smykal's apartment, it was by someone who did not know them.

"But can we keep out of it? Our fingerprints will be there," Clay said. "I imagine there's something in that business of fingerprints?"

"They have to compare them to something," Fred said. "Fingerprints without reference mean nothing, like the exhibition history of a picture you can't find. But we could volunteer, tell them we were in the apartment. If we don't, we set a record that looks like guilty knowledge. If they're going to find out anyway, it's better we tell them now than they find out later."

"How would that help me get that letter?" Clay asked. "I keep recalling the way he strove to rub my face in his photographs! Can I want my associates and friends to think of me in such a place? Still . . . how do we get the letter, with who knows what storms washing around the place? You have many skills, Fred. I am sure you can manage something. It's too bad about Smykal—a tragedy from his point of view. But for us, as you keep pointing out, Fred, the important thing's the Heade. He's clever, and he has great power," Clay said, standing and walking toward Molly's back fence.

It took Fred a minute to understand. He realized that the Vermeer had filled Clayton's horizon again; he was talking about Albert Finn.

"We know Finn's in the game since he's staying in town." Clay looked at his watch. "I have a wedding in Manchester I must get to, Fred. I conclude we should be guided by your judgment, which you have described so vividly using the metaphor of lying in ambush in a swamp. We must lie low and still, saying nothing while we watch carefully ourselves. Let us not allow them to see the water shake."

Fred agreed that they might as well keep silent at least until the auction was played out, acknowledging to himself what Clay did not seem to recognize, that any risk being undertaken according to this plan was primarily Fred's.

In the meantime, Clay suggested that "since we are citizens, and if you can do so without risking the possibility of my painting's being confiscated from me as evidence in a crime," Fred might as well use his many skills to pluck the letter safe and well from this flaming disaster, without letting himself be noticed.

"And if I'm caught, say I don't know you?" Fred shot at Clayton as he turned to go.

Clay pretended not to hear. Ever the gentleman, he said, walking out the side gate to the front of the house, "Please thank the lady Molly for her hospitality, and apologize for me again for my breaking into the tranquillity of your Sunday morning.

"I'll understand if you don't come in tomorrow," he added. "Call. I may have an idea. You may also have something to tell me. I agree with your sage advice, though. Don't lose track of our primary objective: the Heade. Whatever you do, don't ruffle the surface."

Clayton paused in thought, the idea struggling for completion. "What's ruffled will not reflect," he told Fred.

11

There was discussion before it was decided what Fred would do. Molly had changed clothes, the yellow robe supplanted now by pink shorts and one of Fred's white shirts, and they sat at the table in her kitchen.

"It's not the desert. Someone must have seen you come out of the building with that painting," Molly said.

"It was wrapped. It was the day before Smykal was found," Fred said.

"You're damn right. Which you know because you were there just before he got killed, and then right after. Jesus, Fred, you were practically living at that place."

"Smykal was expecting someone," Fred said. "He buzzed the door lock open without using the intercom. He said, when he saw me, 'You're not him.'"

"Who was 'him'?" Molly asked.

"I may have to find out," Fred said.

If they had been married, Molly would have something to say about the situation he was in. And Fred would have to say something like, "Trust me." This present arrangement was more awkward since it didn't provide Molly any legal right to worry.

"Just don't be an asshole," Molly said, taking his arm and giving it a rough shake.

Fred didn't say, "Trust me."

"And don't pretend you don't know what I mean," Molly said. "Someone's been killed. So you're going to poke a stick into a dark place where you can disturb somebody who will kill. You, for example."

They both knew that Molly was thinking about Fred's scars, which looked too amateur to be from surgery: the slash marks on his chest and upper arm and the one along his jawbone on the right side; the puckered, light circle on the inside front of his left shoulder, matched by the larger one from the exit wound on the back.

Fred wouldn't talk about them. When she'd asked him, early on, what they were from, he would only say, "I was acquiring life skills." Then he would talk about artists, people like Caravaggio, who had died violently.

Now he said, "Art itself is violent, like hanging steel girders three hundred feet up, or making anything, really; like breaking eggs. Art requires philosophical defiance as well as the contest with material. The artist's eye is grasping, transforming, destroying. Clay finds art peaceful and can't feel the painter's hot breath as he gets down to the short strokes. There is nothing peaceful in a work of art, any more than the force of peace prevents the moon from crashing into the earth."

Fred talked about this with Molly. He would talk pictures, she would recall his scars, and they mixed in her mind, the pictures and the scars.

Fred added, "Besides, I'm interested."

He began prowling the backyard. He realized that the yard wouldn't long survive that, so he put on shorts and a T-shirt and went for a run by the pond to clear his mind or give it distraction. It was midmorning, already getting warm. Dogs were out, and birds. The sky was blue and clear.

Fred hadn't known that Molly was running, too. They bumped into each other three blocks from the house, both of them sweating, coming from their opposite directions.

They got back to the house and sat on the front steps, cooling off.

"It's true," Molly said. "We are interested."

Fred stretched and turned to go into the house. He showered in the creaky little bathroom all of them shared on the second floor. He dressed for a warm day, putting on a blue polo shirt without the alligator, khakis, and once-white sneakers.

Sam's door was closed. Terry was waking as he passed her open door. He stepped in for a visit. She kept her room in a sweet rumpus. She collected rocks, which tended to get mixed in with homework she forgot to deliver; she slept only in the upper third of her bed so there would be room for the rocks at the foot.

"Sit down," she said, offering him the rock pile.

"Thank you." Fred sat. "Your bed reminds me of the Yukon."

"Thank you," Terry said. "Fred, can you teach me to throw a curveball?"

"I'll show you how it's done," Fred said, "but your coach may want you to wait till your hand is bigger."

Terry followed him downstairs, still in her ragged blue pajamas, and made a lunge for the most disposable parts of the paper in time to provoke a confrontation with Sam, who came in right behind them, still dressed in yesterday's T-shirt and jeans.

Fred did what he could to postpone bloodshed, found Molly still sitting on the front step, gave her a squeeze, told her, "Don't worry, I won't be recognized. Yesterday I was wearing a coat and tie," and took the car into Cambridge to poke around.

Cambridge on a late Sunday morning in spring, warm, not raining, around Harvard Square, was filled with people who were somewhere else. Many were in Paris. They sat at tables next to the traffic and consumed coffee and croissants served to them by kids required by the management to wear berets. But the kids smiled at you, so you didn't get that Paris feeling.

Some people were in New York. In jogging outfits, jangling with jewelry, accompanied by designer dogs, they ran or biked or roller-skated through the streets and on the sidewalks.

Some folks were attending church in Armenia. Some were at a Baptist wedding in Atlanta.

Some were in Southeast Asia still. Even home, they hadn't been able to get home. They lived on vents by the river and panhandled, trying to score the comparative sanity of being drunk to take the place of the demon-haunted nightmares they otherwise frequented.

The parks were full of people. The bookstores, at least half of them, were open, but the places to buy earrings were still closed.

Harvard's buildings loomed, dorms and offices strangling the village that had been here once, where cows had walked down to drink out of the river. Long afterwards, in the same village— now a city—a generation of young people had heard the martyred ghost of JFK urging them to ask what they could do for their country, and some, like Fred, had tossed everything and talked to the smiling suits and opted for a life of patriotic travel and intrigue.

Fred parked near Turbridge Street. The sun was bright enough for him to keep his sunglasses on. Half the people were wearing shades anyway. When he was here before he'd been wearing his working clothes: the white shirt, jacket, and tie. He could sit at a table on the sidewalk on Mass. Avenue, drink coffee, and stare up Turbridge Street, seeing what was going on and expecting not to be recognized. A cop car idled across the street from the café. The cops were drinking coffee, not going anywhere, now and then glancing up Turbridge Street.

Fred bought a Sunday paper and watched. A man he knew only as Teddy, a damaged veteran now living in the Charlestown house, sidled by and looked a question at Fred, asking, Can I know you? Can you know me? He was six-two, rail-thin, and dressed in odd scraps of uniform and mismatched sneakers, his lean face twisted and grizzled with a week's beard.

"Sit down," Fred said, and he went inside and bought Teddy a cup of coffee.

Teddy had come to the place in Charlestown after Fred left it. Teddy was the only name he would give. He sometimes was absent for long periods. He'd got the address from some buddies—nobody knew who—and he wouldn't talk, except about baseball.

Fred believed that Teddy was from Atlanta, though his skin was so black you would have thought him straight Senegalese or Nigerian.

"How you doin'?" Teddy said. "We don't see you."

"Well, no," Fred said. "How you been?"

Teddy closed his mouth tight and shook his head. He was not saying. He looked carefully at the surface of his coffee and left it on the table, untasted.

"You be back, you know," Teddy said. "You hear me, Fred?"

"I reckon," Fred said.

"We all come back, don't we?" Teddy said.

"Drink your coffee while it's hot, Teddy," Fred said.

"Later," Teddy said.

Teddy looked more frantic, less focused, than when Fred had last seen him. He stood up. He smelled a great deal when he moved, as anyone would.

"You staying over at the place?" Fred asked, meaning the place in Charlestown. "You doing okay? Need anything?"

Teddy shook his head, not saying. He was looking in the pocket of his desert camouflage pants for money. He couldn't take anything without paying for it. He found a scrap of foil; it looked like something torn off a chewing-gum wrapper. He laid it beside the coffee he hadn't tasted.

"Don't be a stranger," Fred said as Teddy walked off.

He had some of Teddy's coffee.

He looked up Turbridge Street and speculated. People had been in the apartment. He'd heard a woman's voice. The man with the bike, coming out, letting Fred in—what floor had he been coming from? At 3:30 A.M.? Smykal had been expecting another person. A him. Whoever had been with him ought to have a useful insight into what had happened.

12

Fred drove back to Arlington again on Sunday afternoon and slowed down in front of the house, and there was Sam. He'd combed his hair and put on clean shorts, shirt, and absolutely the most expensive and up-to-the-minute pump-up sneakers in the known world, which Fred had bought him recently. He wore the sneakers seldom, hoping they would last. Fred had forgotten the date he'd made yesterday to make up for canceling his attendance at Sam's game by spending time alone with him this afternoon. He felt terrible seeing Sam's hopeful face at the screen, trying to look cool and show it didn't make any difference that he'd been forgotten.

Sam didn't comb his hair to go to school or anywhere. It was a big honor that Fred had almost blown.

"Hey, buddy," Fred shouted. Sam was coming out of the house slowly, the Frisbee behind him in case it wasn't going to happen. "Am I late?"

"Five minutes," Sam said. He smiled.

"Sorry. I'll go inside and tell your mom we're moving out."

The plan was to do some serious study of the Frisbee. Fred had promised to teach Sam tricks he'd learned back when he thought he might pitch for the Dodgers, before he started doing something else.

Molly, reading the real-estate section in the backyard, glanced up and said, "I would have killed you if you'd forgotten."

Fred made the expression that indicated he wasn't someone who would forget, and he thanked Molly's higher power that he hadn't screwed up.

"I called Walter and Dee's house," Molly said. She was looking worried. "I talked to Dee. I asked them to come by for tea this afternoon. We got talking. She mentioned the murder-robbery in Cambridge yesterday."

"Murder-robbery."

"It's what she called it," Molly said.

Walter was the head librarian at Cambridge Public Library. He'd been at the public high school, in Molly's class, so they were old friends. His wife, Dee, was on the police force in Cambridge—in traffic and parking, but she got around, heard things.

Molly kept track of what was happening in Cambridge, and between her mother (who lived there still), her work, and a large network of friends with telephones, there wasn't much of significance that she missed.

"People who lived in the building said they noticed a painting missing," Molly said. "I thought it couldn't hurt to get a worm's-eye view of what the thinking is at headquarters."

Fred nodded. It was a good idea.

"They're coming at five with the kids, and it could turn into supper, if that's good for you, Fred."

"Thanks. Yes."

"Dee might know other things that aren't in the paper."

"It's good thinking, Molly."

Sam appeared at the side gate, and Fred went to join him.

Fred worked with Sam on the Frisbee in a park near the pond. He liked Sam and wanted his confidence. He'd thought, when he started seeing Molly, that there was one string with him on one end and her on the other, and that she held other strings leading to Sam and Terry. He could keep track of one string, the one between himself and Molly.

But what happened after he moved in was that he noticed one day that he was attached to each of the children, each had a string of his or her own to pull. Fred was surprised at how much he liked that and how lousy it made him feel when something went wrong between them. The kids could just look at you and make you feel like a bastard or a hero.

With Sam it was especially important since he had been the man of the house until this buffalo with scars and big feet moved in and started sleeping with his mother. Fred told Sam he was proud of a man who was prepared to protect his mom. Sam should tell him if anything felt wrong about his being there, because he didn't want to intrude between him and Terry and their mom. That's what Fred said. But he was the one who crawled in bed with her, whose shirt she was wearing in her backyard, reading the paper.

"We can do similar tricks with your geography homework sometime, if you want," Fred suggested on the way home. On the subject of geography Sam did not take up the invitation.

From Walter and Dee—from Dee, really, since it was she who had the connection—they learned not much over iced tea that changed to beer and finally was joined by hotdogs and the works.

Walter was from one of the old families of Cambridge. Dee

was local, too, but descended from more recent, Italian, immigrants.

Dee was a lot of fun; Walter was more reserved. He and Fred had taken time getting used to one another. Fred had thought at first that the fact that Walter was black was making him expect the normal white patronizing hostility, and that he was hanging back, waiting to be offended. But that was Fred's mistake, not Walter's. After they'd shadow-boxed for a year or so on the occasions when they met, Fred came to what should have been the easiest conclusion from the start: Walter was simply diffident and courtly, almost Old World, more comfortable with books than with people. So they'd talk books.

Walter was large and handsome and dressed, like Fred, in the Sunday leisure uniform of khaki twill and polo shirt. Walter's was pink. Dee was little and fast-moving, with black hair and notable breasts that were covered with flowers in a flimsy dress with ruffles. She'd come barefoot. She was as out of uniform as she could manage without being arrested. She'd kissed Fred, reaching up to do it, when he and Sam arrived.

Molly was good at showing excited interest in the Cambridge killing since it wasn't feigned. She stirred the pot as hard as she could without asking straight out or dropping any hint as to why they needed to know about it. What was known did not go far beyond what Fred had gathered in his own quick survey; it was the working theories of the investigators that he wanted to know.

The initial hypotheses confirmed that Smykal had been killed on purpose, with a hammer, beaten to death. Nobody in the building had reported a man screaming.

Dee put mustard on a hotdog with deliberate care and said, "The man was into pornography something heavy, which I don't like, and the detectives are having trouble holding on to the evidence. My fellow cops keep running away with samples. They just take it off the walls. The people I work with!

"I saw some. To me it looks gloomy," Dee said. "I guess it's lucky for the female race, but what men see in women's genitalia, I can't for the life of me—" She looked sideways at Walter, who kept his own counsel.

Dee went on. "A downstairs neighbor who was inside once, to talk about a leak from Smykal's toilet, noticed that a big painting was gone. It looked like an Old Master, the neighbor said. A nude woman. Par for the course. Smykal said it was his grandmother or something. Hah! A woman painted with nothing on. That was no grandmother, A, the neighbor said, and, two, that was a masterpiece, mark his words.

"There is a big mark where the painting's missing from the wall—the nude, the so-called grandmother. That should interest you, Fred."

Molly looked at Fred. A general pause focused on him. The cops had undone the evidence he'd planted.

"I don't know," Fred said. "There's not much future in stealing a painting, Dee. Art is harder than cars or TV sets, since there's only one of it and it looks only like itself. How do you sell it? You might run off with a painting and then find a picture of it the next day in the paper listed as missing, then where would you be?"

Walter had brought the Japanese beer he favored, and opening another for himself, and one for Fred, he told them, "The theory is that the painting is an important masterpiece, stolen for one of those drug lords, secret collectors, who keep a private collection hidden in the basement."

"The invisible Dr. No," Dee said. "The same one who masterminds all the museum thefts they never figure out. Like the one at the Gardner, you recall?"

"Which is a lot of horseshit," Fred said.

"Which, as I was saying to Dee earlier, is a proposition that has never been justified," said Walter. "Or, as you would put it, a lot of horseshit." He smiled at Fred, not born to it but willing and able to speak the language of tea in Arlington when in Arlington.

"I would have thought, with a thing like that killing," Fred suggested, "the pornography—there might be drugs involved somewhere, you know?"

"I guess," Dee said. "Right now our people like the painting as the motive, though."

"It adds romance," Walter said. "Everyone likes romance, even detectives."

Molly turned the conversation in another direction. "It's what I say: a man living alone, he has a shorter life expectancy. Poor fellow. Did he have family?"

Not that Dee had heard of. Nor friends. Only certain people in the building who were used to seeing him.

"Someone to clean for him?" Molly asked.

Fred exploded with an involuntary guffaw that became a cough.

"It's only the day after, and I haven't heard anything since yesterday evening, when some of the officers were talking in the hall," Dee said. "Mostly about what they had taken for themselves, showing each other stuff under their uniform jackets, like seven-year-old kids with a *Playboy*. What do I know? One officer said the victim's apartment made him think of his teenager's bedroom, but with a lot more blood."

Walter and Dee had brought their three children, two girls and a boy who fit right around and between Molly's two, so things went well. Fred and Dee tossed the Frisbee with Sam in the street, and it was late by the time everyone acknowledged that the kids had school in the morning.

Fred put a call in to Clay and failed to get a response. He had tried late in the afternoon also, thinking it prudent that they keep in touch in case of developments on Turbridge Street.

Evidently Clayton's North Shore wedding was progressing. Fred hadn't been happy to hear of the police detectives' concentration on Smykal's missing painting, but there wasn't much to do about that beyond sleeping on it . . .

. . . with Molly's knees and feet and elbows getting into the act, her curly hair smelling of smoky hotdog and marshmallow, the clock ticking in this strange woman's bedroom, and birds too smart to sleep making consultative noises outside. The birds were agreeing with Fred that you can't always think and sleep at the same time.

At about four in the morning Fred was thinking of the gun he kept with his few possessions in Charlestown. He had begun to sweat, visiting with old deaths and terrors not related to his present predicament, and so he slipped out of Molly's bed and went to stand by her window, looking through her gauze curtains across the pear blossoms.

The air was cold on his naked body, and Arlington's black dark threatened to shift into swamp and jungle. His gut wrenched at the thought of allowing the man he was, if that included carrying his gun, into the place where Molly and the children slept.

"Wake up, Fred," Molly whispered urgently from the bed behind him, frightened and barely coming out of sleep. "There's a man in the room."

"It's me," Fred said.

"You all right? You want me to wake up and be with you?"

"No."

"Jesus, is this you sweating the bed?"

"Sorry," Fred said.

"I'm just impressed," Molly said, rolling over to sleep again.

13

By the time Fred was up and moving, having fallen asleep just as the birds were getting seriously into their new day, it was noon. Molly had gone to work. He called Clay and got no answer. Molly had left the paper on the table with the second-day article about Smykal marked. It was on the fourth page and added nothing to the piece of the day before, except to say that leads were being followed.

Being someone who preferred the direct approach, Fred was not happy that his own tangential involvement in Smykal's murder made it essential for him to lie low while he gathered information. What he couldn't do was bull into the apartment building on Turbridge Street, stand people in corners, and ask questions.

He made a breakfast of the picnic leftovers, then put on his working clothes—khakis, white shirt and tie, and tweed jacket— and went into Cambridge. The lunch crowd had been replaced by the afternoon coffee contingent when Fred settled in again at his sidewalk table. The clientele included kids coming out of the public high school next to Molly's library. Up Turbridge Street a cruiser was still dozing in front of Smykal's building, but there seemed to be no other relevant activity.

Fred tried Clay's number a few times and failed to get any answer. Clayton could be such a nitwit that he might take a notion to spend the night somewhere else. He might have taken a trip to the Grand Canyon. The man could be so upset that he wouldn't answer his own phone. It was unusual, though, for him not to let Fred know where he was. His was an organized soul. Fred wasn't happy about the prolonged silence at Clayton's end; it put a strain even on Clay's usual version of security. Because it was silence, it could be read as ominous.

Violence spreads. Like a virus or good slang, it becomes common currency. Sipping at the large coffee with which he was paying his rent on the sidewalk table, Fred realized how the logic of newspaper fiction worked at rumor in the back of his mind. Already one man had been killed in the immediate vicinity of the painting Fred had taken out of Turbridge Street.

Fred drove into Boston. The late afternoon had turned frankly cold. Unattached persons strolled up and down Charles Street, at the foot of Beacon Hill, beginning the evening's search either for an attachment not previously attempted or for something incredibly cute to eat, to complement the new haircut.

Clay's car, a golden Lexus, was in its spot. Fred pulled up beside it, relieved. That much of him had gotten home in one piece, at least.

He let himself into the office. The place was empty. Fred found one of Clay's index cards on the clear space he kept in the center of his desk; on it, in Clay's unmistakable semi-Greek printed hand, was the message, "Whistler. Copley."

That was Clay being inscrutable, using code.

Fred's first thought was, Well, then. So the painting of Conchita is by Whistler after all.

But then what sense did "Copley" make?

Fred wandered around his workspace, thinking, then went upstairs to look in Clayton's living quarters. He didn't go up there often, only when Clay asked him up for a drink after a long evening. They were most comfortable together when there was an issue between them regarding work, their shared interest in Clayton's passion.

Clay's living space was made comfortable with furnishings that Fred was sure had once been attached to the young lady, née Lucy Stillton, who looked out from the silver frame on the baby grand piano that was never played, at least not in Fred's hearing. The piano was draped with a Kashmir shawl. Clay's living area was lined with gilt side chairs, large Oriental pots, and armchairs upholstered in brocade. Some of the furnishings might have come over with the first of the pirate barons who started the American wing of the Stillton dynasty. Fred knew the paintings well and had participated in the care and acquisition of several of them. It was up here that one could most easily enjoy the company of Clayton Reed; here, surrounded by objects that he cared for, Clay seemed a whole person, even one who cared for other people.

Feeling an intruder, Fred looked into the rooms the next floor up. The bedroom where Clayton slept was so plain as to seem almost monastic. It was bare except for the single bed with brass headboard and footboard, a bureau, and a straight-backed chair. It was so ascetic after the refined opulence of the rest of the apartment that it seemed like Clayton's idea of a hair shirt.

Fred would never remark on it, but his guess was that this was Clayton's way of reinforcing the pleasure he took in his collection, and a way also for him to rest his eyes.

Fred looked into Clay's bathroom. His prizewinning collection of toilet articles was not in evidence. There was no need to look further.

Clayton had fled.

The enigmatic notice "Whistler. Copley" was doubtless designed to give Fred this information, revealing where he was and how to find him: a method so much more secure than calling him on the telephone.

Fred went back down to the office and sat at his desk. He stared at Clayton's note. Boston has a hundred things and offices and stores and institutions that proudly bear the name Copley. Dry cleaners and commercial groups. But Fred figured Clay for having sneaked away to one of the two hotels with that name: the Copley Plaza or the Copley Square. There was no Copley Whistler.

Fred called Molly. She'd be home and would have finished supper with the kids. She was not expecting him because he had remembered, before he left in the afternoon, to leave a note telling her not to expect him. He might not be home till late.

Fred could see Molly, finished in the kitchen, in her living room now, all blue and gray, not a pretentious puff in it, books lying around, the walls hung with photographs, mirrors, and posters. She'd have flowers in vases, hyacinths, making the room smell. Thinking of her there talking to him, from the luxury of her domestic simplicity, made his office feel dingy.

"Are you having any luck finding a track to start on?" Molly asked.

"Nothing looks promising at the moment. Clayton's run off. He's apparently staying at one of the Copleys. Copley Square, you may be sure."

"I know," Molly said. "He called me at the library to give you the message. He said he was calling from a pay phone because he thinks they might tap his line, or mine, and so he doesn't want to use either."

"Clay's not used to a life of crime," Fred said, picking up

the index card and beginning to shred it absently, by hand. "Because they *can* tap a phone doesn't mean they do or will. If Clay wants to divert suspicion from himself, it's a stupid move to start acting guilty, staying at a hotel several blocks from his perfectly good house."

"Listen," said Molly. "Tell Clay. Don't tell me. Are you coming back, or what hotel are you going to choose for yourself? Something in Saugus?"

"See you later. Stay awake, or I'll wake you."

"Listen," she said. "Stupid suggestion, but you don't think Clay's done something he really has to hide out for?"

"Don't think so," Fred said. "Really, I don't. He's sticking to his priorities. Number one is Clay. Clay wants the Heade. He wants to keep it simple: no calls, no interruptions. I'm going over there and interrupt."

Fred walked to the Copley Square Hotel. He got through the Boston version of grotesque opulence in the lobby and made inquiries at the desk, discovering that Mr. Whistler was registered in Room 314 and not answering his phone.

For the hell of it, Fred checked out the hotel restaurant, sweeping aside harpist and maître d' and a fleet of incipient waiters. He looked around the room, the chairs and people all done in velvet and shellac, the antique Musak on the harp perfectly matched, everything reaffirmed in the mirrors, and found Clayton behind a large menu lettered by hand in a script chosen to suggest refined complexity rather than comfort in dining.

Clay was still dressed for a wedding, as he had been Sunday morning—as he was every day. A small rose did its job in the buttonhole of his dark blue suit. His angular face was twitching over the choices parading before him. Fred's shadow crossed his menu.

"Ah, Fred. Will you join me?" he offered, looking up.

"I'm not sure this is a good idea," Fred said, sitting across from him on a frail chair speedily offered by a waiter.

"The chef is well recommended," Clay said.

"I mean running away from home," Fred said.

"It's too tense. I can't be where Albert Finn can find me," Clay said blandly. "So I moved. Moved out. Let them infer that I left town." He turned his attention back to the menu. "Will you dine, Fred?"

"I'll have a drink," Fred said. "You go on."

Fred wasn't in the mood to eat anything that took so many curls to write down.

Clay took his time choosing between the *Noisette farcie* and the *Farce noisettée. Sea bass mousquetaire. Abomination d'artichaut.*

Fred let Clay order while he looked the other way. Clay had to ask questions of the waiter, like a nervous king taking a particularly delicate crap. You really wanted to be somewhere else.

Fred didn't listen to what Clay was going to ingest. He ordered a large gin and bitters, "House brand."

These items of importance set aside, they talked.

The waiter bowed and delivered Clayton a kir, smirking as if he'd thought it up himself. Imagine having the wit to mix fruit syrup and white wine in a glass and charge five dollars for it.

Clayton sipped and nodded toward the expectant waiter. Waiter, energized by approbation, drifted back into the wings to undertake new triumphs.

"Also, if anyone should be looking for Arthurian," Clay continued, "then it's fortuitous that I am out of reach. Smykal may have told someone about my incognito visit. From the moment I saw him, I knew he'd be indiscreet. His own art was indiscreet, did you not think, Fred? He opened the door and I heard a voice say to me, immediately, Clayton Reed can't be here."

"It turns out that was a good decision. Was that the first you'd seen him? That Friday?" Fred asked.

"I stopped by Friday morning." Clay put into his mouth something the waiter had brought with his kir, which must be other than what it appeared to be: three dollops of goat shit on a cracker.

Every few minutes the waiter brought something new. They had to keep Clay from getting impatient, breaking furniture, while he waited for them to breed his salmon correctly, bring it up right, and send it to the best schools.

Clay went on, "I introduced myself and was invited in. He denied having any paintings by Conchita Hill, or ever having seen one. All he had left, he said, was that picture—which I had not been prepared for. I asked what it was. He showed me the letter. I told him I'd buy it and asked for a price. He gave me a price. He wanted cash. I went and got it. It was simple, surprisingly simple."

"Too simple," Fred said. "Except as it turned out. There are times, Clay, when you should do some heavy lifting."

"So you say now," Clay answered. "What he told me then was that he wished to make a photograph of the work, to keep as a memento. That being a blood relation of his, how could I refuse?"

He motioned toward a new arrival: rose petals mixed with cucumber and something almost white squirted on the cucumber.

"I'm all right," Fred said.

Fred had a respect for materials. He liked his food to look like food, not like a hat or a boat or a day at the races.

"How did he know what it was, a man like that? How did he know how much he wanted for it?" Fred asked. "Normally, in a situation like that, you don't get in and out so cleanly. You know, Clay, if a person has something like that painting, and you show interest, they right away get paranoid, thinking that if you want it at all it's because you're trying to cheat them. The more you're willing to pay, the more they're sure you want to cheat them."

14

Clay sipped impatiently at his kir while the harpist undertook her revenge on a Chopin prelude.

"I am aware of this, Fred," Clay said. "You request that they supply a figure they consider attractive, and they are stricken dumb. They had believed what they owned was worthless, or priceless."

"It's true? You asked him how much he wanted for the painting, and he just told you?"

"It did surprise me," Clay said.

Clay had now to attend to the wine steward, tasting the Vieux Château d'Antipape, an Avignon rosé, and pronouncing upon it.

"Once you alert them," Clayton said, "the truly unintelligent try to outsmart you. The less unintelligent cast out blindly into the world for appraisals. They run to auction houses and art dealers. They try to set up their own private bidding situation, in the course of which everyone sees the painting, the thing

gets shopped, the price—supposing the painting is truly interesting—fluctuates madly.

"Meanwhile, the owner gets flustered with hope, loses all
faith in the world, and puts the picture in a vault or, better, in
a basement, where it rots.

"By this time my own interest has flagged. The owner must
be left to the tender seduction of the bow-tied functionary from
the auction house, who is the sad result of the ill-advised cross
between mortician and old family retainer."

The waiter presented Clay with his opening course, an *aspect
of saumon fumé d'ambre gris*. Everyone bowed, except the fish,
which was beset by outsize capers split and stuffed. It looked
as if it had died of infected tumors.

Clay nodded. The waiter withdrew. Clay raised his fork.

The simplest way to get a painting away from a Smykal—
and numerous people used this technique well—was to wear
old clothes: the pay-me-and-I'll-clean-your-basement-or-attic,
lady, haul-the-crap-away approach.

Arthurian had done this, but in fancy dress.

"Yes," Clayton said. "I did think it was odd when Smykal
volunteered a price and seemed so comfortable dealing with
me. Of course, I had attacked his defenses by admiring his own
work—the man thought of himself as an artist, remember—
and I also encouraged him to believe I might accept his invitation
to slither in his footsteps. That disarmed him further.

"In the meantime I asked him, 'Since you don't have any
paintings by Conchita Hill herself, will you permit me to purchase the nude?' My excitement at finding her represented in
a painting of such quality was unfeigned. I asked for a price
and he answered straight out, 'Thirty thousand. Cash.' "

"Jesus," Fred said.

That was a solid chunk of money for an unsigned painting.
No wonder Clay wanted the letter. The artist must indeed be
someone of interest. "And here," Clayton said, "I think I did

something that helped settle any reservations Mr. Smykal might have been harboring. I asked if he'd accept three thousand more and let me take the frame also.

"Naturally the price he'd given me included the frame, but he didn't blink. He took the extra three thousand."

Buying and selling are like judo. The winner must be alert to what direction the weight and position of the opponent are tending in and supply the extra touch or feint to allow him to let both weight and movement carry him down. The victor is the combatant who takes best advantage of gravity. Your own weight fells you.

"Will you accept a glass of this wine?" Clay asked.

"Thanks, Clay. I'm driving back to Arlington, so I'll pass."

"Here's what I want you to do," Clay said, business now. "Concentrate on the Heade. This is Monday. The sale is Saturday. Our problem will be Finn."

"Unless Buddy Mangan is a player," Fred reminded him.

"Brute force we can deal with," Clay said. "What worries me is Finn's finesse—and the fact that we can't guess what that devious man might know. It was the lady Molly who reminded me. On the phone, when I called her, at around noon. Assume the worst. I must think about how Finn works and who his informant is."

Fred began shredding a roll for something to do.

Clay went on, "Suppose the informant is a past or present student, a scholar with time for research, endless and grueling. 'Why don't you look at the graduate students?' Molly asked. 'Find out who in the neighborhood is working with Heade, or with Vermeer. Start from the bottom and work up.'"

The way Clay said it, as he began to separate the leaved flesh of his fish, made Fred recall those nature films where the lioness runs the warthog down, getting her first good hold under the tail.

"For the moment, let us keep what advantage we can in the

game," Clay said. "Let us be elastic, versatile. We can change plans where indicated. Let the police do what they do about the Cambridge misadventure. We will respond as needed, doing what we do, if need be."

"Right." Fred rose from the table. As far as the Cambridge "misadventure" was concerned, he would do what he thought was best and safest for all concerned, regardless of Clay's directions.

"Give me a call tomorrow," Clay said. "I'll ask around, too. I'll call a friend at BU who knows who's doing what. Why don't you check Harvard? Go on to Brown if you like. Talk to the guy. Who is it? That book on Mondrian? It can't hurt, as long as we are absurdly careful and—"

"Other than that . . . ," Fred said, standing and watching the servitors become edgy about the large man standing, looking like a potential threat. "Other than that, Clay, you'd best be thinking about what our position is going to be, financially speaking, especially if Buddy Mangan's got his eye on it. As a Heade, the estimate is eighty to a hundred K, already too much for that picture. I'll need to know how far to go on the thing, what the cushion of risk is between what the Heade is worth to you as such and what it might be worth if it's what you hope."

"Not here," Clay whispered. "Don't talk amounts." He looked down, blushing, as if discovering himself unexpectedly, and publicly, naked.

There was plenty of room between tables for private conversation.

"You'll need to think about it," Fred said.

He walked out past the bowing help. He tipped the startled harpist, who was taking a breather at the bar. Her long black strapless gown packaged a cleavage that would easily accommodate five bucks.

15

Molly was awake, reading in her living room. The kids were in bed. School tomorrow. Molly had something she wanted to talk about.

"It meant a lot to Sam, your taking time to be with him yesterday," Molly said. "I can tell him forever how handsome and smart and responsible he is, and how he has to take a shower, but he needs a man to take him seriously enough to play with him."

It pleased Fred, hearing Molly tell him this.

"You're not a man who sets out to hurt people, Fred. But you do approach life like an act of God. You've got Clayton's work to worry about, and the other matter. That's your business, Fred. But you're not good at thinking about more than one thing at a time.

"Both the kids have been hurt before, by their father. I'm not telling you because I'm afraid it's going to happen, but you should know. If it develops that you hurt me, that's okay. It's a risk I'll run, and I won't mind retaliating. But I won't see either of the children hurt again, and the more vulnerable at the moment is Sam.

"Terry thinks the world of you. Your sex is an advantage. If you're going to make a commitment to Sam, don't forget it's important."

They'd come into the kitchen, where Fred was warming a can of beans and making toast for toast and baked beans as an antidote to Clayton's dinner.

"You want bacon with it?" Molly suggested.

Good idea.

"Did I hurt Sam?" Fred asked, defensive. For God's sake, he'd spent yesterday afternoon with the kid.

"On the contrary. You gave him reason to try some trust and affection on you."

"Well, that's good."

Fred got out a beer to go with his late supper, offering one to Molly, who refused it.

"It's good unless it's betrayed. If that happens again, I won't forgive you. Not even if it's not your fault."

A good thing about Molly was that she would give clear expression to so unreasonable an emotional proposition. A bad thing about her was that she'd do it while you were trying to have supper and unwind after an uneasy day. Even if Fred took time in advance to think about it, he couldn't predict what the proposition was going to be, so he couldn't have an answer ready.

Molly's opening gambit could lead to one of two ultimate resolutions: either Fred's sleeping on the couch, where the kids could find him in disgrace in the morning, or a more satisfactorily intimate exchange, to be achieved only by fancy footwork on the part of them both.

Fred could not, himself, opt successfully for either resolution.

The conversation would go where it had to, and then he would go where he had to.

Fortune smiled on him this time, and he found himself in Molly's bed after all, with Molly crying and taking comfort, and then one thing leading to another in the happy, random plunge of the juggernaut of unlogic.

In the morning the kids kvetched and noodled in anticipation of school, and Molly whirled around preparing to go to work at the library, where she could be found behind the reference desk.

Important issues arose concerning the Red Sox game of the previous evening, in the form of a shouting match between Terry and Sam. Sam had the paper and Terry the urgent opinion that contradicted the paper, and Fred was called on to arbitrate. Terry was dressed for school, holding tight to the homework that she was not forgetting this morning and eating Froot Loops out of the box—"for the vitamins, Fred."

"Roger Clemens has milk with his," Fred said, pouring her a glass.

"If I put down my homework, I'll forget it," Terry protested. Fred had to pour the milk into her, Sam watching with envious disdain. To keep a balance, Fred sided with the *Globe* and Sam, and Terry stamped off to the bus mad but still clutching her homework. Sam went upstairs to dress. He would ride his bike today; he liked to skid into the school yard as the bell rang.

Molly was wearing a bright red dress this morning, feeling good. Fred was not fully dressed yet since he'd be the last one out of the house and had to straighten things up before leaving.

"Watch your back, honey," said Molly—her exit line as she headed for the garage and the Honda and the day at work. Sam went out with her, the two of them a couple.

"Won't be long before you're driving your old lady to work," Fred called. Sam didn't look back. He had another fish to fry: his mom.

Start anywhere in the maze and you finish either at the start, or at the heart, or in one of the blind alleys. The best place to be, with regard to a maze, is directly above it, but that was a luxury far from Fred's present circumstances. Despite the threat of attachment to Smykal's ugly body in its bath of violence, he nonetheless determined to keep his attention on Clay's main objective—at least this morning.

He had to find a way through the local crop of professors, scholars, and graduate students in art history and figure out if someone existed who might have put the Heade and the Vermeer together and taken the package to Finn. If this person turned out to be at Harvard, whether grad student or professor, he, she, or it was probably holding a clutch of books concerning Heade, or Vermeer, or—preferably—both.

Academics are trained to despise commerce. The idea of being a merchant is the antithesis of aesthetic intellectual idealism. Take money for things? Horrors! No, no, take money for words, ideas: mouth-temperature air. Live, travel, hump, and defecate in warm tranquillity, supported by money laundered by the sanction of the institution.

Let pirates give their money to Harvard, and Harvard pass it along to scholarship. That way all can console themselves that the ivory tower has nothing to do with dead elephants.

So far were they from recognizing art's proximity to commerce that not many graduate students in the area even knew Doolan's existed. It was outside of town. Students might be aware of what was happening at the museums, if it was in their own particular field, but they spent more time with words than with things, were more familiar with prints of photographs of objects than with the objects themselves. Conversely, brilliance in commercial instinct would not drag a youngster to the drudgery of the graduate student's life and the prospect of an ill-paid career spent counting objects bought by someone else's manipulation of the world.

It was what made Finn so brilliant an anomaly. He continued with one hand to grasp academia by the short hairs while keeping the fingers of his other hand tightly curled around the testicles of commerce.

If a mature Finn existed, Fred reasoned, why not a larval form as well, slowly devouring the bland pap of the academy and looking even now for a safe corner in which to secrete the chrysalis where he or she could blossom into something rich and wonderful?

Fred left his car in the garage under the Charles Hotel. He might be in Cambridge all day, and he didn't want to run back and forth feeding a meter.

At the entrance to the fine-arts library Fred told Joan good morning. She was standing, as usual, behind the desk, looking severe, her rimless glasses glaring, her black ponytail frisking in an independent way, as if it did not know that the rest of the animal was in dead earnest. Joan was as tall as Fred was. Whenever he came in, it seemed she was lying in wait for him.

"Come here, Fred," she said. "Don't be so fast. I want to tell you a joke about Teddy Kennedy."

Fred submitted to the joke, an awful one that could survive only in the forgiving groves of academe. He went back past the reference desk to the card catalog.

It was a Tuesday morning. So late in the academic year, the place was almost deserted, as it had been the previous Saturday. Fred looked first, on the computer, for recent theses about Vermeer or Heade, but nothing local was cooking in this regard.

It would be hard to sell the idea of a thesis on either Vermeer or Heade. The subjects were already well covered. Harvard wants you to study odd, neglected corners of art that have long since kissed their ninth lives good-bye, such as the persistence of the Roman funerary-portrait formula into Byzantine decoration, or how Pontormo's figures can be explained by inferring an extra joint in each limb and digit. The idea is to find something that hasn't yet been said about a pot and say it at enough length to call it a thesis.

It was partly on account of this enforced attention to the inane that Fred had lasted less than a single term at Harvard, whose main contribution to his early career had been to make it impossible for him to go back to the Midwest.

The quiet plan, the first plan, was to go downstairs to the stacks, find a gap around either Heade or Vermeer, and then go back up and ask at the desk who'd taken those books out.

He found no such gap or gaps, no hole in Vermeer's section. Higginson's mentor's book on Heade was safe and well on the shelf with the others, not recently checked out, according to the sheet in back.

As long as he was here, Fred looked around. The place was so deserted that he thought he'd check on what the graduate students were actually up to. This meant simply strolling along the carrels, seeing what books they were using, what little clippings and Xeroxes they had taped to their humble work places.

Someone was studying Scythian influences on the working of leather in medieval Poland. Was it not at this desk that Fred had seen the rotund student dozing so profoundly last Saturday? Another student was apparently seeking to establish how many of Venice's different canals could be identified in all the Canalettos, if you discounted the fakes.

Another, harder project on one desk sought to deal frankly with the question of whether or not surrealism could have existed as a school of painting had it not been 85 percent literature and 10 percent illustration.

Someone was evidently doing a comparison between Celtic bronzes and William Merritt Chase. If Harvard's fine-arts department was letting that happen, it had got a sense of humor suddenly.

Maybe the student just liked Chase and was doing the Celtic bronze for real, or vice versa.

Or . . .

Shit!

Something other than bronze began gleaming in the back of Fred's mind. He sat at the desk and looked at the absent student's collection of books. There were two shelves. On the top was what you'd expect of a normal student's interest: volumes exhausting methods of bronze casting; Roman influences; Celtic influences; trade roots; Iberian history; and Sardinia and Carthage and the Phoenicians. . . . photocopies of twenty or more bronze and clay horses were taped around the area, annotated, all looking pretty much the same.

Shelf two was all William Merritt Chase. Here was the catalog of the sale of his studio's contents and his personal collection of paintings after he died. There were books done during his lifetime and after; collections of works by his students; semi-definitive works by the Chase guy, who was keeping his options open.

Chase was a serious side issue for this Celtic bronze student.

Fred looked around, the back of his neck prickling. He remembered now, when he was down here on Saturday, prepared for bolts of lightning that would reveal who had painted La Belle Conchita. He'd noticed that, in the stacks, there wasn't much on Chase. This was why.

The place smelled of decayed plaster and incipient mold. He turned on the student's lamp that was clamped to the upper shelf and started leafing through the Chase books. He felt that tingle you feel when, half the time, you're on to something.

Chase.

Why not?

Fred picked up one of the books, the way you do, and started through it.

He remembered how the guy had been sitting here, the one he'd seen last Saturday, nervous, tearing his long blond hair—and how he wasn't here any longer when he looked up again. It was a young guy with a mustache, drinking like a bird out of his book.

The books were marked here and there with yellow Post-it notes.

Jesus Pete. Here it was, at carrel sixteen. The painting of Conchita was by Chase. Fred knew it even before he flipped to a marked plate in one of Pisano's books—the 1890 nude, *Study in Curves*, almost the mirror's version of La Belle Conchita. Very Velázquez in its feel.

It made absolute sense. Clay's unsigned painting of La Belle Conchita, from its style, manner, and subject, was a Chase. Chase had been in Paris at the right time; he'd been in Munich already. He knew Whistler, and Duveneck. In fact, he had done a portrait of Whistler, aping Whistler's own work (its reproduction was also marked with a Post-it note), in 1885, before the two had a falling-out. Chase was American. He would have known the other Americans. Chase could paint a hell of a good nude when sufficiently moved, and he didn't like paint so much as to forget flesh, or vice versa. And as far as robbing from Velázquez, Chase had loved Velázquez so much that he saddled one of his kids with it as a middle name. Helen Velázquez Chase.

"Jesus!" Fred said aloud, wanting to crow, so bemused by the accuracy of his inference about the painting's authorship that he did not pick up immediately the other implications of the blond kid's obsession. In spite of murder and danger in the wings, he was seduced by joy at finding the answer to the puzzle, What dead man long ago painted Clayton's picture of a dead woman?

The blond kid knew Clay's painting, had known it when it

was Henry Smykal's: Conchita in the raw, red in tooth and claw. All the marked pages showed the triumphant researcher reinforcing his conclusion as to the painter's identity. If the kid knew Smykal's painting, the kid had been at Smykal's place.

Fred gazed across the dusty stacks.

"Shit," he said.

He realized he was jealous and disappointed. The kid had scooped him—figured it out first. What else did he know?

"What can you tell me, little man?" Fred whispered.

16

Fred started looking among the scraps and notes that lay on the desk to see if its occupant revealed his identity easily. Nothing on the table betrayed the name of its user.

If he asked Joan who used carrel sixteen, he could in time find out not only the kid's name but even his address—it would all be on their computer. The trouble was, Joan was an absolute stickler for routine, and for propriety, and she was also an incurable busybody. There was no way to ask her without setting off a chain reaction that Fred didn't want to risk. Ask a question, leave a record.

The student would come back. He'd have to. Sometime.

Fred went upstairs and emptied his bladder, picked up a couple of magazines to look through, took them back down to the stacks, and chose a place to wait where he could keep an eye on the kid's desk.

He'd dressed that morning in unostentatious academic fashion, in sport jacket and plain green tie with blue button-down shirt. He sat at carrel eight, leaned back, put up his feet, and waited for four hours.

Enforced inactivity can lead to strange expansions in one's fund of knowledge. A long period in a Greyhound bus terminal had once produced, for Fred, an understanding of the relative merits of seven different methods of depilation. After his magazines were exhausted, he occupied himself with the chosen subject of carrel eight's tenant, studying the reserved copy of *The Shoulder Bust in Sicily and South Central Italy: A Catalog and Materials for Dating.* As it turned out, you could date the shoulder busts according to hairstyle.

At two forty-five the blond student came down.

Fred lifted *The Shoulder Bust* and looked at the student from behind it. The book was big and red, perfectly designed for the purpose. His quarry was one of those men who had grown taller faster than they expected in their youth and who try to make up for it by tiptoeing flat-footed, using the walk that goes with loafers. He was tall but skinny, with a bow tie fluttering in advance of his throat. Papillon. Otherwise he dressed like Fred in his academic mode. Perhaps his natural look was furtive, obsessive obeisance. Furtive he surely seemed.

He shouldn't be a hard man to corner. But Fred found that cornering, like guilt, was seldom the best way to get an eager flood of information from a person. He'd wait and watch. He had the advantage; why waste it by making himself known?

Carrel sixteen's occupant did not sit, wasn't settling in today. Fred would have a chance, then, to stretch his legs. If the gods were merciful, the kid would go for lunch.

Fred watched him. What the kid did next was gather together all the Chase books from his desk, think a moment, then take the pack of books to the stacks and arrange them on the shelves as if they'd never been out. He made sure to put them in order by call number. Obsessive he was also. Then he headed for the exit. He was nervous, looking like a guilty songbird with hawks around.

Fred scribbled a note, which he dropped on the kid's desk as he followed him out of the stacks.

> Carrel 16, would be interested to discuss the Chase with you.
>
> *Fred*

The kid took off down Prescott Street toward Mass. Ave. Going to Bartley's? Fred could join him in a burger. But the kid turned left, walking hastily. He was still on foot: a graduate student with no vehicle, poor but honest. He was heading toward Central Square, therefore in the direction of Turbridge Street.

But no, the kid, moving right along as if he had a plan, an appointment, crossed to the other side of Mass. Ave. Fred trailed behind him, on the other side of the street.

The kid talked to a woman for a moment, a young-looking student type whom he bumped into by accident—blond and tall, wearing jeans and a blue sweater for today's cooler weather and carrying a leather satchel. Two minutes later, they told each other good-bye. The woman kept on toward the square, and the kid turned into a video store, Video King. Maybe he'd find a video to help him study his Celtic bronzes.

Fred waited outside, across the street, for the kid to emerge. Inside, he'd be noticed. The kid might recall seeing him in the stacks earlier, or recognize him later. But who would stay in a video store for almost an hour? Had he picked up that Fred was behind him and found a back way out? It was no great loss since Fred knew how to get hold of him again, but it would be a blow to the ego, and a pain in the ass, or both.

Fred decided to risk letting the kid see him and walked in the door. The kid was behind the counter. He worked here.

Fred ducked out fast. Poor but honest, the kid was putting himself through grad school by working at the local video store.

So here was another place Fred could count on finding him again. The kid looked well installed. He would be working part-time, which meant a four-hour shift at least. There'd be time for a burger, and to call Molly and then Clay. Fred went for the burger first.

Bartley's wasn't crowded. Lunch was long over. The rough women in red T-shirts let him sprawl in a booth and get around a Burger Deluxe, complete with onion rings. Fred took his time over coffee, looking through the day's paper to see if something had happened in the world at large or if there were developments that he might want to know about in Smykal's misadventure on Turbridge Street.

What next? Fred wondered. Should he stop the kid in the street and talk to him? Should he follow him home?

He picked up some subway tokens in case the kid came out of work and hopped on the T. He went back and checked to make sure he was still behind the counter at the video place, and then, using a nearby pay phone, Fred called and left a message for Clay at the desk of the Copley Square Hotel, saying he'd call again at eight-thirty if he could: he was working on something. He suppressed a desire to have the note signed Mr. Chase and used a simple "Fred" instead. Then he called Molly.

Ophelia wants us to have dinner with her."

"I don't think so," Fred told her. He described what he was doing and what he'd got so far. "I have to keep with it."

"If you think that's your killer," Molly began, "be careful, Fred."

"Not a chance." Fred laughed. "No, it's the other piece. This guy is one of the meek. A student. However, he knows something about Smykal's painting, now Clay's painting. It's by Chase, by the way. I'm anxious to find out what else he knows."

There was a silence while Molly thought about it, rehearsing the image of La Belle Conchita in her mind.

"Chase makes sense," Molly said. "Poor Jimmy Carter, who couldn't get away even with lusting in his heart—his favorite painting was a naked back by Chase, too, wasn't it? A female back. Pastel."

"About which Clarence Cook wrote at the time it was exhibited," Fred said, "and I quote, 'No piece of flesh painting has been seen in these parts that could approach the performance of Mr. Chase.'"

"So where does this student lead you?" Molly asked.

"At the moment, I am keeping an open mind," Fred said. "And my eyes open as well. He's in a video store, behind the counter. I am not committing to dinner engagements."

That made sense, Molly agreed. But this was something special. At the Ritz.

"What the fuck do I care about dinner at the Ritz?" Fred exploded.

"I'm teasing," Molly said. "I know you're a big enough boy to grind your own pepper. Ophelia has landed a guest and wants us to help entertain him."

"For God's sake," Fred said, "Don't tell me. She's still got Albert Finn by the short and curlies?"

"That's what it sounds like. I told her Finn is married. She says good, that's one thing she doesn't have to think about. AIDS is enough worry as it is."

"That's class. Shack up with married celebrities at the Ritz."

"So, Fred, what do I tell her? I jumped at it because it seemed to be a chance for you to stay close to him. Ophelia's desperate for help. She exhausted her knowledge of art after the first hour with him—even that was pushing it—and says you can't talk indefinitely about sex with a man, his mind wanders, his eyes glaze over. He's thinking about the next big deal he's going to do in business, and you're making the sex so easy for him that it's not a challenge. So she needs us."

"I get the idea," said Fred. "You and I talk art with Finn to keep his mind on Ophelia while she does to him, under the table, what the waiter does with the pepper grinder in plain view."

"Smart fellow."

"It isn't Finn using Ophelia to get hold of me, is it?" Fred felt suddenly suspicious. "To see what Clayton's interest is in the Heade?"

"Ophelia's more devious than I expect, but I don't think so. Don't think so," Molly said.

"It is important for me to keep an eye on Finn," Fred said. "But this guy I'm behind should help resolve the more immediate threat. I'll stick with the student. Tell Ophelia yes. You go, and I'll meet you if I can. Make it late. Eight o'clock. Is that all right?"

"Ophelia said half past eight," Molly said.

"Even better. If I can't make it, can't leave this guy, I'll get a message to you, maybe join you for coffee. I'll try to," Fred promised. "I just don't have any idea where this is going."

It was five-thirty now. Fred hurried back to Video King. Talking to Molly had taken longer than he wanted. He wouldn't be happy if he'd lost the kid.

He looked in the front window. The kid was still in place. Turbridge Street being so near, Fred drifted in that direction, looking up the street. The cop car was still parked out front.

When he got back to Video King, the video heir apparent was just stepping out. He started walking toward Central Square. Fred ducked quickly into the store.

"The guy that just left," Fred said to a girl behind the desk in a red-and-white-striped shirt, a black ponytail, and beads.

"You mean Russ?" the girl said. "He's gone. A minute ago. You can probably catch him."

"When's he on again?" Fred asked. "In case I don't catch him."

The girl looked in back of the desk at a sheet. "Three tomorrow," she said. "But I bet you catch him."

It was six o'clock now. But it was warm outside, and pleasant. Fred felt he might have been inside all day long. It was good to stretch his legs and make up space between himself and Russ, who was moving at a good clip.

Did the kid speed up or fart liquid when he passed Turbridge Street? Not so that Fred noticed. But that he had intimate knowledge of Smykal's apartment Fred had not a doubt.

The modest parade moved past Ellery, Dana, Hancock, Lee, Clinton, Bigelow Street, Inman, the big Post Office. They went on into the middle of Central Square, then turned left on Prospect toward Broadway, where Russ went into an ecologically correct supermarket. The student had not looked back once. Fred was sure he'd not been seen, but he didn't follow the kid in. He waited across the street, took off his tie, and put it in the pocket of his jacket. Then he hung the jacket over one shoulder, to change his profile. He looked into a restaurant window up the street until Russ came out again, now carrying a bag of groceries. The bag was made of paper covered with signs proving to the world, as Russ walked back to Central Square, that it had been recycled already and was going to be recycled again, forever. The same was also true of the celery waving out of the top of the bag. The same was true of the kid, Russ. And of Smykal.

They turned left again on Mass. Ave., crossed Mass. at Pearl, and went down Pearl toward the river. Russ went into a three-decker apartment building with a street door that wouldn't close and three mailboxes set into the wall and busted out again.

Fred, entering behind him somewhat later, gave him time to go up to where he was going and had a look at the names of the building's inhabitants on the mailboxes: D. Brown & S. Botts; Saul Lazare, Esq.; Russell Ennery.

Russell Ennery, then. Harvard grad student and Video King employee. He'd see what he could do tomorrow with that name. It wouldn't hurt to get information, perhaps even think, before he moved further. He'd rather know the lay of the land before he had a chat with Russell. Russ could be found when Fred wanted him: here at his home, at the library, or at Video King.

Fred had time to go back to Molly's, shower, and change. He'd go on to goddamn dinner at the Ritz with Albert Finn. Molly and he could go together. It could be a double date.

17

Sir Albert Finn was in great form, dwarfing the Ritz dining room. Set off by blue velvet and gold, he loomed and floated, both, like a tethered balloon on whose string clung a delighted female child whose perfect natural breasts struggled to ascend to visit the inflatable.

The perfect breasts were Ophelia's, at the summit of a sheath of pink velvet. Ophelia's blond hair was coiled in Continental fashion, confused by strands of pearls. Her neck and chest were bare in order to accentuate both pearls and breasts. Attendant pearls and gold fawned on her ears.

Ophelia rose from the table as Fred and Molly came into the dining room, saying, "Oh, Fred, I was so hoping—you remember Fred Taylor, Al?"

The risen Finn in deep blue suit was wearing, in his buttonhole, a carnation filched from the bouquet on the table, to match the color and shape of his face. That was Ophelia's touch. Finn spread his arms in welcome also. They looked like a pair of extremely successful scarecrows.

Molly had put on the same black dress, with the moonstone necklace Fred had given her on her last birthday. The moonstones, transparent on her skin, complemented her oval face and challenged her green eyes. Her skin was the smooth, light pink you thought could exist only in paintings.

Fred had selected a gray suit with matching pants and matching jacket and no vest: the suit he had. He had let Molly put a bow tie on him, of a color she described as "runcible" or "mufti."

They'd made a game one Sunday evening of describing the colors in Michelangelo's *Last Judgment* as newly cleaned by the Japanese, using a selection of descriptive words available in current clothing catalogs: cerise, melon, jungle, surplus, and— Fred's favorite—outfit (the color God was wearing).

"Of course I know Fred Taylor," Finn beamed and boomed. "Clayton Reed's man. And the beautiful Molly Riley, of whom Ophelia speaks with such affection."

Finn's kiss made Molly wince, but Finn was used to that, the wince of homage.

Finn and Ophelia were drinking colored liquids from wineglasses.

"It's my party," Ophelia said. "I've chosen the menu, and you'll have to love it."

The dining room was filled. The evening's patrons looked like businessmen traveling on expense accounts and pairs of women celebrating birthdays they would rather forget. There were also a couple of those families whose children consent to dress. You wouldn't catch Sam and Terry letting anyone put leather shoes on their feet, or shirts with Holly Hobbie collars or whatever those were.

"Well," Molly said to Finn. "And what brings you to these promiscuous parts?"

"Kipling," said Finn. "Ha, ha."

"Yes, but what Kipling?" said Molly.

Ophelia stared back and forth as if attending a tennis game.

"I'll give you a hint. 'The great gray-green, greasy Limpopo River,'" Molly said.

"Aha," said Finn, "'all set about with fever-trees.' Got it. 'The Elephant's Child.'"

This started them (all but Ophelia) in a broadly literary fashion leading to Kipling's startling and individual graphic style and its relation to the trends in book illustration coming out of the *Yellow Book* and the decadent nineties, until Molly did a quick turn and added, "I'm so rude, I asked a question and then didn't allow you to answer. Is it another book you're researching? Or what does Boston have to hold your attention?"

Ophelia looked deeply smug and changed it to a blush as she noticed Finn's sidelong glance. "Sir Albert says something's gone wrong with a project," Ophelia said. "But I like to think—"

Finn nudged her. "There is a matter I am engaged on, but it is confidential," he said.

Fred, as deftly as possible, starting from the preponderance of blue velvet in the room, brought the conversation around to the China trade, the Fitz Hugh Lane of Captain Apthorp's clipper ship the *Hester Prynne*, and sea slugs.

He watched to see if Finn betrayed familiarity with the Apthorp diaries or alarm that Fred was familiar with them.

"Apthorp," Finn said, nodding. "The same family as had the Heade, I suppose? I trust the Lane is of superior quality. I don't mind telling you that I find the Heade, even for an American picture, indifferent at best. I have said as much in certain quarters."

"Dried sea slugs," Ophelia said. "Oh, goodness, right after they bring in this lovely pot roast?" She gave Fred a merry moue.

This took the conversation to dehydrated foods in general and how to cook them; they followed that track until Fred went too far, bringing up a favorite recipe of his that he suggested accounted for the ill humor of the Mongol warrior in the time of Ghenghis Khan: "It's simple. A slab of dried horseflesh is placed under the saddle at first light. The warrior spends his day riding, raping, and pillaging, never dismounting; in the evening he pulls out the slab, which has by this time softened and absorbed sufficient moisture as to be palatable."

Finn was too old a hand at this game to let anything slip in conversation. Fred had caught Clay in his room, by phone, beforehand, and told him that he might have another line to follow toward the letter Chase had written. He'd listened with great pleasure to Clayton's dismayed pause at having the remainder of his secret laid bare, then continued, "I decided, since I was in the stacks anyway, that I'd try to nail down the date when Chase painted La Belle Conchita. What's your thought, Clay? Eighteen eighty-five or so?"

"Ah," Clay said. He'd had time to recover his telephone aplomb. "You do not disappoint me, Fred. You recognized Chase's hand once you were free to concentrate."

Fred told him about the young man, Russell Ennery.

"You think he has the letter?" Clay asked, excited.

"I only conclude that he has knowledge of the painting," Fred said.

"If that youngster has my letter, I'll buy it from him," Clay went on. "Tell him—I don't know, whatever will impress him. A hundred dollars? Perhaps I will telephone him."

"I'll follow this up," Fred said. "Leave it to me, Clay. Don't mess with it. It's complex, don't forget."

Clayton was not thinking about the broader implications. He was forgetting that they were monkeying around the edges of a murder and that they wanted themselves isolated from it.

Ophelia's dinner sparkled on, a triumph of Yankee international cuisine served by omniscient waiters of an Italianette persuasion, whose dexterity with the pepper grinder—lobed and long as Fred's forearm—was applauded under the table by Molly, kicking Fred's ankle.

The telephone waiter appeared at the same time as the dessert, asking for Finn, who listened to the receiver, grunted, "Not now," listened some more, said, "Not here," listened some more, said, "No," and then, "I'm working on it," and hung up.

"Excuse me. Confidential," Finn assured the table. He was as impenetrable as the German chocolate cake they were presented.

They got through the meal. Fred had to accept coffee but refused brandy. Ophelia was grateful. She turned down Fred's offer of a ride, simpered, and hung on to Finn's arm. Finn was attended by tuxedoed waiters as if he were the Second Coming. A couple of them, big ones, even seemed to follow him.

"You don't think that ridiculous man is traveling with bodyguards?" Molly said after they had left their hostess and her companion at the Ritz door and were walking down Newbury Street toward where Fred had parked his car.

Fred shrugged.

He enjoyed Newbury Street after the galleries closed. You could look in the windows. Paintings are bought and sold like stamps, or stocks, or sofas. Of a sofa, people need to know, is the color right, and will it fill the available space? Of a stamp, is it genuine? what number of this issue were circulated? what's its condition? Of a stock, is it going up or going down? But paintings that you look at on the street, you have to see with a different eye than you cast on those in institutional captivity. On the street they are a complex, floating form of currency. This is true not only of pictures by dead people (now limited in number by the truncation of production); some living painters can be marketed in the same way. Their dealers make the artists exotic, limiting production, keeping it even and predictable, like the issuing of stamps, once the painter hits on a formula people will buy.

They took their time getting back to the car.

It was cold. The temperature was more fitting for late April. Molly shivered. Fred put his arm around her shoulders, and they walked that way.

"Let's look at the place in Central Square," Molly said. "You can show me what you did all day."

They parked in front of the building on Pearl Street. It was a scruffy, seedy neighborhood, partly defined by drugs and crime and children up late and, now and then, blood on the sidewalk. The children were visible even now, but the blood, drugs, and crime were occult.

It was a part of Cambridge where rent should be more supportable than in safer surroundings, perfect for the poor but honest student.

"That's where our Russell lives," Fred said, pointing across the street with his chin. "Tomorrow I'll find out what he's up to."

18

At first light Wednesday Fred heard the paper hit the door, untangled himself from Molly's pleasant limbs, put on pants and shirt, and went down to have coffee by himself. It was five-thirty.

He put water on the stove and pulled the paper in.

There was trouble in the former Yugoslavia.

Local scandals in banking had to do with mortgages.

The Red Sox had won a game without Clemens.

There'd been a murder in Chinatown.

Birds sang outside in a light rain. It was going to rain all day. Fred put the boiling water into the drip pot.

A paragraph under the headline TRAGEDY ON TURBRIDGE STREET read:

> In connection with the slaying, police seek to confer with the collector Arthur Arthurian, to assist them in their inquiry.

Fred called Clayton's incognito, Mr. Whistler, at the Copley, making the desk keep ringing until Clay picked it up. He was furious at being aroused before six, then frightened when Fred told him, "Developments. I'm coming over."

"What's wrong?"

"I'll be there shortly," Fred said. "Wait for me. Stay in your room."

Fred poured a cup of coffee for the ride into town.

He stopped in Charlestown first. Someone was always awake there, at the door. Nobody could sleep if someone wasn't watching. It was Bill Radford this morning, reading the *Herald*, drinking Coke, and eating potato chips. Radford sat in back of the desk they'd put in the front hall. His large, pasty torso was encased in a leather vest, and he wore a Vietnam Vets cap over his long gray curls. He looked like a Hell's Angel, his bare arms covered with tattoos.

Bill nodded to Fred's " 'Morning, Bill."

"Teddy's in your room," Bill told him.

"It's okay," Fred said. "I don't need it."

"How do you like Clemens this year?" Bill asked.

Fred made some answer. He never had liked Bill Radford much. He thought the guy could be working, should be working, by now. Radford had a wife and children somewhere with no news of him. But it took some people a long time to get evened out; some didn't make it at all, and some didn't want to. The best they could do for each other was mind their business. They were brothers, and what did Fred know? It was hard to get in life again.

Fred went in back to the kitchen, got his lock box from the cabinet over the sink, opened it, and took out his .38, the shoulder rig, and some rounds. He'd have it with him in the car, anyway, where he could get to it if he needed it. Not knowing where Russ Ennery might lead, he wanted it. He hated to go armed but would hate worse to blunder, without reasonable force, into

Smykal's friends. Bill Radford saw him take the gun but didn't ask if he needed help—any more than Fred would have asked him if their positions had been reversed. They knew, these people, where to draw the line, and they were all of them holding that line as best they could, even poor Teddy upstairs who didn't dare drink a cup of coffee in the open.

Fred drove over the bridge to Boston, Boston waking up now, the river smoking in the rain and strands of mist blowing. It gave off that general feeling of expectation you get when it's cold and rainy and too early in the morning. He left the gun in the car and parked near the Copley. It wasn't hard to find a space this early.

Clayton was sitting in his room, that dressing gown on over blue silk pajamas. His face was pinched and white, the white hair agley.

"I ordered coffee for you," Clay said. "What's up?" Clayton was excited, awake, hopeful!

"The police want Arthurian," Fred said. He put it to Clay straight and fast. He wanted to be certain that he understood that this could be about more than a picture.

Clayton went from white to gray. "There is no Arthurian," he said.

"No, but there is a person—yourself, Clayton—who is known to exist, who operated using that name. The police want him in connection with a dead man."

A stealthy knock troubled the door. Clay jumped. Then he said, "Coffee. For you. I don't require stimulants. And my breakfast."

Fred took the tray at the door and put it between them on a glass table that reflected, in the morning light, the blues and golds of the decor.

Clay pursed his lips and gestured toward the plated pot of coffee, poured orange juice and Perrier into a glass for himself, and said, "The police having that name, and looking for that person, Fred, does place us in an ambiguously anomalous moral position."

He'd been rehearsing that.

"You get a prize, do you," Fred said, "if you say it fast perfectly five times?"

Clay took a sip of his chosen beverage.

"I've got a line that may give me entry to the back door of the Smykal story," Fred said, "in this Russell Ennery, who was doing research on your painting of Conchita Hill. But we can't afford games anymore, Clay, since the cops want you, and they assume Smykal was killed for that painting."

"That's ridiculous," Clay said. "People aren't killed for paintings! He didn't have the thing. I have it. I bought it."

"Their theory is that you are Dr. No," Fred said. "If they have a chance, they'll prove it. If they connect you to Arthurian, it will take them about five minutes to get a warrant to go through your place and find the painting—and about a half hour more to track you here. Since you paid cash, you can't even prove you bought the painting. It was a huge amount of money, Clay."

Clay twitched and suffered. He didn't want anyone knowing his business. He must be fun for his accountant.

He said, being reasonable, "I know, Fred."

Fred looked at it. "It's not too much to kill a person for, though, Clay. It's an attractive prize, money like that. Much more attractive than a Smykal. At the same time it's not much, would you say, for a Chase of that period, of that subject?"

"It's unsigned. And it's what the man wanted." Clay was now on territory he understood. He spread marmalade on a roll, tasted, and nodded to himself. "In fact, he got three thousand more than he wanted. And he held out a significant portion of what I paid for, don't forget. He cheated me of the letter, which I still lack."

Right. The welsher deserved the hammer treatment.

"Without that letter, I'm going to have a time convincing Pisano it is by Chase," Clay continued.

"But how did anyone get your name?" Fred mused. "The Arthurian name. If the police have it, who else does? Now, obviously, everyone who gets the newspaper."

Clayton went green. Marmalade trembled on the end of his knife. Fred pulled his chair closer and made Clayton look him in the eye. "One thing, Clay, is, on the off chance that someone outside the benevolent forces of the law connects you through that painting to the killing, we have to worry about your neck as well."

"That may be," Clay said. He put his knife down and fingered his neck absently.

They looked at each other.

"Short of publishing our business," Clay said, "what do you suggest, Fred?"

Fred said, "I'm going to lean on that kid, to see what he knows, who he knows, and how he knows it."

"Before you leave, Fred, I should tell you," said Clay hesitantly, "this new development may impinge negatively on a small independent effort of my own."

Fred, standing to leave, turned back. "What have you done now, Clay?"

"A ruse occurred to me by which I thought we might safely obtain my letter. I could not just sit idle. This was before you put your finger on the student yesterday."

Clay sipped from his beverage and almost smiled. He leaned back in his chair, folding his hands, doing his imitation of the *Brahmin* by Gaugengigl. "I placed an advertisement that may bear fruit."

"Advertisement, for God's sake?"

"In the personal columns of both this morning's *Globe* and *New York Times*: 'Wanted. Artist's autograph letter of value only to me. Cash reward. No questions asked. Reply in confidence. A. Arthurian.' The only problem I see is with my having used that unfortunate pseudonym again."

Fred stared.

"Don't worry," Clay said. "I arranged that all and any replies should be forwarded and held for Arthurian's arrival at the Ritz. You will make suitable arrangements about that later."

It was a move of such grotesque stupidity that Fred could only admire it as one would a winged turd: a natural wonder, but who needs it?

"Clay," he protested. "For God's sake, stay out of the cloak-and-dagger business. You haven't been to the right schools."

Clay set his jaw.

"Don't leave this room," said Fred. "Don't arrange any more surprises. Don't, for God's sake, go near the Ritz. Let me take care of this part of the operation."

He stormed out before he killed the idiot himself, hearing Clay call out behind him, "Be careful, Fred. Watch out for yourself."

The rain was colder, heavier. Fred drove through it into Cambridge. He had the .38 under his arm now. He hated to do it, hated seeing the stakes raised like this over a goddamn picture.

It was a beautiful goddamn picture. Representing perhaps forty dollars' worth of materials in its day and some daring good times for a couple of young artists, La Belle Conchita and Chase, this labor of pleasure, faith, and love, liberated from the fumbling grasp of a half-assed residuary legatee of a pornographer, was still on the outskirts of a trade in squalid adventure.

He thought of Molly and of how sometimes, when they were making love, she'd fondle one of his scars absently until she recollected what it was. Then she'd draw in her breath and look wounded. He couldn't stand to be at Molly's while he was carrying a weapon. He didn't want to be around her kids with the gun. He did not want, over there, to be a man of violence. He'd feel he was betraying all of them.

Meanwhile, he needed a place to work from where he could have a telephone, get messages, and have a dry space to operate. He booked a room at the Charles Hotel. He paid in cash and registered as Fred, a simple alias. He didn't want to be at Clay's to answer questions if anyone connected Clay to the Arthurian name.

They gave him a large pink room from which he could look out onto the river. He called Molly. He told her what he was doing and why and asked her to bring some of his clothes to the library with her, and he'd pick them up later.

"I can't bring a weapon into your house," Fred said, meaning, I can't be in your house myself because I'm danger and ashamed of it. But he wouldn't say that.

"Sorry," he added.

Molly said she was sorry, too. Maybe she'd see him when he came to the library for his things. Please take care.

19

Fred was working the secretaries at Harvard by nine o'clock.

Russell Ennery was indeed a graduate student in the fine arts, studying with people in archaeology as well, doing a thesis on Celtic bronzes in Iberia. Russell was twenty-four and had a home address in Maryland. He had attended New York University as an undergrad. Fred confirmed the address on Pearl Street and jotted down the names of graduate advisers. He couldn't get access to a transcript but could infer, reading between the lines, that Russell hadn't qualified to be a teaching fellow. Hence the job at Video King, which paid better and likely gave him access to a better class of people.

Fred now had enough to take over to Pearl Street. He drove to Central Square, the wad of lethal metal itching under his left arm. He'd look like law down here with his sport coat, his necktie, and the bulge.

Fred parked where he could watch Ennery's building. Pearl Street was busy and multiculturally seedy. Less in the way of blossoms, saying spring, put up a front against generic trash. At about ten, nobody having come out of the building and with nothing else of interest developing, Fred went in. Russell Ennery's apartment was on the third floor. The stairs were wood and chipped linoleum, smelling of mouse and roach and disinfectant and several varieties of smoke. He reached a dingy hall at the top of the stairs, with brown paint, a flaking ceiling, bike tires in the hallway, and a tray of kitty litter. Some extra had been generally kicked around the floor and squeaked under his shoes.

Fred knocked on Ennery's door, using a brisk, competent knock, like a narc's. There was no answer.

Fred called, "Russell?"

No answer. He tried the door. Nothing. He could come back and pop it later if he had to.

Fred went down one flight to the second floor and knocked. He heard movement inside the apartment, a scattering scramble and the sound of a toilet flushing. "Just a minute," came a hoarse voice from within: female, he thought.

He stood on a green rubber mat that told him he was welcome. He looked at the sprig of dead hemlock on the door at eye level. The toilet flushed again inside. Footsteps came up to the door. A flicker of movement clouded the spy hole hidden in the hemlock. Fred stepped back and smiled. The hoarse voice, definitely female, said from inside, "Who is it?"

"I'm looking for Russ Ennery," Fred said. "He lives in the building, upstairs. He's not home."

The door opened narrowly on a chain, making enough space to reveal a young woman in a green terry-cloth robe. Her black hair was wet, and there were beads of water on her face, hands, and bare legs.

"You have something for Russell?"

"No," Fred said. He waited.

"A message, anything like that?" the girl asked.

Fred shook his head.

"I can't help you. Sheila can help you," the woman said. "Maybe. I'm Dawn. I can't."

Dawn shouted, "Sheila," turning her head. She held the green robe closed. The room behind her was dim. Its furnishings were rudimentary and gave the impression of having been passed from one generation of students to another. The smell of pot was definite but mild; to Fred, from past association, it was the smell of mortal panic.

"Sit down," Dawn said. "If you want. On the stairs, buddy. A guy looking for Russ," she shouted into the apartment behind her, closing the door on him again.

Fred sat on the top step, listening.

"Sheila will be out in a minute," Dawn said, opening the crack in the door again and releasing the chain. "You might as well come in. If you're a friend of Russell's. Are you a friend of Russell's?" She looked doubtful.

"Not yet," said Fred, following her green robe inside.

The room was sparsely furnished with yard-sale clutter and dingy carpet. A double futon lay in one corner, with a dirty Indian-print spread across it, and tumbled blankets. Clothes were piled next to it in a heap. A closed door on the left had water running behind it. Bathroom. Shower. To the right the room opened into a small passage kitchen, which must lead to another room. Sheila's bedroom? Aside from a large mirror, there was nothing on the walls at all, other than old tan paint on top of wallpaper.

"My futon's the only place to sit," Dawn said. "I don't care if you don't. I'm not here much. I'm late."

"Students, are you?" Fred said.

He sat on an edge of the futon. Dawn raised the blinds on the room's two windows and let light in—not much of it, since the next building was only an arm's length away. She held the green robe tightly together when she moved, as if she were naked under it.

"Sheila was, I guess. Maybe still is. I dance," she said.

"What kind of dance?"

Dawn stood looking down at him, leaning against the wall between the windows. "Modern dance," she said vaguely. "Like Twyla Tharp? Gestural. Something like that."

"It's a hard life, dancing."

"So life is hard, the man says. What else is new?" Dawn turned toward the bathroom door and called again, "Sheila! I have to go."

She chose articles of clothing from the heap next to Fred—blue jeans and underpants—and put them on, carefully, primly, under the robe. She turned and let Fred see a glimpse of naked back, dropping the robe and shimmying into a black sweatshirt. She stepped into black boots with high heels.

"I'm leaving," Dawn shouted. She pulled a shoulder bag out of the heap of clothing and, running out, told Fred, "She'll be with you in a minute, buddy."

Fred listened to the shower running, enveloped in the aura of untidy female.

In five minutes Sheila and a cloud of steam came out of the shower. She was the blond girl Fred had seen yesterday talking to Russell Ennery on the sidewalk near Video King.

She had nothing on except for a pink towel wrapped around her hair. She had long legs like a horse's and reasonable muscle tone, breasts round as fruits, and skin pinker than beige.

"What the fuck . . . ," she said, seeing Fred. She doubled back into the bathroom and came out again wearing a long-sleeved shirt, a man's, with blue stripes and a button-down collar. She'd taken the towel off her head and left her long wet hair straggling.

"Jesus Christ," Sheila said, looking at Fred. "What do you want? Fucking Dawn let you in?"

Fred stood up.

"Don't touch me," Sheila said, backing into the door.

"I'm looking for Russell," Fred said. "That's all."

Water commenced staining through the shirt, showing the upper contours of her breasts, and their nipples.

"You want Russ, go to his place," Sheila said. "Upstairs."

She moved toward the apartment's front door.

"I want Russ," Fred said. "But for now you'll do, Sheila. Russell's not home."

Sheila fidgeted with the bottom of the shirt. "Let me get some pants on, for God's sake." She looked skittish.

Fred said, friendly, "As long as I can't find Russ and you're his friend, I'd hate for you to disappear before we have a chance to get acquainted."

"I put pants on before we get acquainted," Sheila said. "Unless you got a better idea?"

She looked at Fred. Fred waited.

"We'll both concentrate better," Sheila said, moving toward the kitchen, the shirttail cleaving to her damp backside. "You couldn't talk to Dawn? She knows Russ."

Fred stood to stay next to her, then realized that there was no other way out of here except by the back kitchen door, and Sheila was heading the other way, toward her bedroom.

She turned and said, "Don't fucking follow me, all right? When I come back, you tell me what you want to know and why I should tell you, and who the fuck you are anyway."

Fred sat on the futon, watching the kitchen. Sheila came in again wearing jeans with the shirt tucked in, and she stood looking down at him, her eyes narrowed.

"What you want with Russ?" she asked.

"I need to talk with him."

"Russ took off last night," Sheila said. "But that's enough about me. Let's talk about you."

"Russ is in over his head. He's going to get hurt."

"Go on," she said.

Fred said, "Maybe I can save us wasting time. I don't have any reason to hurt the guy myself."

"I thought you were the cops," Sheila said. She backed across the room and looked Fred over. "You look like a fucking narc. That's a piece, isn't it, under your arm?"

Fred nodded.

"What's the gun for? You want to show me some ID?" Sheila said.

Fred said, "Call me Fred."

"Okay, Fred," she said. "Fuck off, Fred." She opened the apartment door. "About Russ I know from nothing."

"You looked pretty close to Russ yesterday," Fred said, "talking together, the two of you, in the street. I'm telling you, Sheila, people could get hurt." He leaned back against the wall, comfortable, ready for a lengthy visit.

Sheila looked at him a moment, thinking. She closed the door. She crossed the room and squatted on the floor near him. "Tell you what. Let's us you tell me more and I'll see if I can help."

"Russell's in grad school at Harvard. In art history," Fred said. "I'm doing research that overlaps a project of his."

"You're in art history?" Sheila exclaimed, surprised.

"I'm working on Chase," Fred said.

"Chase. Cut to the chase. So?"

"Russ needs to know," Fred said.

Sheila leaned back, arching. Her hair was starting to dry toward silver. She took a brush out of a hip pocket and started brushing it, then said, "I wouldn't know Russell's business. You're wasting your time."

"Russ knows a painting I'm interested in. By Chase. It's missing."

Sheila stopped brushing and looked at him. Her tongue appeared at the corner of her mouth. Her eyes stayed carefully uninterested.

"He said that got completely screwed up," Sheila said. "Whatever it was. How does he get in touch if he wants to, if he calls?"

"It got screwed up, all right. Tell him to call me. Fred. At the Charles Hotel. I'll write down the number for you."

"I'll pass the message on," Sheila said, "if he calls, or if I see him."

"Tell him the letter is worth money," said Fred, standing.

"And you're connected to that?" Sheila said. "Money. A letter. Right?"

"I might be."

Sheila said, "If he calls, I'll tell him. I don't know if he'll call."

"Is there someplace else I might find him?" Fred asked. "Where he might be during the day?"

"I wouldn't know."

Fred got up and walked across the room toward the apartment door, noting that Sheila did not mention Video King. He wondered what else she was not mentioning.

Sheila stopped him. "How much money we talking? So I can tell him."

"Why don't you tell him to call," Fred said. He grinned in a reassuring manner.

He took the car back to the hotel and parked before walking back to Video King. Russ was scheduled to start work at three. A fat guy with a blond buzz cut and a pink Video King T-shirt chewed gum at him a minute in response to his question, thinking, then looked at the list in back of the desk, said, "He's finished with his shift at seven," and chewed some more.

If Russ didn't telephone him, Fred could come back at three-thirty and talk to him. Unless he'd left town. If he had, this would be harder.

Fred took portable coffee and a paper to his room. Sitting and looking across the river, he started thinking about Smykal's place on Turbridge Street—Smykal's place and Smykal's art and Smykal's body. He wanted none of it to be his business.

$\mathbf{F}$red called Molly at the library.

"I have your clothes, Fred. I'll bring them if you want to do lunch."

"You're on."

"Listen, Fred? Will you call the kids and tell them why you're not around? They think we had a fight. I know they think so because they won't say it."

"I'll call tonight. Come at noon-thirty. We'll do lunch in my room."

20

Fred went out and bought materials to make sandwiches, doing the errand fast in case Russ called, and then he sat at his window again. How well did they know each other, Russell Ennery and Sheila? Something about the painting had got screwed up, Sheila said. Had Russ been trying to buy or sell the painting? Suppose he had set something up with Smykal and Arthurian had scooped him? Russell comes back looking for the painting, and it's gone. Russell . . . someone had better talk to Russell soon, and it had better be Fred.

But Fred couldn't visualize Russ Ennery's managing to do to Henry Smykal what he had seen accomplished on that body, not even by accident. The idea was ludicrous and impossible.

Fred called Clay, told him where he was, what he was doing, and said, "Don't move."

"Wait," Clay said. "Before you hang up. You're neglecting our main concern. You didn't report to me about your dinner with Albert Finn last night. What have you learned?"

"Finn's gone Hollywood. He takes phone calls in the middle of dinner. Does it in monosyllables. I couldn't get anything out of him."

"Or Molly?"

"He's surrounded by a confidential aura. He signals that the Heade is of indifferent quality. Draw your own conclusions. I can't. Ophelia believes he's staying in Boston for the nookie. Hers."

"Nookie? Is that a painter? I seem to recall—an English sporting painter? Ophelia has a Nookie? Can I see it?"

"You can ask her. Ophelia has one, but it's not a painting. There are other things in the world, Clay. Be good."

Fred took a shower, leaving the door open and listening for his phone. Russell might call. Half dressed again, he lay down and shut his eyes to wait for Molly to come and wake him.

The telephone rang at 12:10. It woke Fred out of a sleep that wasn't prepared to finish for twenty minutes more.

A trembling male voice spoke. "Mr. Fred? Fred?"

"This is Fred. Russ Ennery?"

"You left a note on my desk?"

"Yes, that was mine."

There was a pause. Fred waited.

"Was that a joke?"

Fred waited.

"I guess not. You came looking for me. You came to my apartment. You talked to people, yes? That was you?"

"You got my message about the Chase painting," Fred said.

"Sheila says you mentioned money," Russ said. "Can I trust you?"

Fred said, "What did Sheila think?" and let that hang.

"You're not going to the police with—well, you're not . . ." The voice petered out.

His voice came again, frightened: "That thing, the other thing—I don't know anything about that."

150

Fred let that, too, hang. Nobody had mentioned Smykal or Turbridge Street or a body beaten until it died. Russ was putting out a feeler. Let it wave in a worrying void.

"Before I make a move, I want to talk with you," Fred said. "If that can be soon."

"I'm—well—pretty far out of town. But I'll come back if it's . . . I should be at work in a couple hours. You can meet me after."

"I'll be there at seven," Fred said. "Video King."

"You know where I work?"

"I know where you live, I know where you're from, I know where you work and when you get off. I'll meet you."

"Can we meet at your hotel? Maybe someplace quiet. Like— does the Charles Hotel have a bar?"

"It's called the Quiet Bar," Fred said. "I'll see you there at seven-fifteen?"

"That's great. That'll be great. About the money—"

"We'll talk."

"Yes. Talk."

Russ Ennery was sounding grateful, even relieved of his burden. Help was on its way.

Then Molly came for lunch. They picnicked and fooled around. Fred kept the .38 and its rig in the bureau beside the bed so neither of them would have to think about it.

Molly wore a white shirt of Indian cotton, a red cardigan sweater, and a green corduroy skirt. She was healthy and fragrant, like a good loaf of bread, and he told her so.

She said, "See, Fred, you do have domestic instincts."

"I'll call and talk to Sam and Terry," Fred said. "I will. I can't stand being around the kids carrying a weapon."

"It's nothing to be ashamed of," Molly said. "Just so you tell them something they can make sense of. Otherwise children always think it's their fault."

151

"I know," Fred said. "We all do. It won't be long. I'll call and tell them."

Fred hated the waiting. With Molly gone, he hated the waiting. The kid, Russ, made him uneasy. He was a slippery kid under pressure. He had seemed too grateful, too compliant—too willing, given the tiny amount of pressure Fred had brought to bear.

Whatever he thought he had going with Smykal's painting, Russ was out of his depth. Learning that the man had been murdered must have worked on his nerves. He was already nervy last Saturday when Fred first saw him in the fine-arts library, before the news got out. He was moaning and tearing his hair even then.

Fred walked past Video King a couple of times during Ennery's shift and saw that he was there, in back of the counter, wearing that bow tie. He hadn't lost his sense of style.

At seven Fred went to the Quiet Bar and looked around. At the Charles you got comfort with your class. They offered individual tables and big chairs. Fred took a big gray foam armchair beside another empty one, on one side of a table across from two more. A waitress hovered next to him until he asked for coffee. He watched for Russ.

In a few minutes, as the coffee was placed before him, he heard a damp voice claiming, "I've seen you around."

Fred turned to a vision of denim and the open-necked checked shirt of Buddy Mangan. Mangan stood next to him, studying him. The short blond curls faltered, and he grinned.

"This seat taken?" Mangan asked.

"I'm waiting for someone," Fred said. He took a sip of his coffee.

Mangan sat in the chair across from him.

"Let's say I represent him," Mangan said. "Friend of a friend."

He beckoned to the waitress, who approached him with reluctance. In this costume Mangan would give them all a bad name.

"Bring me a beer," Mangan said.

"Sir, we have Sam Adams on draft, or Beck's Dark, or—"

"You choose, hon," Mangan said. "You mind? We're talking."

"You're Fred," Mangan continued. "That all?"

"My wants are few," Fred said.

The waitress leaned over with Buddy Mangan's beer, a dark draft, and a dish of cashews.

"I've seen you around," Mangan said again. He took a drink of his beer and popped a nut into his mouth, using his thick fingers with a delicacy that made Fred think of pinning insects.

"I have a client for the Chase," Mangan said. "I take it you control the picture?"

"Control is a relative concept," Fred said.

"What's on your mind?" Mangan asked. "I presume we can get something together."

Fred said, "It's complex."

"So we stick to the point and don't get suckered into irrelevant side issues," Mangan said. "Then it's not relative and it's not complex. It's easy if you think of it like this: You have something. I want it."

"Side issues," Fred said. "Like bashing in a guy's head."

"And cunt pictures and whatnot have you," Mangan said. He scratched the thick hair that was struggling to escape at his open neck. "I heard about that. It's distracting, an unfortunate coincidence. I'm not worried, if I get the picture."

Fred said, "Suppose we are both looking for a Chase painting."

Mangan leaned toward him. His face reddened. The beer on his breath was Beck's, and dark. "Listen, you fuck. I want the picture."

"Let's not make a scene," Fred suggested. He motioned

Mangan to sit back, allowing his two big hands to rest near Mangan's on the table. "Your client is Arthurian, I take it?" he asked.

Fred watched more people come in. The singles stood at the bar, hopeful. Groups took the tables. The waitresses herded and served gracefully. It was a perfect world, the peaceable kingdom.

Mangan looked poleaxed. His jaw dropped. His body language expressed confusion. "The kid said you work for Arthurian."

"I do not have that honor," Fred said.

"That fucking recluse!" Mangan said, all command lost. "Who is he? Where is he? My client, hell! I never heard of Arthurian. Nobody has. Arthur Arthurian? The Arthurian collection? Nobody's heard of any of it. Ask anyone."

Fred signaled a waitress for more coffee. Mangan finished his beer.

"I know I've seen you around," Mangan said.

"Apparently my guy wants the same thing yours does," Fred said.

"In that case, fuck you," Mangan said. "You are wasting my fucking time."

The waitress brought Fred's coffee. She looked a question at Buddy Mangan. Mangan nodded. He thought a minute, smiled at Fred, and made the "fuck you" into a joke, retroactively.

"We both want something, right?" he said.

Fred nodded.

"The same thing."

Fred nodded again.

"This Arthur Arthurian. According to the paper, the cops want him, too. We want to find him first. We can work it together. I don't know. If we get the painting for my client and you keep your guy out of it, there'll be something in it for you."

"So I help you find Arthurian's painting," Fred said. "Tell me about the commission."

"Five thousand dollars. How's that sound?"

"Maybe we get a better price from my guy," Fred said.

"You find that painting, get in touch with me first," Mangan said. "My people do not like to dick around. You know what we're looking for, I presume?"

Mangan reached into the bib pocket of his overalls and pulled out a card for Buddy Mangan Fine Art, with the Cohasset address and phone number. The waitress delivered his beer. Mangan threw a twenty onto the table, hauled out of the same pocket.

"There's one thing bothering me," Fred said.

"Don't worry about the dead guy," Mangan whispered confidentially. "The stuff I hear he was into, I assure you he was asking for it. It makes it harder, though, don't it? What a business we're in! 'Complex,' to use your own well-chosen word. And relative as all shit!" Mangan laughed and swallowed his beer.

"You want to be careful just the same," Fred said. He stood.

"Keep in touch," Buddy Mangan said. He waved toward the waitress.

21

Fred walked out. He had to decide whether to drop this right now.

Russ was hunting with Mangan, acting as his jackal. Russell was a dangerous fool. That academic arrogance. Triumph of the mind. Russ was a kid with no conscience, no center, no understanding of the world. Perfect for a career in Celtic bronze. As far as working with Buddy Mangan—you don't outrun a waterfall. You don't stand and argue with it, don't try to appeal to its sympathy. Either it batters and drowns you or you find your way around it by land.

When Fred got back to his room, he called Molly's and talked to the kids for a while. Mostly he talked to Sam, man to man. But he feared Sam wasn't believing him. Fred tried to explain that he was doing something that meant he had to be closer to town. He'd maybe see them Saturday, or Sunday.

Then he realized that the reason Sam didn't believe him was that he was lying. That was fair.

"Look, Sam," Fred said. "I should level with you. The fact is, the work I'm doing has started getting risky. I'm thinking it might make a dangerous situation around your house, for your mom and you and Terry."

"I know," Sam said. "She'll be pissed if you're hurt."

"I will be, too," Fred said. "I'll be careful."

"Good," Sam said. "Mom says you have your gun. I'll put Terry on."

"Miss you," Terry said.

It was good, over the phone, almost as if he deserved it, having two children, one saying she missed him, the other one thinking it would be better if he didn't get hurt. It was a problem, though, because it meant he had to be careful.

F red had the evening free. He wasn't going to lean on Russ, or follow him, or push him any more. He knew now where the Russ theme led: to Mangan. And at the moment he wanted no part of that. If Clay had the painting and Mangan the letter that authenticated it, that was an interesting problem made still more so by the corpse lying between them.

Fred called Clayton and reported that he had found a loose end to pull but wasn't convinced it was a good idea since there was something nasty on the other end. Clayton should sit tight, do nothing.

Clay was remarkably docile. "I'm reading Proust," he said. "It's what I always thought I'd do in prison."

Fred took off his shoes, sat in the hotel's chair, and put his feet up on the bed, looking out over the hotel's darkening river. It should have swallows darting over it, but it was still too dead.

Buddy Mangan. Prior to this Fred had only seen the man throwing his weight around in the auction room. He acted as if he'd had a deal with Smykal. Presumably he had the letter Clay needed. Had Smykal been fool enough to sell the package twice—to deliver the painting to Clay and the letter to Mangan—and then run? He might have believed he could diddle Clay, but hardly Mangan—unless he'd met only Russ.

Fred thought about it, wondering whether it would be worth it to find Russ and sit down with him. Or should he leave this where it was and tell Clay to take the loss?

Meanwhile, the tail end of Smykal's avocation flicked from under a rock Fred hadn't turned over: the photography he had been making when Fred came back for the letter, of which no evidence remained when Smykal's body lay there not long after, starting to cool in its blood and sweat.

It was a troublesome fact to know about and not resolve if Fred decided to let it be his business. His urgent instinct was to leave it.

Fred called Molly and asked her to come into Cambridge. Maybe she could take in a movie with him.

"Sam has a Spanish test I have to study for," Molly said. "I can't be gallivanting around with you."

Fred would sleep awhile, let things settle in his mind. Then he'd find dinner if he felt hungry.

He was uneasy. He wanted something to unravel the tangles in back of his eyes between what he knew, what he didn't know, what he didn't know he knew, what he knew he didn't know, and what he didn't want to know if he could help it.

He woke sometime after one, startled. Was there noise? Someone in the room? Something out in the hall?

He recalled Molly's waking in fear some nights ago to find him standing naked in her dark window. How could he not be the thing she rightly feared?

He'd wakened as you do when the phone rings, adrenaline pulling you out of sleep like a diver hauled too fast from the deep. He listened, looked into the dark. Nothing else was breathing here. Pulling open the drawer of the bureau, he slid the gun out and paced through the room. Faint light reflecting off the river came through his window. He listened at the door, opened it quickly, and stared into the empty corridor.

He was awake for certain now and wouldn't sleep again.

He went to the window. The sky had cleared. The glass was cold.

Molly had packed a sweater with his clothes. It was wool, navy blue. He put that on over a heavy shirt, with his jeans and sneakers. Smart Molly to think he'd want them. He could call her, wake her, and thank her. Then the shoulder holster and the jacket. It was a tight fit, but warm.

He eased through the hotel, still active in the bars and lobby with people putting off going to bed. He'd leave the car in the garage and walk down to Pearl Street, stretch his legs, maybe check on Russ; just take a look.

Walking through Harvard Square, still fitfully merry with stragglers, he wondered, was it sympathy that had wakened him? His feelings about Ennery had changed, as if they'd been pushed off a high cliff. He had the kid in his mind and was feeling sorry for him. Whatever his business with Mangan was, Russ was outclassed, out of his depth, suffering a big loss and trouble he could only start to guess at. On the telephone he'd come on bravely, doing his best, trying to scramble long enough to retrieve something out of the ruin. If Russ was reporting to Mangan, Mangan was calling the plays.

Fred didn't want to despise Russ. He didn't want to see him hurt. He didn't want to see that silly bow tie, so naive and defiant, so newly out of its chrysalis, smashed into permanent submission.

What had awakened him was a feeling of danger for Russell. Fred wanted to take care of the kid.

He'd have to be careful, then, and see to it that he didn't allow his judgment to be pulled out of focus by his instincts and emotions.

Outside the square, traffic, vehicular and foot, thinned out fast. Fred stretched his legs, warming up, almost everything closed now along Mass. Ave. Video King was dimly lit but empty. Cops dozed in their cruiser on Turbridge Street in front of Smykal's building. The Irish pub on Hancock Street was open. Someone was working behind closed doors at the Post Office, a few lights on. Central Square was brighter, friendlier. More people were out. It was a different population here, with more variety of color, shape, and size. It was more truly cosmopolitan, with Indians, Haitians, Arabs, blacks, Puerto Ricans, Chinese, and the multitudinous immigrants of the European countries.

Fred spotted a place still open that did barbecue, and indulged a sudden hunger. He had coffee with his sandwich. Seven or eight people were in the storefront, a couple of them drumming on a table. It was lively. The walls were painted fire-engine red. A pair of cops walked in, in uniform, joking with the people behind the counter. No two people in the place were the same color.

Fred thought, I'm playing bachelor. He'd been knocked off track by the seductive affection that had come over him in his sleep. If he'd had a son back when he was first old enough to have one, that son might be Russ Ennery's age now. Was that it? Was Fred the bull cow looking for his calf? A sympathy like that was irresponsible. You could lose men that way.

Well.

He paid the guys at the counter, told them good-night, nodded to the cops, and went on to Pearl Street. It was three in the morning now. The front door of Russell's building sagged open, as usual. No lights were on in the apartments, but one bulb burned in the stairwell. Someone was sleeping in the back of the first-floor hallway. It looked like an old lady back there, curled up. She snorted in a toothless way when he looked down at her, and curled tighter in her nest of plastic bags, stuffed with what she owned.

You couldn't tiptoe up these stairs, but people who conspired to leave their street door flapping open wouldn't be surprised by heavy footsteps on the staircase at any time of the day or night.

Fred climbed to the top floor. The kitty litter outside Russell's door had been changed. There was a saucer of milk out. Russ was in residence. Fred stood listening at the door, but he knew there shouldn't be anything to hear if Russ was sleeping.

He stopped on the second-floor landing and stood outside the apartment he'd been in this morning, talking with Dawn and Sheila. Anyone who saw him standing here would take him for a middle-aged geek, a peeper.

"Jesus Christ!" Fred said almost aloud. "What did I throw away?"

He hurried back into Central Square, found an all-night convenience store where he picked up a tiny flashlight, batteries, and heavy gloves, and headed back toward Harvard Square.

"Goddamn," Fred said. "When's trash day?"

The night was darker and more deserted than before. The cops were still sleeping in their cruiser in front of Smykal's place on Turbridge Street, lulled by the companionship of their radio, voices, static, and the occasional flickering shadows of passersby crossing the streetlight. The insides of their windows were fogged by their breathing.

The barrels stood full, even brimming, next to Smykal's building. Piled next to them, and heaped on top, were soaked cardboard, a mattress, a busted baby stroller, and the rest. Fred put it through his mind and called the image back, selected the second barrel in from the sidewalk, figured how far down he ought to have to go, and pulled the gloves on. The street surrendered enough ambient light for him to see what he needed to.

"I'm not the only person in this town combing through people's trash to look for cans and bottles," Fred muttered. "And watching out for needles."

161

If the cops in the cruiser woke and saw him, it wouldn't cause a moment's question.

I guess they found enough to go through in his place, Fred thought, surprised that the Cambridge detectives had not sorted through the building's trash.

"What do I do for Clayton Reed?" he said aloud. "You'd call me a curator, madam."

Two feet down and relatively dry, he found it: the Kinko's bag he'd tossed early last Saturday morning on his way to visit Smykal's corpse.

L I G H T S °° C A M E R A S °° A C T I O N and the rest of it. L I V E °° M O D E L S and the number.

Fred put one of the posters in his pocket. Alone outside the dead man's place, he felt a wave of dismal kinship moving toward him: the wary fellowship of the lone man.

Live Models. A thing of beauty is a joy for about a moment. Fred had taken a thing of beauty from this place, a thing that had a genetic link with the dead man. Conchita Hill, that charming young woman, naked and frank as an apple—what had become of her? Where were the paintings she made? Her wedding dress? The basket of pins and ribbons she used, her glasses and false teeth? How had the energy and beauty of the woman, launched into the world, come to find itself finally cornered hopelessly in the dead end that was Smykal?

That thing of beauty, Conchita—everything she had done or made had vanished utterly.

Fred sat in his room and watched the sun think about lifting itself to ride over the river. He laid the poster next to the phone. He looked at the phone number. He looked in the book; Smykal was not listed. He looked at the number and dialed it. Four-thirty in the morning. He listened to it ring until it clicked into a cheerful recorded voice: "Lights. Cameras. Action. Our models are busy but willing. Please leave your name and number. We'll get back to you."

The voice was Dawn's.

Fred tasted the fecund air of the outdoors. Mangan nagged at him. He wasn't going to sleep. The man had had the gall to hand his card over as if he were an insurance salesman. Mangan was up to his eyeballs in Fred's business. In Smykal's killing, too, maybe—not Fred's business. But it was Fred's business if Mangan had the letter, the Chase autograph. He itched to drive to the South Shore, take a look at Mangan's famous spread, walk in and look around. A move like that would have to wait, though, until after the auction. Fred should at least follow his own advice and not risk making waves until the issue of the Heade was settled. Wait. Let it wait.

Let Russ be. Forget Dawn's voice on the machine. It's not your problem, Fred. Interesting, but not your problem. File the following observation, though: Buddy Mangan is more than a loud noise. He's dangerous.

Telephone.

It was Molly's voice in Fred's ear. He put the gun down.

He'd picked the gun up when the phone rang. That was instinct working: old habits; nerves.

"Miss you," said Molly. "You awake?"

"I'm awake." He looked at his watch. It was eight o'clock. He'd slept again. "I miss you, too. Did you do good Spanish? Let me talk to Sam. I'll try to egg him on."

"He left already. I told him you wished him well."

"Let's have lunch. We could go to a place," Fred said.

"I liked how we did it yesterday," said Molly. "It makes me feel egregious. I'll bring a snack. See you—what?—around one?"

"Check. Meet me in the Quiet Bar. It's my new hangout."

"Be in your room," Molly said, "because that's where I'm going."

"Fair enough."

"I want to warn you: Ophelia may call you."

"How come?"

"She wants your opinion. I couldn't think what to say about why you were at the Charles, since I won't tell her your business."

"God, no."

"Say whatever you want. Ophelia has the impression there's a rift between us. I didn't deny it since, with Ophelia, there's no point."

"If she calls," Fred said, "I'll try to be decent with her. Is she still with Finn?"

"She said she has to talk with you," Molly said. "We didn't talk about her sex life."

"Ghastly thought. I'll see you, Molly."

"Believe it."

22

Fred showered and dressed for the day, putting on white shirt and tie. He put the gun under his arm and pulled on the sport coat over it. He went downstairs for a paper and breakfast. The hotel's dining room was filled with the clean and blessed. He sat. Two minutes later, behind the headlines, Ophelia materialized. She was all business in a blue suit and exhibited elaborate surprise at seeing him.

"Fred! What are you doing here? Breakfast at the Charles! La la. Alone? Or are you meeting someone?"

Ophelia was content to trade an hour's scandal for her sister's well-being.

"I'm having breakfast. Alone, as you see. Until now. Molly said you'd call."

"Oh, you talked to Molly?" Ophelia said, disappointed. "I'll join you, may I?" she said, sitting, her tail end used to being warmly received wherever she presented it. "I want your opinion, Fred."

"So Molly said. Let me order."

He asked the waiter to bring pancakes, and coffee as soon as possible. Ophelia ordered coffee also, "as long as I'm here."

She leaned across the table, her hands clasped, a gleam in her eye. "I decided I must see you this morning. Fred, I need your advice. About an idea."

She paused, waiting for Fred to bite. He drank coffee and waited, looking at her.

"You are the first person I'm talking with. I haven't even mentioned it to Sir Albert. Al. Al Finn."

"Do you want something to eat?" Fred asked her.

Ophelia shook her head. "I'm excited about Al's potential. He knows so much, though, it intimidates me. I'm afraid if I talk with him prematurely, he'll laugh. I don't want to go off— pardon my language, Fred—half-cocked."

Ophelia looked at Fred, waiting.

"Why should he laugh?" Fred asked her.

"He doesn't believe in TV, but I think he's a natural ham, and you know I have an instinct for the medium." She leaned back, awaiting Fred's approval.

"You want to get Finn on one of those 'Be Happy with the Body You Have Already' things?" Fred asked. "It would be great to see the old boy in a white leotard, pontificating."

"No, no. It's a new series I'm developing, trying to bring to the proposal stage. Totally new idea. I produce it and appear as hostess since people want to see me. But my idea is to have Sir Albert as, well, the artistic director."

Ophelia gleamed.

"Al and I get on so well," she went on. "We are almost inseparable, except when he's working or—"

"What's the plan?" Fred interrupted.

"*The Great Collectors*. A series about the interesting art collectors. Al knows them all and helps them with their collections. He knows where the bodies are buried." Ophelia's merry laugh sounded as if she'd spent far too much time already in the company of A. Finn.

"The idea is, we film the collections. We go all over the country together. WGBH pays for it. Albert can do a spinoff book without even thinking. You do the shows to sell the books. Sir Albert introduces each show in his beautiful English way, he talks to the collector for ten minutes, then they show the collection. Albert and the collector talk, with my help. It's made in heaven. It's never been done."

"I'll tell you right now," Fred said. He occupied himself with his pancakes. "Clay's such a private cuss, you won't get to first base with him."

"With Clay?" Ophelia looked perplexed. "Oh, you mean your boss. No, no, heavens." She vouchsafed a peal of laughter. "My plan is to have Sir Albert talk with people of importance, not locals. Some of the persons he advises. A few chosen others."

She leaned across to where she could almost strip a bite of pancake from Fred's fork. "Some of these collectors have never consented to be interviewed before. Al's reputation, and the growing momentum of the project, will bring them on board. You'll never guess who I'm thinking of to do the kickoff."

"I never will," said Fred. "Listen, Ophelia, I've learned to love the body I have. Do you want my last pancake?"

"No. Thanks. I'm serious. I heard Al talking about him last night, very excited, you know how he can be, and it came to me, the whole thing. We'll lead the series—*The Great Collectors*—with Arthur Arthurian."

"You're joking."

"I knew that would impress you," Ophelia said. "From something Albert let drop late last night or early this morning—I lose track of the time, he's so exciting to be with—he's going to write an introduction for the catalog of the Arthurian collection."

She reached out, took Fred's remaining pancake, lathered it with butter and syrup, and started eating.

"I wondered," Ophelia said with translucent innocence, "because you know so much about it and I know so much about other things instead, before I start talking the project through seriously with Al, what can you, Fred, personally tell me about the famous Arthur Arthurian?"

Finn had been in town for what, three days? four? and already his network had caught the scent of Arthur Arthurian. He must be going crazy wondering about this collector he'd never heard of.

Fred signaled for more coffee while Ophelia sharpened her attention. Let her wait for a change.

"One only hears rumors. He's not your Onassis type," Fred told her, "nor your Gulbenkian. From what I hear, Arthurian abhors the light of publicity, the beaten track."

"Wait a minute," Ophelia said. "Let me take notes."

Fred obliged. Ophelia found a notebook in her Hermès handbag, which she'd put beside her on the table so the room could see she had one.

"Don't breathe a word to anyone," Fred advised, "until you have Arthurian's permission."

"Of course not," Ophelia said. "But since you're telling me, it will save the great man's time later."

Fred had an uncomfortable suspicion that Ophelia was here not as what she seemed but as an ambassador, looking, on Finn's account, for information that he couldn't get himself because it did not exist. If that was the case, Fred would send back smoke. Clay deserved a gesture of revenge.

"The art world is a small world, and Arthurian a very private man," Fred said.

"I understand. But tell me, for example, where does he live?"

"I hear he has become a recluse."

"Became a recluse where?" Ophelia said.

"I know nothing I can guarantee," Fred said.

"Where is he?" she asked. "Where's his collection? Albert knows, but I hate him to think I'm ignorant."

"I can only tell you what I've heard, and none of it may be true. I only tell you in strictest confidence," Fred said. "Because what Arthurian owns—the paintings alone, when I tell you—naturally you are familiar with *La Gioconda.*"

"Of course," Ophelia said. "Just . . . remind me."

"The *Mona Lisa.*"

Ophelia nodded and smiled. She loved that. "Yes, by da Vinci. The mystery smile!"

"Its companion piece, her husband, facing toward her—*L'Arcigno*—that belongs to Arthurian."

"My God. Will he let us film it?"

"You'll have to ask him," Fred said.

"Where is he to ask him?"

"He travels."

"Would your boss know?" Ophelia asked.

"He stops in Boston when he can," Fred said. "I gather he was here last week. He was to leave for Kansas City, by train. He travels only by train."

"He was in Boston last week?" Ophelia repeated.

"That is what I heard. It may not be true."

23

Fred drove into Boston.

He would not assume indefinitely that Clayton's home and office must remain a no-man's land. There had been no sign that any connection had been made between Clay and his snowballing imaginary friend Arthurian. If the police had put the two together, they'd also know the way to Clayton Reed was through Fred, who was not hard to find.

Fred, ever since he'd picked up the gun, had been watching his back, as a matter of old habit. Nobody seemed to care about him. The day was clear and would be warm again, spring already waning. There was no traffic to fight. Rush hour was over except for executives starting late.

He parked a couple of blocks from Clayton's and walked over, looking for unusual interest in the house and finding none. He went in, picked up the mail, and put it on his desk to take to Clay later.

Fred pulled out the Chase and looked at La Belle Conchita.

He hadn't had a chance to enjoy the painting since identifying its author. It was Chase all over. As to La Belle Conchita herself, she looked an energetic kid, amused at her own daring, knowing herself in the hands of a young master, in the company of Goya's *Maja*, Titian's *Danaë* or *Venus* (whatever their names were), Courbet's and Whistler's Jo.

When Chase had finished work and washed his brushes, had Conchita rolled over, hopped up, and said, "Okay, Will, my turn. I want to do you. Drop trousers and recline. Allow me a long gaze at that precious fanny. Or no, face me. We'll see if my brush can catch the indigo accent on the testicles against the crimson of your waving thingy!"?

How had they talked to each other of such things in those days? The painting, as formal in its way as conversation recorded in novels of the day, drew down the curtain of discretion before the slippery moments started.

The painted nude of the period had not much to do with sex and rather more with monuments. It allowed a stripping-away of evanescent fashion, a concentration on what was permanent: a form that a succession of humans continues to fill. It was unlike the pornographic photo torn out of *Penthouse* in that pop pornography, to maintain its narrow focus, must exhibit a contrary fillip of current fashion. The boots, the smile, and the hat in the photograph all emphasize the thesis that the sum of a woman is smaller than her parts.

The telephone rang. Fred left it. He'd let Clayton continue to be unreachable since that was the plan. When it stopped, as long as he was here, he called Clay at the Copley. Was there anything he could do? Feed the cat, take in the milk, water the plants? It wasn't that kind of house. Nothing was alive in it but Clay, when Clay was home; and Fred, and the paintings.

"Thank you. As long as I have Proust, I want for nothing. You might collect the mail, in case of something urgent. I called the Ritz, by the way, and learned that Albert Finn remains in town. Therefore he has his eye on the Heade, either as a Heade—in which case I shall outbid him—or because he knows what we suspect."

"I'll come over," Fred said. "We can talk about it. Not only is he in town, but Ophelia says he's talking about writing an introduction to the catalog for the Arthurian collection."

"There is no Arthurian collection," Clay protested.

"We'll talk about it," said Fred. "I'll be right over."

Normally he would have enjoyed walking to Copley Square, but he'd stick with the car today, not knowing where he would have to go next. This part of Boston looked nice in the spring. Trees were putting on heavy green. Daffodils, tulips, and magnolias were established in the small plots of yard allotted to the old buildings. In a week all bloom would be gone from the magnolias.

"What's this about Finn and the Arthurian collection?" Clay asked as he let Fred in. Fully dressed and groomed, he had a green volume of Proust—in French—closed on his finger, so he would not lose his place. "Is it a joke? I do not feel like joking. I don't relish living away from home. I own a new painting I have barely seen. I don't wish to be Mr. Whistler. Proust I can enjoy equally well in my own flat, except for the distractions. I begin to think of this, Fred, as my period of exile."

Fred sat in one of the armchairs. Clay kept his room so neat you could barely tell it was being occupied. Suitcases had been emptied into drawers and closets, the cases themselves sent down to the baggage room to be stored until he was ready for them. Nothing was left lying on chairs or tables. The *New York Times*, already read, was folded again.

"It's no joke," Fred said. He handed the pack of mail to Clay as he sat in the chair, the two of them on either side of the round table in front of the window. "No joke. Finn heard of Arthurian, possibly from someone who read your advertisements. More likely he read it himself in yesterday's paper and

172

is itching to learn about this potential pigeon. In any case, Ophelia—you recall Molly's sister, Ophelia?"

Clay shuddered. Ophelia had made a determined play for him at that disastrous Christmas party at Molly's. "It's not that I fail to appreciate women," Clay had confessed later, apologizing for his precipitous departure, "it's just—I am preoccupied with other matters, and they are so complex!"

"Ophelia," Fred continued, "came to see me at the hotel to pump me for information about Arthurian."

"You told her nothing, surely?" Clayton needed to be reassured.

"She's no wiser about Arthurian than she was," Fred said. "The thing is, I don't know if Finn sent her to ask me."

"You think Arthurian is definitely after the Heade, then, do you?" said Clay.

"Clay, climb out of the Proust a minute. *You* are Arthurian, remember? There is no Arthurian."

Clay said, "Did I say Arthurian? I meant Heade. I mean Finn."

Fred said, "The police want Arthurian to help their investigation. Ophelia's in on the act, with Finn. Do you think it may be time to simplify this? Break cover, tell the cops who you are and what's going on?"

He had decided not to mention Mangan. That can of worms, as long as he himself did not know whether to look into it, could be opened later if it had to.

"What day is it?" Clay asked.

"Thursday."

"Stay with the plan. Sit tight until the sale. I cannot think about two things at once. Finish one thing first, Fred. The main objective."

Clay crossed his legs and held the stack of mail in his right hand, gesturing with it. He went on, "The stakes are high. Sitting in this room, having time to contemplate—and let me tell you,

Proust is a great aid to contemplation—I have been looking at the Vermeer. Let me show you."

He rose and went to the desk supplied by the hotel, set in a window overlooking Copley Square, with its churches, parks, and homeless. He opened the top drawer and pulled out the catalog of Doolan's sale. The Heade, placed late in the sale—a tactic to keep the buying audience present and alert through the doldrums of the earlier part of the sequence—was illustrated in color. An oblong almost square, 26 × 27 inches, it sat on its long side. A landscape by Heade should be more horizontal, so as to take advantage of its shape and lead the eye out to the horizon on both sides.

Clay brought the catalog over to the window and held it sideways. The Heade was now tipped on its side, so that the haystacks pointed east, like the breasts of Renoir's Wertheim *Baigneuse*. Beside it Clay held the photocopy of the drawing made from the Vermeer when it was shown at the Mass. Mechanics Hall in eighteen-whatever.

Clay said, "Heade wouldn't have had time to lay down a coat of white lead to obscure the earlier painting. The work was done on the spur of the moment, and white lead would take a week to dry. Heade had to paint directly onto Vermeer's image, on top of whatever dirt and varnish had accrued, which will be our good fortune.

"He'd have known that over time his oil paint must become more transparent and allow the underpainting to show through. Contrary lines would appear from below, challenging his forms. And so, where possible, he let his new forms correspond to the design on his support."

Clay gestured with the eraser of a yellow pencil, tracking the lines on the two images. "See here? The line at the base of the haystack corresponds to the vertical edge of the window. This shadow-line falls along what would have been the bottom edge of the window. Those hard edges would be the most difficult to conceal.

"But the shoulders of the principal haystack, here—do you see?—adapt the curve of the woman's arm, down to the table, and a river line in the map, and so on. I've studied the two, and the fit is quite extraordinary."

"It's a convincing argument," Fred said. He held the color print from Doolan's and the drawing together and looked at them.

"I think of those two young people," Clay said. He sat down again and gazed out the window. "Young townspeople, full of life and hope, on the brink of great adventure, condemned to a century of bucolic obscurity."

He was talking about the characters in the picture, the fine, flat smudges and glazes of oil and light: the hours of careful edging, the slow resolution of harmony and contrast. He thought it was a puppet show.

"And," said Clay, "naturally I think about Vermeer also: his work held hostage. Look at the Heade, for heaven's sake! Any moment a cow could splash through that swamp!"

"If Heade could draw it," Fred said.

"Of course Heade could draw it! Someone who can do a magnolia that delicate?"

"A joke, Clay."

"In poor taste," Clay said.

"But you plan to dissolve the Heade, don't you?" Fred asked.

"If it comes to that, I will make a determination based on the higher good."

"Survival of the preferred."

"Something like that," Clay said, immune to irony.

"I'll be off," Fred said, rising.

"Yes, of course," Clay said absently. "I leave this in your hands, Fred. Wait, look at this." He pulled a note out of an envelope. Fred had leafed through the mail and noticed the envelope addressed simply to Clayton Reed, without stamp or address—therefore delivered by hand. It was this that Clay had opened.

"It is from Albert Finn. Listen, Fred. The man covers the world, like a miasma."

Fred had undergone a surfeit of Proust.

Clayton read, "'Dear Clayton, you are evidently out of town—in search of something wonderful, I trust?—because the telephone fails to raise you. I must postpone my departure from Boston a few days and wonder if you might care to visit about a matter of common interest? Albert Finn.'

"On a sheet of Ritz notepaper, as you see. That tears it," Clay said. "Finn wants to do a deal. You talked too much, Fred. He knows what's under the Heade."

"You won't know unless you talk with him."

"Talk with that pirate again? I'm out of town. I cannot receive his missive." He snorted. "No talks. No deals. No quarter. I'll call my bank and see how much we can allocate to the Heade. We'll not compromise."

Fred left Clay preening in his dove gray suit, sitting in the window, the Proust falling open again to where his finger marked it, his eye picking up where he'd left off.

24

Fred drove back to Cambridge. He had decided, after reflecting on it, to keep Russ in his sights. He hated to go near this again after hearing Dawn's voice on the recording. It smelled like the edge of a rat's nest. But someone ought to watch Russ.

As he reached the second floor of Russell's building, the door of the apartment opened and Dawn came out dressed as he'd seen her last, in jeans and sweatshirt, the sweatshirt pink today, her big green bag swinging.

"Fred," she said. They were old friends now. "They told me that's your name. Russ said he talked to you. He came back last night. He's out again, but he wants to meet you at your hotel. The Charles? Same place as yesterday. About eleven, he said."

"Right."

It was almost eleven now.

"He called your hotel, he said."

"Right. Can I give you a lift somewhere?"

"My mom said don't go in a strange man's car," Dawn said. "Especially one as big and sexy as you."

She gave a brilliant grin, excellently crafted.

"Not even if they want to talk about *Live Models?*" Fred said. "*Lights—Cameras—Action?*"

"Oh, shit," Dawn said, leading him down the stairs to the sidewalk. "You're one of them. Pussy photos. Shit. I should have known. Okay, buddy. What's your game?"

"Where you headed?" Fred asked.

"I'm not crawling into any fucking car with you," Dawn said. "You think I'm crazy?"

They paused while an old woman carrying groceries passed between them on the sidewalk.

"Your voice on the tape. How did the rest of it go? Tell me about Smykal," Fred said.

"Oh, fuck," Dawn said. "That cheap asshole. Jesus, that man was worse than he smelled." She shuddered and looked at Fred, the two of them standing on the Pearl Street sidewalk, traffic trudging past, dirt blowing around their ankles.

"Smykal died," Fred said.

"He couldn't smell worse now," Dawn said. "So what if he used my voice? What's your angle, buddy? Everyone's got an angle. Crotch shots."

"Not on the sidewalk." Fred opened the passenger door and held it.

"Fucking gentleman," Dawn said, climbing in.

"I'm going up to the T." She locked her door. "Ride me to Central Square. Say whatever you want on the way. You don't have to threaten me. I'm ahead of you, buddy."

"I need information, that's all," Fred said. "So I understand how it works." He started the car and eased down toward the river, Pearl being one-way heading away from the square.

"You don't fucking know? Central Square's the other way."

"If you have time," Fred said, "we could sit somewhere. And

talk. You and Russ and—was Sheila in this thing?—you are looking at a lot of trouble."

"That jerk-off Russ, what did he tell you?"

"Why don't we talk it over with him?" Fred suggested. "We'll pick him up at the Charles. If you have nothing better to do." He looked sideways and saw the sweat of consternation on Dawn's face as she thought. Reaching the river, he turned upstream, toward Harvard and the Charles Hotel.

"Shit," Dawn said. "Fucking Russ. He promised me our troubles were almost over." She stared out Fred's window, across him, at the river and the cherry trees blooming along the bank.

"I can help fix it for you," Fred said. "If it's fixable. But first I have to know what's going on."

"Shit," Dawn said again. "What do we do, talk in your fucking room?"

"Maybe that's good," Fred said.

"With your cock in my mouth, right? So I enunciate better?"

"Why don't we not bother shocking me with the frank intimacies, Dawn? I'm serious," Fred said. "Get Russ in the Quiet Bar and bring him up. I'll park the car."

It was almost half past eleven.

Fred dropped Dawn at the front of the hotel.

"I'll bring him," she said, slamming the door.

Fred watched her sail past the doorman. If only Ophelia could see that long, athletic stride, the young woman with the dancer's body climbing out of Fred's car at the Charles Hotel. That would offer a year's supply of grist for her salacious mule.

Fred drove down into the hotel's garage and parked the car, and two large men started beating the shit out of him as he was halfway out.

They were big. They were ready, seasoned, and able. One grabbed Fred's left arm as he opened the car door and stepped out. He pulled while the other chopped, punched, and jabbed Fred around head, shoulders, and kidneys. His right arm free,

Fred whirled, grabbed the ear of the second man, twisted, jabbed his eyes, and punched at the face of the first while kicking shins and knees. He ducked and twisted in a flurry of fists, crimson, sweat, and cologne.

He felt his left arm gripped so hard he had to twist and dive to avoid the hammerlock and get his arm back. He got a good punch in on the nose of the first man—thin and dark, with long hair—and saw blood. Then he tried for the eye and connected. Harvard jacket on him, crimson: *veritas*.

The gleam of a blade showed the knife in the hand of the second guy. The blade moved flat, low, side-to-side, held to stab upward. It was a big, ugly camper's knife. The lights of the garage ceiling winked off it. The man knew what he was doing. You look at the blade first, swinging, then at the man—large redhead, black clothes, big arms; smell of cologne coming off that one. The other one, the dark-haired one, then, was carrying the old sweat smell.

"We have questions, buddy," the knife said. The first was going for the gun under Fred's arm. Fred ducked, his hand there first. He motioned the skinny man back, his hand under his arm, ready.

"Just questions. Don't worry about it, buddy. No big deal," the knife said, swinging to make that paralysis of fear a knife likes to establish in its victim, if it can, before it chooses a spot.

Fred felt bruises growing on the cheek next to his right eye. He had blood there that was not from the first guy's nose.

The brunette, weasel-quick, moved in.

Right hand on the gun butt, gun out, Fred raked hard across the face, nose, eyes, twice, of the weasel, whose face already was filling with blood. He stepped back, hurt, shaking his head.

"Shit, the man's fast," the weasel said. "For a big guy."

The redhead was a problem. He held the knife in front of him, ready to make his run, his partner out of the way. "Just some questions, buddy. Don't get sore."

Fred drew back, leaving room between himself and his visitors. The redhead crouched lower.

"You finished with that left kneecap?" Fred asked, pointing his gun in that direction. The redhead was a big man with freckles and zits and curly sideburns. He hadn't shaved today. He grunted, chewing gum. His wide arms sported tattoos and coarse hair, set off by the black knit shirt. He started moving forward.

"Shit," he said.

Fred took a look at the weasel, the thin, dark one to the left. He was rubbing at his face with his cuff, getting the blood out of his eyes.

"Kid said he had a piece," the weasel said.

"Stoopid kid, what did he know? Who knew?" said the redhead.

"Stay where you are," Fred said. The two moved toward him.

"You're not going to fire that," the weasel said.

"Depends," said Fred.

"Asshole," said the redhead.

"Hey, asshole," said the weasel. "There's a guy wants to talk to you."

"Tell me about it," said Fred.

"Tell you shit," said the weasel.

Fred's shoulders, neck, and head were starting to throb. Did nobody need their car? Did nobody need to come down around lunchtime to take a car out and go someplace?

"Somebody wants to talk to you. Which he believes you have something he paid for," the redhead said.

Fred asked, "Buddy Mangan can't call?"

The redhead spat. "Buddy Mangan hell," he said. "Buddy Mangan, you wish!"

Fred looked at them and waited. The redhead stood upright and shrugged his big shoulders, loosening them.

"He told us to bring you in," the brunette said.

"That does not seem practical now," Fred said, reminding them of the gun. "Who wants to talk to me?"

"Where's the pitcher? Where's the broad, the nood?" said the redhead. "Which you have."

The weasel made a move toward the pocket of his crimson Harvard windbreaker, on which the splotches of new blood would not show.

"Try me," said Fred. He gestured with the gun.

"Kleenex," said the weasel. "You mind?"

"Be my guest," said Fred. "Slow."

Way back in the dark behind the weasel he saw lights from an elevator door opening, and people, a couple, getting out, walking this way.

Fred watched the weasel pull the pack of tissues out of the side pocket of his windbreaker, demonstrating innocence, all sweetness and light. "See?" He selected one and started work on his face.

The weasel moved a step; Fred motioned him back. The couple was coming closer.

The redhead watched, still threatening.

"Put the knife away," Fred said, motioning with his head. The guys could hear footsteps behind them now.

The redhead's knife went into his right pants pocket. He had a sheath in there. Fred held the gun in his jacket pocket, hoping he wouldn't have to shoot through the tweed.

As they neared, the couple looked at the three men uncomfortably, not wanting to intrude; they were a man and woman in their sixties, wearing raincoats and hats, dressed for springtime in Boston whatever the weather. The weasel's face dripped copiously. The couple walked on into the cement dusk, looking for their car.

"We don't know for certain it's the guy," the redhead said.

"It has to be," the weasel whispered. "We picked him up at

the kid's place. He looks right. He's staying at the Charles Hotel, like the kid said."

"Where's Russ?" Fred asked, a chasm of alarm opening up in him.

The couple drove slowly past them, he at the wheel, she looking at the three men, still interested. She lowered the window. She and the old man had been arguing about it. She was telling him to slow down. She couldn't forget the blood on the weasel's face, and some blood on him, too, Fred thought.

"Is everything all right?" the lady asked bravely. The three men were facing each other, tense.

"How about it?" Fred said. "Everything all right?"

The two men nodded.

"My friend fell down," the redhead explained, snickering.

"Thanks," Fred said. The car drove off. It was a small, modest new black Cadillac. The driver was now telling his wife, "See, what did I say?"

"This is the guy, or the kid lied," the weasel said. Fred noticed that his face was pockmarked.

"Where is he?" Fred asked again.

"This isn't going anywhere," the weasel said.

"Let's call your guy, if he wants to talk," Fred said.

"You want to call while I wait with him?" the redhead asked his partner.

"Shit, you know we can't call. We have to fucking drive back so he can turn the fucking radio up, lean over, fucking whisper in our fucking ear, fucking drive all the fucking way to fucking Providence for fucking permission to fucking go to the goddamn motherfucking toilet?" said the weasel.

The elevator doors were opening again. A woman stepped out with two young children dressed like Easter.

"Tell me about Russell," Fred said.

"The kid?" the redhead said. "I forget where Russell is. You remember, pal?"

The weasel shook his head, his congealing ringlets making jerky arabesques. "In case you care, buddy, he's healthy, and he might stay healthy. You never know." He slipped the pack of tissues back into the pocket of his red windbreaker.

The redhead bent down and slashed the left rear tire of Fred's car with his knife. The two men turned.

"One'll do it," the weasel said. "We don't want to make the guy mad. Just slow him down."

"As long as the kid's healthy," the weasel said to Fred, "why don't you stay in this nice hotel garage a few minutes and let us make, like, our getaway, so we don't anybody worry about the kid."

"Why don't you tell your friend to telephone me here at the Charles," Fred said.

"Asshole," the weasel said.

"Stay in your room," the redhead said, "in case he calls. He don't like to call for nothing, you hear what I'm saying? If he calls. If you don't hear by five, he's not calling, is my guess. He'll send someone." He smiled and shook his shoulders like a fighter.

Fred watched the men swagger out of the garage the same way the cars came in, up the ramp.

The woman and her children, a boy and a girl—perfect; six and eight?—came up to him. The girl, older, pointed at the rear tire and said, "He has a flat."

"Never mind," Mom said, hustling them along. This was supposed to be a nice hotel.

Fred took the stairs up, disregarding the stares of his fellow lodgers. There was no sign of Dawn in the Quiet Bar. She was supposed to take Russ upstairs; not finding him, she'd hightailed it out of here, Fred had no doubt. He went up to his room and confirmed it. Dawn was slick. Could she have set this up with Russell's friends from Providence, who were missing a painting that someone down there had paid for? In the meantime, they had Russ himself as a consolation prize. The pieces Fred saw now were plain enough. Russell, having identified Smykal's painting, had initiated a process that led to Buddy Mangan—and evidently, now, to some disappointed backers whose money Mangan had been representing.

Fred was basically uninjured—only bruised and grazed. The bright blade had kept its distance. He ducked into the bathroom and pulled a long bath. Molly was due in less than an hour. She was going to see him roughed up, and he wanted to reduce the evidence as best he could.

He couldn't leave the room, since they had Russell.

While he waited for the tub to fill, he called the number listed on Smykal's poster. L I V E °° M O D E L S. It gave him only Dawn's recorded message. Fred told it, after the beep, "Dawn, Sheila, this is important. Call Fred as soon as you can." He left his number at the hotel.

He called the number on Buddy Mangan's card. No answer. A ring, but no machine to take the message he would have left: "I can get you the painting."

Fred climbed into the hot water and listened for the phone. For a situation that he wanted not to be his business, he'd got into this one pretty deep.

Providence would call unless he decided to send someone—someone better than the redhead and brunette tag team.

Fred lay in the tub, bruised in spirit. That was the necessary consequence of allowing domestic instincts purchase. Old as he was in this world, Fred was surprised at feeling betrayed. Russ had sold him out to buy time, or they had scared it out of him. They had the kid stashed, likely in fucking Providence. Fred had been mooning around outside his door last night, intending to offer him protection, going easy on him, and first chance he got, the kid sold him out.

Fred fixed the features of his two assailants in his mind. He wouldn't forget them. He could find them in mug shots in fucking Providence when the time came.

While they had been picking him up at Russell's and following him here, Fred himself had been noticing nothing but what a stud he must look, having that good-looking young woman, Dawn, in the car with him and at his mercy. He, dazzled by pussy, had been set up by the oldest trap in the world—well, no, the oldest but one. The oldest trap was a person's native hope.

Hot water eased the bruises. There were abrasions but no cuts of consequence. Fred's knuckles were banged and skinned; his cheek was skinned, too, and his mouth bruised. He wouldn't get a shiner. In the art business you stood out with a shiner. Even flashing a gun for the most part wasn't done, though Fred knew of at least one Boston dealer who wore one on his premises.

He stretched his legs a last time, then got out of the tub and toweled off. He was feeling better for a little exercise. Wrapped in the towel, he lay down.

He tried Mangan again. They wouldn't let up on the kid until they had that painting—though what the muscle behind Mangan wanted with a painting, Fred couldn't imagine.

Lying on the bed, he played back the grunts and ejaculations of the opposition during their conversation, the bits of information they had dropped. They hadn't even been sure, those two, that Fred was the man they wanted.

Fred rose to a knock on the door.

Up off the bed with the hotel's towel tucked in, gun in his right hand, Fred moved quietly to the door. "Who is it?"

"It's Molly, you goof! Who do you expect?"

He threw open the door and closed it behind her, tossing the gun on the bed. He hugged her around her arms full of groceries and kissed her bright face.

"Jesus," said Molly, seeing the gun bounce. "Kinky."

Then she saw Fred better. "Fred, you all right?"

"Sorry," Fred said. "Some people came to see me who leapt before they looked. I'm all right. I should have called and told you not to come."

"And miss this?" Molly asked. She pulled his towel off and had a look.

"Nothing important damaged."

25

After they'd eaten, Molly called work and told them, "Something came up."

"Cute," said Fred. "Clever. Original." He was wishing he still smoked.

Molly waved him quiet. She kept on with the phone, saying she'd be late getting back.

Fred was in the bed. Molly fidgeted around the room, worrying. She was pleasant to look at after rough exercise had scared some thugs back to Providence, and while you were waiting for a telephone call concerning, perhaps, ransom demands on a worthless kid who had betrayed you.

"I don't like violence," Fred said. "Although I'm good at it."

"I'm going to take a shower," Molly said. "I'm sure yours is better than mine at home."

"I like yours better, though it's worse," Fred said. "Please be my guest."

Molly said, "Want to call down for coffee while I scrape off?"
Fred tried Mangan's number first. No answer.

With Molly there, Fred organized things in his mind. He laid out as much as he knew. Molly listened, wrapped in the hotel's towels, sitting by the window, drinking coffee.

"So you figure," she said, "Mangan has the letter Clay wants?"

"It makes sense if Smykal tried to sell the package twice, giving the painting to one buyer and the letter to the other as an opening gambit. It would be very stupid, but he probably had no inkling who he was dealing with. Having seen only Clay, how could he guess Fred? And if on the other side only Russell was visible, it must have looked like child's play."

"Mangan or his backers want the painting."

"Right."

"Russ, whose hide you hope to save, in order to save the same miserable hide told his pals in Providence—sorry, *fucking* Providence—that you could help them with their problem. Because first Russ, then Mangan, concluded you hijacked the picture."

"I guess so."

"Mmm," said Molly. "I'm not sure I like it, any of it. Except I liked the painting."

"It is a good picture, isn't it?" said Fred. "All this hoorah, you forget."

"If it's the mob behind Mangan, why would the mob buy a painting?" Molly asked.

Fred said, "You can launder money that way, but this particular painting seems an odd choice, being unsigned and all."

"Unless they have the letter."

"Yes."

"Which apparently they do."

"Right."

"Let me think about this," said Molly. "How does it work? The laundering?"

"You have cash that you can't afford to account for but you want to be able to. Otherwise, anything you buy with it, if you're nailed on a RICO, goes to the government. If you buy something of value for cash under the table—like a painting you might have inherited or picked up at a yard sale for nothing—and then you sell it on the open market, that transfer generates income you can be seen with. You can buy cars and dancing girls or whatever," Fred said.

He sat by the window with his coffee. Molly, finished with hers, was putting herself together, heading for work again. She was dressed in black stockings, a blue jumper and a white blouse, and the red knitted cardigan: her housewife-librarian outfit. She looked very sexy in it, her brown curls still damp, drying. The room was festooned with wet white towels.

"You should see Clayton's room," Fred said. "He makes as much impression on it as a ghost."

"Obviously you're planning a straight trade," Molly said. "The painting for the kid. The kid doesn't deserve you, Fred."

"If I can get through to that attractive nuisance Buddy Mangan," Fred said.

"Good luck with your phone calls," Molly said. "Call if there's something I can do. Or if . . ." She faltered. "Or if you plan to go somewhere."

"I'll call," Fred said. "And thanks. For not saying it again."

"Not saying what?"

" 'Don't be an asshole,' " Fred said.

"I felt that went without saying," Molly told him.

It was three-fifteen.

Suppose Russ Ennery deserved whatever they were doing to him? Fred couldn't calmly let it come. Even though it was not his business, because a life was at stake and salvageable, Fred's instinct was, as Molly had guessed, to engineer a straight trade: La Belle Conchita for Ennery. But Mangan didn't answer his phone, and the anonymous friend from Providence was not calling. Fred would find another way to float a message down.

You think of those cartoons where there are twelve little fish swimming, and in back of them six bigger fish with their mouths open, teeth; behind those are three bigger ones looking really hungry, and behind them, the biggest, smiling, lazily swimming, keeping track.

You want to get word to the big guy without having the messenger get eaten.

Fred was friendly with a couple of people in the art business in Providence. The smartest of them, and the one he liked best, was Harriet Raskin, who had a one-person operation downtown. Fred called and found her.

"Look, Harriet," he said. "I'm working on something and I want to talk it over."

"You want to come down?" Harriet asked.

He could see her, lean as an ostrich, smoking continually, sitting in her little gallery in a cloud of blue smoke, a bunch of nineteenth-century landscapes on the walls, with the tree, maybe the cow, the piece of water, the mountain, the sky.

Two bullterriers slobbered beside her.

"Let me just talk a minute, Harriet."

"You want to give me a general idea of what you want to talk about?" Harriet asked. Fred heard her cough and strike a match.

He said, "There's been a mix-up up here."

"Has there?" said Harriet. "What kind, if you want to say?"

"Apparently a person in your part of the country arranged to buy something that didn't get delivered. Something in your field."

"I wouldn't know," Harriet said.

"I didn't think you would. This person is naturally disappointed, and I may be able to assist."

"Yes or no: do you know who you want to talk to?"

"I thought, asking around, you might find out and let me know."

"I can ask. Is it urgent?"

"I get the idea the person is pretty disappointed," Fred said.

"Let me see what I can stir up," Harriet said. She asked how she could reach him.

Fred gave her his number at the Charles. "Don't stir too hard," he said. "There are delicate objects involved."

"I know delicate objects," Harriet said. "I'm in the picture business. Sit tight. I'll see what I can do.

"By the way," she went on, "while I have you, what can you tell me about a collector by the name of Arthur Arthurian? Sounds Armenian. I never heard of him."

"I wish I never had either. The person I want to reach is likely the one who wants to know about Arthurian."

"Stay there," Harriet said. "I'll get on it. You'll be at your phone?"

"I'll be here."

26

Fred called L I V E °° M O D E L S again and got the machine. Then he called Mangan's number.

He had nothing to read. To occupy his mind with white noise, he turned on the TV and watched a painter working— an educational painter. He did a whole picture in a half hour, a 1990s version of the landscapes Harriet sat in front of in her Providence gallery, though hers had taken longer to make. A thick round bush of hair grew on this educational painter. Fred wanted to rub the painter's hair in the art he was making. You'd get a nice little effect that way, on both the canvas and the hair.

The painter with the hair blessed the world and disappeared. Fred did not want to learn how to build a new antique table out of a condemned barn using only seven thousand dollars' worth of power tools. He turned off the set.

Clay had Proust in his prison.

What was Russ reading? Had he been carrying something with him when they picked him up? Was that where he'd been a couple of nights ago? In Providence? Or had he been hiding from them, too?

Fred called Sheila's again. His phone didn't ring until almost five. It was Clayton, wanting to know, "What's going on?"

"Nothing. I don't know. I have to keep the phone free. I'll call you when I have something."

Five-twenty. Telephone.

"Fred." It was a man's voice.

"Yes."

"Wait a minute. You got more name than that? These guys balls everything up." There was whispering on the other end.

Fred waited, holding the phone to his ear. He couldn't make out any words.

The voice tried again: "This the Charles Hotel, Cambridge?"

"Yes," said Fred.

"You want to talk about some money we are missing?"

"A painting," Fred said.

"Got in too deep, didn't you, asshole?"

"I know where the painting is," Fred said.

"Wait a minute."

More whispering.

"We don't want the fuckin' thing. We want our money. You want to bring it down?"

Fred said, "Let's talk a minute and see if we're going to be able to put a deal together."

"Put together a what?" The voice was offended, outraged. "Put our money together and bring it, that's what you put together. The fuckin' pitcher, do what you want."

"Let me talk to Mangan," Fred said.

"He's out," the voice said.

Fred said, "The money. How much you missing?"

"Twenty-five grand, asshole."

Smykal had done a silent auction. Offered twenty-five thousand by Russell's pet shark Mangan, he had told Clayton the price was thirty. Then Clay had paid him thirty-three: a quick profit of eight grand over the first offer. But apparently the money on Mangan's end had actually been delivered as well.

"Look," the voice went on. "I'm standing in a fucking gas station talking on the fucking telephone and you want to play fucking guessing games? You going to deliver the fucking money, or not?"

Fred said, "Maybe I can. There are a couple of other things I'll need to talk over, Mr.—do you want to give me a name?"

"Do you want to eat your own fucking nuts? Fuck you. What else you got to say?"

"Two things," Fred said. "There's a guy I want to see, maybe you can help me with, who's been detained."

Pause.

"Oh, the kid. I hear you. No problem. We have the money, we don't need him for anything."

"And I want the letter."

There was an exclamation of amazed disgust. "He wants a fucking letter? Personal visit isn't enough? Phone call won't do it for him? What am I, the fucking federal government, put my business on paper? You fucking crazy?"

"The kid knows about the letter," Fred said. "Or ask Mangan."

Pause. Whispers. Was Mangan in the room, next to the voice Fred could not see?

"Mangan knows about it," Fred said. "Maybe he has it."

Another pause.

"Have to call you back."

"Hold it," Fred said.

"Have to talk to a guy. Talk to another guy. That's gonna maybe take time."

"I have to go out," Fred said. "I'll be out for an hour at least."

"Listen," the voice said. "Wait a minute. I was you, I'd wait a few hours, maybe someone calls you. If you don't hear by eleven, I didn't reach him. Then I'll call you tomorrow morning, set something up, okay?"

"Everything cool until then?" Fred asked.

"Stay near your phone."

"Okay," said Fred.

"We'll get someone to fix your car. So you can drive down tomorrow."

Fred said, "It's your business, but your guys—you think they can change a tire?"

"Fucking comedian. I'll tell them take it one step at a time," the voice said. "Talk to you, if I don't get back tonight, in the morning. First thing."

"What time is first thing?" Fred asked.

"Like ten, ten-thirty, eleven. In there."

Fred stood up and stretched. Stay in his room, the guy had said, the voice of Providence. Wait for the phone.

They didn't want answers. They didn't want the painting. They wanted their money back. That would have to come from Clay. It was going to cost an additional twenty-five thousand to get that letter. He'd have to see how Clay felt about it.

27

Nothing stirred in the corridor when Fred edged out at midnight. Clay had called back five times, furious, confused, perturbed, exasperated, repentant, even intrigued. Why was it going to cost so much? Why, when Fred didn't know who had the letter or where it was or even if he could get it for certain?

Fred had explained as well as he could without bringing in Mangan's name; there was no point in starting Clay thinking in terms of turf wars. The extra money amounted to ransom, but since Clay wouldn't see any reason to buy back a kid he hadn't met and didn't want, Fred did not emphasize that argument. Instead, he reminded him of the value of the painting of Conchita Hill.

"If you get that picture for a total of fifty-eight thousand, you're stealing it, Clay. You're buying it at a third of its market value at auction. Personally, I'd estimate it higher, wouldn't you? A Chase that good, that early, of that subject? Having the letter with it, and the story, and the provenance?"

"It's not a story we're going to publish," Clay had said.

Clayton had kept insisting that the painting's monetary value was beside the point. Why should he buy the letter twice? It was the principle of the thing.

Fred had given up. "Tell you what," he had said. "I'll give you till tomorrow morning at eight to make up your mind. Smykal's dead, and your deal died with him. If you don't buy the letter, I will. You'll have first option to purchase it from me at cost. Let me know by eight. It'll take time to put the money together."

And by God, he had realized as he hung up, he'd do it, too, though at the moment he had not the faintest idea how. He had no money of his own put away. He was not comfortable living like that, keeping things. What money he had he'd put into the house in Charlestown. He could sell his share of it— but not fast. He'd manage something.

He'd still not had an answer or a call back from the phone at Sheila and Dawn's. Mangan's phone did not answer. Waiting in his room, he had been planning, once the midnight deadline was past, to go down, change his tire, and drive to Cohasset to look at Mangan's place. But it would be more prudent not to make a stir anywhere around the outskirts of a business most of which he did not understand. There was nothing more he could do about Russ tonight without adding to the kid's danger. He'd see what the opposition's bid was in the morning, "first thing"—around noon.

In the meantime, his disquiet was growing at the lack of response at the women's Pearl Street apartment. Fred put his sweater on under his jacket, changed his tire, and drove to Pearl Street. The same old lady slept in her nook under the stairs. He knocked on the second-floor door and got no answer. He waited and listened to the building's creaks and silences before he let himself in.

Fred was sitting cross-legged in the darkness on Dawn's futon when Sheila came in at two. She didn't see him and was moving through Dawn's room toward the kitchen. She was dressed in black—jeans and a black jacket—her blond hair swinging and a black leather bag over her shoulder.

"Russell's in trouble," Fred said.

Sheila jumped, gasped, backed against the wall, and turned to run. Fred, up fast, took her wrist.

"It's Fred," he said. "Be smart. Where's Dawn?"

Sheila said, "I know fuck-all about Dawn. She let you in? Let go, will you?" She pulled against him until she remembered that she knew him already.

"Russell's in trouble with ugly people," Fred said.

Sheila dropped her bag on the floor and looked defiant. She stared around the room. Fred released her wrist.

"Dawn fucking took off?" she said, noticing that the majority of Dawn's things were gone. Fred had reached the same conclusion.

He sat on Dawn's futon again. Sheila gazed down at him, her hands on her hips. She was simultaneously bleary- and bright-eyed, high on something.

"I'm not afraid of you," she said.

Fred waited.

"I've fucked with worse people," she said.

Fred waited.

"I'm going to smoke some weed," Sheila said, kicking her sandals off and closing the apartment door. "So I can think."

Fred nodded for her to go ahead.

"I can sell you a joint if you want," she said.

"I'm fine," Fred told her.

Sheila smoked. She dropped her ashes onto the mangy carpet and rubbed them in with her bare foot.

"The people Russ is in trouble with," she said, "was something he's doing on his own, giving Dawn and I the runaround. As far as Russ is concerned, we're just rental pussy."

Fred watched the red glow work against the ash. The smell was that of before dawn, while you wait for them to come for you from the other side of the clearing. The fools around you, frightened, numb their senses to trick the death they fear toward pleasant adventure.

He said, "Dawn told me Russell said their troubles—his and Dawn's—would soon be over. What did he mean?"

Sheila thought. Her lean face focused on the operation of the joint until she finished it, then she stood and went to find a saucer in the kitchen to stub it out in. She dropped the charred end into a tin from her bag.

"I guess Russ has something going with Dawn," she said, "is what it sounds like." She shrugged her shoulders and came back and sat on the far end of the futon. "Whatever you want, let's do it. I'm tired."

"Tell me about Smykal's operation."

"Oh, God," Sheila said. "That's why Dawn ran off. You're taking over. Fuck you, Fred. I'm finished. That bastard screwed us blind. Fifty bucks an hour? To let the geeks and creeps crawl all over you, taking their pussy pictures? I'm through, unless we're talking a real different financial arrangement."

She giggled and went on, "God, the creeps they rounded up. Lean over, honey, get that effect there of the flash, abstract, you know, I just thought of something. Let's grease it, make it shine; there's twenty extra if you let me do it myself.

"And all the while that geek Smykal's filming from the next room, with video. A secret hole he has. He's getting tapes of the geeks sweating and fumbling, maybe drinking, doing lines— he sells them coke if they want it, makes them feel like studs, they need all the help they can get—and trying to get lucky;

getting lucky sometimes with some girls, it's up to us, we want a bonus, if the guy doesn't look sick.

"Jesus, men are ugly."

Fred sat and waited. He had no argument at the moment, though he'd be inclined, himself, to broaden the subject of her sentence to include a larger segment of humanity.

"Okay," he said at last. "Suppose I take over, run it better."

"You kill the old man?" Sheila asked, studying Fred. She started to tremble. "You're shitting me."

"How does it work?"

"Smykal's thing—the models and art photos—was a scam. The deal for the girls was setting up the marks, see, because Smykal would choose a mark and follow him to the precious little home in Belmont, or the sacred glass office on Beacon Street with the view, or the vestry at Old North Chapel— whatever—and he'd offer to sell his film, which, Jesus, half the time the guys aren't doing anything."

"A honey trap," Fred said.

"That's me," Sheila said. She stretched her limbs and yawned. "All honey."

Fred said, "How does Russ fit in?"

"Sweet Russell's the fucking pimp," Sheila said. "Smykal was too much of a fucking artist."

"Smykal met Russ at Video King," Fred said. "Around the corner from his apartment. Right?"

Sheila nodded. "That's where Russ recruits the marks. Which Smykal called unfulfilled talent. Russ pulls them in, and we fulfill them. The people who rent porn, you know, they want to do porn, do all that stuff they rent to look at, but they're scared. Smykal provides a setup they think is safe. Russ has their address and credit-card number and phone number, work number, everything, from the Video King computer, which he sells to Smykal."

Sheila scratched the inside of a thigh and lay back on the futon. "Fifty bucks an hour," she said. "A bonus if we get the guy's little dick out of his breeches to where Smykal can film it, and the guy's face showing so Smykal can nail him—dicks being pretty much alike—and the girl. That's all we normally do. Smykal took it from there. Sometimes, though, he'd put one of us on the phone."

"Lights, cameras, action," Fred said. "That was Dawn's voice."

"A girl's voice on the phone at the guy's house, Sunday morning—'Hi, I'm Dawn, remember me? Is this a bad time to call? Who's that answered the phone? Is that your wifey?'— sometimes that got results. A girl's voice on the phone, or a girl's pants coming off—these guys sometimes go to pieces." Sheila giggled.

"So what are we gonna do about this, killer?" she asked Fred. She ran her fingers through her hair, starting underneath and moving upward, fanning it outward.

"It figures Smykal was killed by one of his marks," Fred said.

"He never hit them for all that much," Sheila said. "You can see from how the guy lived. The asshole kept us all poor. Still, some of the geeks he got—you never know. Maybe one of the girls. So you can do better? If you can, maybe I'm interested, and maybe I'm leaving for Omaha in the morning."

She looked at Fred in sudden, tardy, genuine alarm. "What happened to Dawn, anyway? Where's Russ?"

"Where did Smykal keep the answering machine?" Fred asked. "I didn't see it at his place; it's not here; it isn't upstairs."

"I wouldn't know," Dawn said. "Upstairs? You've been up-stairs?"

"I gave myself a house tour while I waited for you. Russ had Smykal's file box of records," Fred said.

Sheila stood poised, off-balance, on the futon. "Russell has Smykal's records? You serious?"

"Had," Fred corrected her. "I'm taking them, and his compu-ter disks. In case he has stuff on them I want."

"Jesus," Sheila said. "Fucking Dawn, she told you her and Russell's troubles are over? She and Russ cleaned him out? Russell? They popped him? Russell was going to run the business for himself?"

"That's what it looks like," Fred said.

Sheila stooped, picked up her bag, and started toward her bedroom. "They played me for a fucking fool," she said.

Fred reached out and held on to the bag.

Sheila tugged, but without much energy or hope. "Oh, what?" she said, disgusted.

"Take your clothes off," Fred said. He kept holding the bag.

"Shit, are you kidding?" Sheila said. She pulled harder at her bag. Fred stood up.

Sheila turned red, then gray, with anger.

"Put your clothes on the floor. Come on," Fred said. "I don't have a whole hell of a lot of time." He pried the bag out of her fingers and dropped it behind him. Sheila stared.

"Or you'll take them off," she said. "Right?"

Fred nodded.

"Take off the clothes," he said. "I'm searching you, that's all."

"Jesus," Sheila said. "Right. What's the big deal, another rape. Don't hurt me, do you mind?"

"Do my best," Fred said.

Sheila peeled the black sweatshirt over her head. Champion, it said. Under it she was wearing nothing but a narrow gold chain around her neck. The skin on her upper arms rose in goose bumps. Her breasts were as round and firm as if they had been painted in about 1450, by the Master of Flemalle, to be offered one at a time to a large-headed baby.

"I don't have anything," Sheila said. "Whatever there was, Dawn and Russ have it. Now you. Russ wouldn't have the balls

203

to do it, but I guess Dawn has enough for both of them. I mean doing Smykal."

She dropped the sweatshirt and opened her belt buckle, businesslike, slid the jeans down, and stepped out of them. Then the black lace underpants, designed for show: young body, tired, with hints of flab establishing a toehold at belly and buttocks.

"Turn around," Fred said.

Naked, the woman had the same dramatic power as a man in uniform.

"It's what I have to sell," Sheila said with a smirk, turning until she faced him again. "Whatta you think, Fred?"

"It's good, but just the same I wish you'd spend more time working on your curveball," Fred said.

"What?"

"Something to fall back on," he explained. "I was distracted. In fact, I was thinking about someone else."

"Thanks. I don't want to use Dawn's futon," Sheila said, standing in a slouch, making no effort to mitigate her nakedness by posing.

"Put something on if you're cold," Fred said. "I wanted to make sure not to miss anything."

"You've been through my fucking apartment, too, haven't you?" she said.

Fred started looking in the pockets of her jeans. She stared at him. He laid out Certs and change, a comb, subway tokens, a ticket stub from the Loew's in Harvard Square.

"You want to search the body cavities, too?" Sheila said, standing there naked.

"Nope." He began working through her bag.

Sheila charged him, fighting and striking at his face with her nails until he rolled her into a red blanket and more or less sat on her. His face was tender enough from the previous day's attentions, thanks.

He found it in her bag, among the tissues: the Sony videocassette she was carrying.

Sheila sighed and went limp. Fred put the tape in his coat pocket. He stood up.

"We can work it together," she said.

"I'll be off," Fred said.

"That's mine. It's all I got."

"It's mine now," he told her. "The works."

The woman rolled out of the blanket and came toward him, fragrant with effort. "Tell you what," she said, persuading. "It needs more than one person. I was thinking of going with Russ, but it needs a man. Fuck Russ. Him and Dawn. Think they can cut me out? He's out now anyway, according to you.

"You'll see, we can work good together. I was there that night. This guy showed up while I was working, said he was coming back, and he did. In spades." Sheila shuddered. "I figure I'm not going back there again and I want some protection. So I rip the tape off."

She noted both that she was cold and that her nakedness was a useless tool, and she stooped for the blanket, wrapped it around her. "Seeing what happened, it's gotta be worth big bucks. But if you get this guy and put the squeeze on him, keep me out of it. He scares me."

"I'll be in touch," Fred said.

28

Fred drove to the house in Charlestown. He was relieved, given the nature of Pearl Street, that the material he'd taken out of Russell's apartment—the computer disks and the two cardboard Porta-file boxes that Russ had taken from Smykal's place, and the video camera (after the man was dead, and before Fred got there? that didn't sound like Russ, but it wasn't Fred's concern)—was all still in his car.

Dawn, the one with balls, was also the smart one—smart enough to know, yesterday morning, after looking Fred over, that it was finished, and time for her to get lost.

It was four in the morning. The city of Charlestown was not dark, but its buildings and its Bunker Hill monument made silhouettes of black against a sky in which light was struggling to establish itself.

Teddy was at the desk, on watch, his eyes wide. He was dressed in a black suit, looking like a Mormon missionary, but missing shirt and tie and haircut. Here, in the safety of the house and with sentry duty to give him focus, he seemed more like himself.

"I'm in your room, Fred," Teddy said. "I told you you'd be back. You carryin'?"

Fred nodded. Teddy, alert, was referring to the gun under his arm, not to the file boxes.

"I'm on until eight," Teddy said. "So go ahead, sleep. It's your bed anyway."

"Gotta work," Fred said. "Bill Radford still got his TV stuff in the kitchen? I have to look through some tapes."

Bill Radford was inclined toward brief, expensive hobbies.

Teddy nodded, saying, "Don't tell him I told you."

Fred took the things upstairs. They had the whole three-decker, but it was a small one, with a total of only ten bedrooms. Some people bunked together; the normal population varied from five to thirteen. The only rules were no drink, no stealing, no women, mind your business, and it helps if you play chess.

Teddy made little more impression in the room than Clay made in his.

Fred had looked into the file boxes already, before he took them from Russell's neatly arranged apartment. The lighter one held cassette tapes labeled with names and dates. The other was divided into compartments for individual clients, with names, addresses, prurient stills, and, in some cases, notations of collections made—in surprisingly small amounts. Smykal had been a cautious man, bleeding his people in two- and three-hundred-dollar increments at intervals of several months. The quick impression was of an operation going back three years.

Fred recognized several names but dismissed them as not his business, unless one had done for Smykal. The man had wanted to have a Clayton Reed—or Arthur Arthurian—folder, too, not content with the windfall in an amount much larger than what he was used to.

Fred would study the client list if he had to, but only if he had to. He had no doubt that what he wanted was on the tape Sheila had been hoarding for her own purposes.

He dropped Sheila's cassette into Bill's machine and rewound it, sitting on the floor next to his mat, which now smelled somewhat of Teddy. The tape presented segments, bits and pieces, filmed surreptitiously from a position in Smykal's bedroom (if he recalled the layout correctly), from which the camera had the advantage over the studio, its bed, its doorway, and—through that—the front door, visible when the studio door was open.

What Smykal got was depressing: portraits of men intent on deluding themselves into a parody of art that was also a parody of sex. A microphone hidden in the studio collected sound. It was ugly and pathetic, with occasional flashes of sadism or bravura. The women worked, exhibiting their limbs and parts, responding and suggesting, and seducing their clients into further creative invention. "I know, why don't we take your clothes off, too?" "Twenty bucks more and you can put that camera down and put your head up in here instead."

A running date and time moved along with the image on the film. That would be useful.

"Honey, what did you say you were doing at eleven twenty-two P.M. on the evening of April second?" the little woman asks.

"I was at that PTA thing. It ran late."

"Funny, I just got this tape in the mail that shows you being sucked off by a girl with red hair," she says, confused, handing him the pipe and slippers. "You wanna talk about this?"

Aside from Sheila and Dawn, three other women appeared. Some segments were brief and others as long as ten minutes. The show was worse than the educational painter with the hair. Smykal himself seldom appeared, though on occasion he would step into the frame to give suggestions or reassurance—"It's all right, they are professional models, this is art."

It was mostly sleazy, soft-core stuff—like mud wrestling— but it was sufficient, on the Boston scene, to inspire guilt and terror in carefully screened men if publication was threatened. It was enough to ruin lives and plenty, if the victim was timid, to form the basis for extortion.

It took an hour to reach last Friday night.

The TV screen showed Sheila in the studio, on the white bed, in front of the vague roses on the wallpaper, naked, curled on her side, reading a magazine. Beyond her, in the same frame, the studio door opened on the view across Henry Smykal's living room, to the inside of the front door. The sound on the tape was of a phone ringing, which Smykal did not answer.

Smykal, wearing that suit, entered the room, Pentax around his neck.

"I don't want to miss this guy," the dead man said, his voice clear on the microphone. "You lying here, him coming into the apartment, first thing we see is him seeing the first thing he sees, which is your crotch, right?"

"Lie here with my legs open," Sheila said. "I'm not brilliant, but I can understand that, I guess. What else is new?"

"Not much," Smykal said. "Let's not drown the guy. There. Just enough so he thinks, Hey, I got an idea."

"When is he coming?"

"He'll be here," Smykal said. He walked out of the room, and shortly afterward the tape went blank, then started again to show—across Sheila, now striking a pose of lascivious welcome on the bed—Smykal going to the apartment's front door, opening it a crack.

Hot lights burned, and the telephone was ringing.

Smykal said, "You're not him," and the camera showed his back as he tried to force the door closed. There was a voice on the other side of the door that Fred couldn't hear precisely. Sheila lolled.

Smykal said, "I'm filming," as he pushed against the door. "What letter?"

A foot in Fred's shoe was stuck in the crack of the door.

Fred heard the sound of the name Arthurian, spoken in a voice he recognized.

Smykal said, "You can't come in. It's art film. I guarantee privacy."

There was a murmur from the far side of the door.

Smykal said, "You can't come in, not now."

Sheila posed, increasing the welcome, lifting her legs.

Smykal pushed at the door, saying, "Just get out." Then, softer, "It's not here."

Fred got the reprise, the Smykal's-eye view of his first visit of Saturday morning, until he pulled out his foot and Smykal, in his shiny suit, closed the door again.

"Forget it, Sheila," Smykal said, walking out of the picture. "Knock it off."

The screen went blank. Fred put it on pause.

Sheila had said, "The guy came back."

That was the part that interested Fred. He started the film forward, the picture focusing on Sheila tossing her magazine to one side and assuming her position again. Smykal came into the picture, going to the door, listening a moment, taking off the chain.

"Now," Fred said.

Smykal's door was pushed in. Buddy Mangan, in the man-of-the-soil outfit, shoving Smykal backward past the studio, gave the naked woman a glance, said, "Get lost," and pushed Smykal off camera.

Sheila rolled over, scratched her backside, picked up her magazine, and said, "Shit."

She stepped out of the camera's frame, and there was nothing to see but empty rooms. Mangan's voice, hard to make out, came from somewhere else: "What do you mean telling my guy the deal's off? Where's the fucking picture? What's wrong with my fucking money, Smykal?"

Sheila, now in jeans and sandals and a pink sweatshirt, carrying the black bag, walked into camera range and out of the studio. A loud slap sounded, and Mangan's voice again: "What's wrong with my fucking money?"

The picture stopped. It was over.

Fred stared at the machine.

He looked at his watch. He could afford to sleep for an hour, in Teddy's bed.

29

There's heat and pain and solitude. Their first aim is to assault the spirit, which, in each of us, can finally be broken: don't fail to believe it. Afterward they start gnawing on the soul.

Curious moral quandary when they say, speculatively, "We'll shoot one and ask the other questions. Which shall we shoot, the big one or the fat one?"

Fred lay in Teddy's dusky room, smelling the discomfort of distressed male and recalling the cramped agony of weeks of confinement in their bamboo cage, hearing again the drone of his insistent envy for the fat one, whom they had selected as the one to shoot, believing Fred's size would promote a heavier fall when he gave in. While they rested between sessions with him, they failed to provide him with a copy of Proust—which, in any case, he could not have read in the total darkness underground.

Whatever he did afterward, forever while he lived, he owed a life. He'd never even learned the fat one's name.

Relentless malice and the drip of blood through jungle

splashed with rain made Southeast Asia in this corner of Charlestown—a pocket of horror unresolved that had so many fellows throughout the country, Fred knew, that the character of the country itself had been permanently altered.

He wondered what form they had chosen for the boy's torment. Fred had a chance to pull him out if he was rested. He stared at the black windows and forced himself to sleep.

Fred woke at around seven. He telephoned Molly from the kitchen extension.

"Where have you been?" Molly asked. "For God's sake, are you all right?"

She sounded frantic. God, he hadn't told her anything since yesterday afternoon.

"Sorry," Fred said. "I'm okay. I'm working it out. I couldn't go back to the hotel till I took care of something."

"You're all right, then." Now Molly could replace mortal worry with what sounded like close to mortal mad.

"I should have called," Fred said.

"Tell me about it."

Fred said, "I talked to the guy in Providence, and it sounds like it's going to work. Listen, I called to wake you up."

"Who was asleep?" Molly asked.

"I'm sorry," Fred said. "Thank you for worrying. I'm stupid. I didn't think. I'm not used to thinking. . . ."

"No sob stuff," Molly said.

"I wanted to catch the kids before they go to school."

Terry was bright and able first thing in the morning. Sam was grumpy, grumbling, waking up. Fred said hello, he missed them, have a good day, work hard in school.

There was no sign of movement from his roommates. Dirty light came in through the windows. Sam hung up the phone as Fred was saying, "Okay, then, see you, Sam. Can you put your mom back on?"

Fred had to call back and tell Molly, "I should be back this evening."

"See you then," said Molly. She was still pissed.

The cassette in his pocket, Fred told Teddy he was leaving some things in the room for a day or two.

"If you want to wait until eight," Teddy said, "and if you want backup—so people see you got friends—you want me to ride with you? People see me, bein' big and black, it might give you a better edge."

Fred thought about it a moment.

"Thanks, Teddy," he said. "I better say no this time. The people I have to see, it's better if I don't scare them. I appreciate it."

Terry nodded and watched the door as Fred closed it behind him.

Fred drove back to Cambridge. It was brisk in the early morning. It would be a bright day: spring. He cut across the bridge and took the long route, skirting the river on the Cambridge side, watching the trees, dogs, joggers, and students on the river in their sculls.

He grabbed a muffin and coffee and carried them with him to the hotel. He picked up his messages at the desk: four calls from Molly, at 1:30 A.M., 3:30, 5:00, and 6:45. She'd been worried, and he was a shit.

A message from Clayton: "Go ahead." Good, Clay was his partner again.

He had the coffee and the muffin in his room, took a shower, and put on the clean shirt Molly had brought yesterday with lunch. He called Clayton at eight-thirty. Clay was an early riser. He'd be in his room, completely dressed or in that dressing gown, mixing his Perrier and his fresh orange juice, his *New York Times* finished, ready to start the day's Proust.

"I got your message," Fred said. "It was too late to call back."

"It's highway robbery," Clay said. "But it is the only way to get it done. How do you want the money?"

"Why don't you have a cashier's check made out to me, and I'll endorse it after I'm sure everything's copacetic."

"Nothing's been copacetic for years," Clay said. "Not since nineteen twenty-five." He was feeling better. He agreed to have the check drawn up and sent by messenger.

"I'll tell you when I think it's safe for you to go back home," Fred said.

"I'm not here for my safety," Clay exploded. "Have you completely lost your sense of priorities? You insist on going off on tangents while you leave me to concentrate alone on our main effort?"

The Heade. Yes.

"Finn wants to rope me into some slimy maneuver," Clay said. "It's the only reason he'd have sent me that note. He thinks he can knock me off the Heade. I've talked to my bank. Maybe it means I don't buy another picture for five years, but we're going to bid on that thing until we buy it."

"I'll keep in touch," Fred said.

He couldn't expect a call from Providence until the end of the morning. He called Video Shak and arranged to rent what he could, buy the few components he couldn't rent, and have everything delivered to his room.

The boys who brought the stuff, who should have been in high school, took his credit-card imprint, made him sign papers, and left him the two VCRs, the jack to connect them to the room's TV, and cassettes and connector inserts. They took five bucks each for a tip.

Fred had decided before he slept that his object would be for the complete tape never to be seen or used. His second object, if the first did not apply, was for the majority of the tape never to be seen. He didn't relish the idea of testifying in court to what he had been saying behind the door Smykal pushed against while the camera played across the reaching legs of Sheila.

However, the tape—or at least the last part of it, the entrance of jolly Buddy Mangan, complete with the recorded time of that entrance, 1:17 A.M.—was evidence of murder. Fred made two copies of the last six minutes, then he rewound the tape and started to copy the whole thing from the beginning. Evidence that important, given the unpredictability of life, you couldn't have just one copy of, not if you wanted to be sure you could produce it later.

Providence called at about noon. It was the same voice as yesterday.

"Fred?"

"Yes," said Fred.

"We think you are Arthur Arthurian."

"I know that," Fred said.

There was a pause.

He waited.

"You have the money?"

"Twenty-five thousand, as agreed," Fred said.

"Why don't you come down and we'll work this thing out," the voice said. "You seem like a guy knows how to do business without fucking around."

"So do you," Fred said.

Another pause.

"You know what I want," Fred said.

"We'll make it work."

The voice described the location of a gas station off Route 95, south of Providence. "I'll be here two-thirty, three. After three I won't be here. I said I'd get your car fixed, but the guys couldn't find it."

"I moved it. Two-thirty, three, then," Fred said.

"After three it's too late," the voice repeated, and the hand behind the voice hung up the phone at that end.

Fred called Clay and told him he was heading for Providence with the payment, which had arrived safely. He thought of calling Molly and telling her, warning her. There was a distant chance he might not come back. But if he didn't, that would be time enough for her to know. Instead he called and told her he hoped to be back for supper, he was sorry she'd worried, he felt terrible that she'd been calling all night, and, he reaffirmed, he'd been a shit.

"See you tonight, then," Molly said.

Fred wrapped one of the complete tapes and addressed it to himself; he'd leave it at the desk of the Charles to be picked up later. He put one of the two six-minute segments in his jacket pocket, packed his meager belongings, and checked out of the hotel.

The other complete tape, and the other segment, he'd take to Charlestown and stash. Fred put the tapes he wanted to keep safe in his lock box and told Bill Radford that if he didn't call or come back for them by, say, Monday at the latest, Bill should turn them over to the police in Cambridge.

It was a nice day for a drive. Fred took the expressway south, then 95.

30

The Gulf station off 95 was small and seedy, set back on a desolate lot half a mile down an empty road through scrubby fields. There was nothing around but roads and green vacancy. An old mechanic in brown coveralls was working on a tire in the garage, and nobody was in the office. Fred drove into the lot and parked his car next to the building. The mechanic came out, looked at Fred's car, and checked it against what he was expecting.

"He'll be here shortly," the mechanic said. He smelled like a cigar butt. "Why don't you wait in the car?"

Fred went back and sat in the car while the mechanic strolled into the office and made a phone call. He went back into the garage without saying anything else to Fred. Fred put his gun under the front seat and waited.

In twenty minutes a Silver Spur Rolls Royce swept in. The redhead and the weasel climbed out of the backseat, looked the terrain over, and nodded toward the driver. The weasel's face was bruised and puffy, and he had a bandage on his nose. Fred opened his car door. The redhead walked toward him. Fred got out. The weasel—he'd washed his hair, had to, to get the blood out—had on a clean white windbreaker today, and black pants. The redhead was dressed the same. It was a uniform. The redhead said, "Let's have your piece."

"The piece," Fred said, "is in my car and stays there." He slammed the car door, locking it. He held the key while he allowed the redhead to pat him down, feel that the shoulder rig was empty. The redhead felt the cassette in his jacket pocket, pulled it out, looked it over, and put it back. Nothing dangerous there.

"Okay, Champ," he called to the Rolls.

The man who got out was young—about thirty, Fred guessed. He was dressed as elegantly, or at least as expensively, as Clayton, but with more ostentation, more lilt and élan to lapel and shoulder pad, more *suggestion de maquereau* in the cinch at the waist of the blue suit with white stripes. He wore his black hair slicked back with no part. He was clean-shaven, with a hard, boyish face and square jaw. Fred walked toward him, and he beckoned toward the office, which Fred entered first. That left the redhead and the weasel standing outside looking like a couple of hit men.

"Sit in the car," Fred's host yelled at them as he closed the office door. He sat behind the cluttered Formica table, Fred on the other side.

"I expected Buddy Mangan," Fred said.

"I give a fuck what you expected. The money," the guy said. "You have it?"

"It's here," Fred said. "Check." He reached toward the inside jacket pocket on the right, opening the jacket as he did so to demonstrate the flatness of its contents, but the guy wasn't worried.

Fred handed the check over. The guy took a look.

"It's a cashier's check," Fred said.

"I see that," the guy said. "It's made out to Fred Taylor. Who's Fred Taylor?"

"That's me."

"They call you Arthurian."

"I can't help that," Fred said. "They call you Champ."

The guy slapped the check down on the desk, disgusted. "This is shit. I can't use this."

"It's as good as cash when I endorse it," Fred said.

"So endorse it," the guy said. He took a nail clipper out of his jacket pocket and started clipping his nails onto the surface of the desk.

"After I have what I came for," Fred said. "The kid and the letter."

"Why don't you go sit in your car a minute," Champ said.

Fred left the check sitting on the desk with nail clippings falling on it. He walked outside and over toward the car. The redhead and the weasel were looking alert, their doors in the back of the Rolls opening, the guy in the office motioning them impatiently to stay where they were.

Fred watched Champ pick up the phone, punch numbers, talk, wait, talk, wait, talk, wait maybe four minutes, talk again, and hang up. Champ beckoned him to come back in.

"Okay. It's like this," Champ said, still clipping. Fred noticed that the blue-and-white paisley handkerchief in the breast pocket of the man's suit matched his tie but was the inverse of it.

"Yes?" Fred said.

"The guy you want to meet, that kid Russ, he's waiting for you. At the airport, the Green Airport, five miles south of here. You know it?"

Fred knew it: a little airport for the capital of a little state.

"Pick him up. Come back. Endorse the check. Fred Taylor, how the check is made out, right?"

"The kid's at the airport?" Fred asked.

"In the waiting room. He's supposed to wait for you. We think he will."

"And that letter," Fred said. "Maybe I'll have a look at it before I go. Make sure everything's copacetic."

"Copacetic?"

"Like, okay," Fred told him.

"The letter," the guy said. He looked carefully at his nails, left hand, right hand, before he put the clipper back in his pocket. "There's a problem with the letter." He raised his hand to calm any objection Fred might have. "A problem, but we're working on it. I'll tell you about it when you get back."

"Should I be talking to Mangan?" Fred said.

"Put it this way," Champ said. "I'm the guy that's here."

"When I get back with the kid," Fred told him, "I want to talk with Mangan."

"Mangan is shit," Champ said, and he spat.

"Or the guy Mangan works for," Fred said. "That happens before the check is good."

Champ stood, shook out his pants creases, dusted his lapels. "You know twenty-five grand is not a lot of money for this kind of aggravation?"

Fred said, "It must be the principle of the thing."

"When you bring the kid," Champ said, "leave him in the car, down the road a ways. The kid's not smart. We'd as soon he doesn't see me or my car. You understand business. He never will. That's my opinion. The other matter, you talking to another party, I was you I wouldn't hold my breath."

"Tell you what," Fred said. "Take this tape to the guy that does the deals. Only him. Tell him to play it. Only take him a few minutes. We'll see if he wants to talk."

"Give me an hour," Champ said, looking at his watch and shrugging his shoulders. He dropped the cassette into his coat pocket and smoothed the bulge before he walked to the office door, Fred following. The redhead and the weasel came to meet him like dangerous puppies, leashed back.

The redhead, bulging and weaving, hunched next to Fred, menacing. "Anytime you want, buddy," he said.

Fred told him, "See you around."

"Fuck you," the redhead said.

"Shut up," Champ told his assistants. "Get in the car."

The mechanic came out of his garage and went into the office again.

Fred drove to the Green Airport and parked. He left the gun under the seat. He looked at the airport entrance. It was a public place you could get to easily, fast, unnoticed; it was also a place where a gun battle was less likely to develop than in a private home, say, in Cranston.

The Green is a small but pretentious airport. It has everything you could want, but just one of it. Just one Russell sat in the waiting area. Nobody was waiting with him or even watching. He looked subdued and forlorn. He wore his student outfit still, a green tweed jacket and khaki pants, the red butterfly looking slept-in and the white shirt very dirty.

Fred sat down next to him. "My name is Fred. We've talked."

Russ looked over and said, "It's you." Then he more or less crumpled. Fred put a big hand on the kid's shoulder.

"Okay," he said. "Let's go, Russ. We're halfway home."

Nobody followed them out. Fred got Russ into the passenger seat up front, put the seat belt on him, and locked the door. The kid was in shock and barely moving. Fred walked around to the other side of the car and got in. He looked at Russ looking blank, told him, "Hold on," and went back into the restaurant snack bar for a couple of coffees. The guy had said to give it an hour. Fred put milk and a lot of sugar into Russ's coffee, sugar being good for shock. Some take alcohol, but it's sugar they want.

222

Fred sat beside Russ in the front of the car, drank his own coffee, and made Russ drink some of his.

"What are you going to do to me?" Russ said.

"We're going to get through this, and then you are going to go back to the Celtic bronze. Get that Ph.D."

Russ shuddered.

"So you can be some kind of pimp all your life," Fred said. He watched a big plane land behind the airport building just as three little planes took off. It looked like a circus trick, the big plane breaking on a bounce into the three little ones.

Cars drove in and out of the parking lot. Russ drank some of his coffee and continued to shiver.

"That other business, blackmail and photo models and all that," Fred said, "it's finished."

Russ trembled and shivered. "Dawn found him in there dead," he said. He gulped, as in the period of agonized reflection that precedes a long spell of puking. "God, it's the worst thing I ever did in my life, sneaking past all that, that dead man, and taking out his stuff. But he wasn't going to use it, and he owed me. He screwed me. He sold the painting to another guy, this Arthurian. I was just going to get enough to see me through grad school—me and Dawn. Then stop. God."

Russ puked, Fred steering his head in time out the passenger window. Russ hung his head out, gasping.

"Did they hurt you?" Fred asked.

Russ shook his head. "They said they would," he said. He rinsed his mouth with coffee and spat. He brought his head back into the car again. "Two guys, a big one with red hair and a knife—they thought I had the money. I never saw their money. I told them you were Arthurian. You had the painting. You had the money. You had everything. What could I do? They would have killed me." He was miserable, looking straight ahead.

"Well," Fred said, "here I am. My next question is, what about the letter?"

"The letter," Russ said.

"From William Merritt Chase to Conchita Hill. It went with the painting Smykal had."

"I was right. I knew you were Arthurian," Russ said, his voice bitter, sullen.

"I'm trying to save your ass," Fred said. "And it's not much of a prize. I want the letter, too."

"I can't talk about it," Russ said. "They said if I talk they'll cut out my heart. And then go and find my mother," he said, "and make her eat it."

"Suppose *I* cut your heart out?" Fred said.

"You wouldn't," Russ said.

He might talk later, when his fear and shock diminished, but for now he was letting his animal instincts fear most the greater potential evil.

"Tell me what happened," Fred said, "what went on between you and Buddy Mangan."

"Buddy Mangan?" Russ asked. He trembled. He started drooling and fell over on his side. Fred went around the car, pulled him out, and laid him in the backseat. Russ curled there in a semi-doze, his eyes wide, snoring.

Fred drove back to the gas station, went past it, and parked up the road, off the edge, in some bushes. He told Russ, "You're all right here. Stay down. I have to go buy you from these people."

He'd do that even if the letter didn't appear, would cover it himself if he had to. He'd have nothing to show for his trouble except Russ, but Russ's mother would prefer it this way.

Fred put the gun back under his arm. He didn't want to leave it in the car with Russ and have it be there when the guilt hit, if Russ was capable of that, or of the massive feeling of worthlessness that follows failure and captivity.

Fred walked back along the fields until he reached the gas station again. He went into the office. The mechanic, behind the table with a newspaper, his feet up, was going to try to make him wait outside, but Fred told him, "I'll stay here."

The old man scratched the white whiskers on his cheeks, then shrugged and offered Fred the sports pages. Fred didn't need them. He would look out at the sky. Birds were out there. A hawk was way up, circling, celebrating nature—the innocent state of nature.

Fred watched the Silver Spur pull up again. Champ got out. The backseat was empty this time. Champ came into the office and motioned with his chin for the mechanic to get out.

"I have my piece on me," Fred said.

"I don't give a smoking shit," Champ said. He didn't sit down. He laid Fred's check on the desk. "After you sign that, leave it," he said. "Put something on it so it doesn't blow away. A guy wants to talk to you."

Still standing, he punched out a number, shading the buttons with one hand. He got an answer, said, "I'll get him," and handed the phone to Fred. Then he stepped out and went back to the Rolls and sat out there.

31

The voice on the telephone was one Fred didn't know. It was that of an older man. He had a warm, slow manner, accustomed both to persuading and to going uncontradicted.

"Arthurian?"

"My friends call me Fred," Fred said. "Thank you for calling."

"I received what you sent."

"Yes."

"It was a surprise."

"I thought it might be," Fred said.

"Mangan said you must have killed the man when you took the painting. And my money."

Fred said, "Forgive me, but I would not, myself, want to be guided by what Mangan says."

"I appreciate your returning my money."

"So you're under no delusion," Fred said, "that was never your money. It's money to buy the life of a stupid man. I don't know a thing about your money. But I'm surprised you would use as ostentatious a front for your investments as Mangan."

"I don't discuss my associates or my investments with you. Wait a minute," the man said.

Fred could still see the hawk from where he sat. The bird was sailing, enjoying the thermals and the press of hunger that would be satisfied.

"You vouch for this film?" asked the man.

"I do."

"Mangan says Henry Smykal was dead when he arrived."

"Well," Fred said, "the tape shows Smykal moving pretty well for a dead man. My theory is that Smykal made the deal with Russ and Russ told Mangan when to deliver the money, while Smykal himself was waiting to see if my guy would come through with a higher bid—which my guy did. Then Smykal informed Russ that the deal was off, and—after I picked the painting up—your boy Mangan turned up at Smykal's to discuss it with him."

There was a short silence. Fred waited.

"How do you happen to have that film?"

"Let me ask this," Fred said. "The letter I am looking for—the agreement I made with the person in the Rolls Royce? Do you stand by it?"

"I stand by my agreements. There has been a difficulty."

Fred waited. The hawk could move while it waited.

"For the time being, on account of a misunderstanding, I am not able to send anyone for the letter." The man paused. "I like things simple," he said. "This has not been simple. I listened to bad advice. Bear with me."

He paused again. "Why did you send the videotape to me? I imagine other copies exist?"

"Of course," said Fred.

"And your plan is . . . ?"

"I felt a responsible person might wish to take action, and the first responsible person I thought of was yourself."

"I see," the man said. "You know who you are talking to?"

"Not necessary," Fred said. "But I started to wonder where your money might be, and it occurred to me—pardon me, wait a minute."

He was being confronted by the mechanic, who was standing outside the glass door, gesturing. Fred understood the old man's gestures to mean that he wanted to come in and use the men's room, which you could only get to through the office. Fred made a gesture back that meant, Use the bushes, for God's sake. We're in the middle of the countryside.

"Sorry," Fred said. "Where was I?"

"It occurred to you . . ."

"Not to beat around the bush," Fred said. "Mangan seems stupid enough to try something. Smykal had thirty-some thousand from my guy, and Mangan was carrying twenty-five more of yours—that's enough to play games for. Not that it's my business."

"Mangan was stupid enough to lie to me about Smykal," the man said. "Maybe I'll ask him about the money."

There was a pause, a long pause, about five minutes' worth. The hawk circled slowly beyond where Fred could see it. Ten minutes. Champ, in the Rolls, had his clipper out again. He was doing his nails, holding his hands out the window so the clippings would fall outside and not mess up the upholstery.

The voice of Providence came on again. "Please keep the check."

Fred put the check back in his pocket. "And the letter?" he asked.

"The letter will be delivered to you at your hotel in the morning."

"I have left the hotel," Fred said.

"I can't change the arrangements now. What will happen is this: a messenger will come to find you tomorrow morning in the dining room of the Charles Hotel. That's the deal. He'll be there at eight-thirty. A waiter will page you."

"I'll be there," Fred said.

"The film," the man continued evenly, his voice conveying no pressure, only mild, comfortable persuasion. "Have you thought what to do next about the film? I presume you have taken precautions should anything, God forbid, occur on the highway?"

"I am aware of my mortality," Fred said. "I, like you, prefer things simple."

"Not only your mortality, but that of your loved ones also," the voice said. "Suppose I assure you that as a person of responsibility, I will see that the issues raised by the film, and associated with it, are efficiently dealt with? They will be, in good time."

"That makes sense to me," Fred said.

"The film, then?"

"Will not be permitted to embarrass you."

"We understand each other. You realize you have only my word on my part of the arrangement?"

"You have my word also," Fred said. "It's as good as yours."

"Please have my nephew take the phone again."

"The one with the Silver Spur and the nail clipper, or the guy who runs the store?"

"We were getting along so well. Don't ruin it by being funny."

Fred went to the door and beckoned the nephew to come in out of the Rolls. He walked back to his car, stopping to use the bushes himself on the way. The hawk circled back into view, patient.

Russ, still curled in the backseat when Fred got to the car, slept all the way back to Cambridge.

Fred left Russ in Sheila's apartment, still curled up, sleeping on the futon. Fred had half carried him upstairs.

Fred pulled Sheila out into the stairwell after him. "Let me talk with you a minute, Sheila," he said. "Russell had a bad time."

Sheila looked him over speculatively, nodded, and answered, "I see that." She had let them into the apartment, wearing a Georgetown sweatshirt, her legs bare.

"People connected to the tape you gave me had him. They kidnapped him, threatened him."

Sheila nodded again, her eyes interested. "That was fast. How much did you get?" she asked.

"Just Russ," Fred said.

"Shit, that isn't much."

"I have to agree with you."

"How do I know you're not cheating me?" Sheila said.

"You don't," Fred told her. "About Russ: it's going to be hard for him when he wakes. If you're at all a friend of his, I wouldn't leave him alone for a while."

Sheila clasped her hands, thinking.

"He's not all that much to me," she said. "I mean to say, who needs him? Everyone's an island, you know?" She pulled the sweatshirt down, noticing the chill breeze on her legs, standing out in the hall. Fred started down the stairs.

"I've decided I'll work with you after all," Sheila said. "I like your style."

"Maybe I'll call you," Fred said.

"What are you doing with my film?" Sheila asked.

"I'm doing a Rose Mary Woods on it," he said.

"A what?"

"I'm going to just chuck it."

As soon as he left the apartment on Pearl Street, Fred felt the Heade rush in. He was tired. Tomorrow was the big day, the auction. He'd have to get Clayton on the phone and start laying out their tactics. After the sale was over, however things turned out, he thought, maybe he'd take a few days off—except he'd prefer to go somewhere with Molly, and she wouldn't leave the kids. They had school. So maybe he'd go somewhere on Sunday with the kids and Molly, like a family. It wouldn't be a rest, but it would put him back on track toward his main objective.

He sat in the car on Pearl Street, thinking there was something he should do before he drove to Arlington. Yes, he'd left that tape at the Charles, the backup. He shouldn't let it sit there. His bag with his clothes was there, too.

Boston's rush hour was starting to spill over into Cambridge. It was after six. Fred found a meter open in the garage across from the hotel, noticed a flower store, and bought a big bunch of irises to give Molly. Fred liked irises. They wouldn't last. He got a bunch of daisies, too, which Molly liked and which would last. He put them in the car, then thought to himself, You've been away, you're bringing back a present for the mom, what about the kids?

The kids liked chocolate. He bought a box for them and put it in the car, then bought another so each could have one.

He went in and picked up his bag, then headed to the desk and asked for his package. The woman behind the desk gave it to him, along with a couple of message slips.

"She called twice," the woman said. Fred looked at her. She had red hair in curls as big as fists. She was middle-aged, plump, and brimming with excitement. "Ophelia Finger. We're not supposed to notice, but is it *the* Ophelia Finger? She wants to see you? Here?"

"Yes," said Fred.

"She's meant so much to me," the woman said, beaming. "Her book? Her show? Everything?"

"She wants to meet me for breakfast tomorrow," Fred said, looking at the messages.

"I know," the hostess said. The tag she wore indicated her name was Fran. "We're not supposed to read the messages, but I was excited. See, on account of Ophelia Finger I have all my

self-confidence. You know? 'Learn to love the body you have'?
I did it, and it works! Now I have this new job and everything?"

Poor Fran. She wasn't going to last long at the Charles.

"Glamorous people come through all the time," Fran went
on. "You have to be on your toes because they don't always look
glamorous. Like yesterday, I caught Harriet Voyt? Her you don't
mistake, a beautiful woman like that. I got her autograph. But
imagine Ophelia Finger! If she's here when I'm on in the morning, will you ask her to sign my book?"

"Sure," said Fred. He turned away and started moving, noticing someone who looked like management approaching Fran
at a good clip.

He crossed the lobby to a pay telephone and called Molly
to tell her he was running late.

She sounded glad to hear his voice. "How'd it go, hon?"

"It's going to fly," Fred said. "Most of it is worked out. I got
Russ back. You don't have to worry about me. I got Clay's money
back. The extra money. The ransom."

"Fred, that's terrific!"

"I guess so." Fred looked out across the lobby at the excellent
outfits walking their people around.

"You don't sound terrific."

"Maybe I'm letting down," Fred said.

"Come let down in Arlington," Molly suggested. "Terry's got
a game. She'll be finished around eight. I told the kids we'd
have dinner together if you were back. What do you want, send
out for pizza, or get barbecue, or bring back fish and chips?"

"I don't know," said Fred. "Which would you like? What
would the kids prefer?"

"They want you to decide," Molly said.

"Let's sit in the kitchen and throw fish and chips."

"You're on. I'm going with Sam and pick up Terry's game.
You want to meet us at the park?"

"You're on."

He called Clay, to have this business finished. Clay was about to go downstairs for kir and dinner with Marcel Proust.

"I can barely concentrate," he said. "It's not like me. The stakes have never been so high. I feel as if I have been chosen to rescue a hostage."

"We *have* rescued a hostage," Fred said.

"My dear man. Concentrate. The auction is not until tomorrow. In fact there is not one hostage, but two: the lovers. They have been imprisoned for almost a century."

Oh, the Vermeer. Clay was talking about the painting, the one that might exist behind the other painting of haystacks. Clay was not ever going to know what it was like to be imprisoned, and there was nothing to do about that but forgive it.

"And were you successful in your mission?" he asked at last.

"Some snags," Fred said. "I've been promised I'll have the letter in the morning."

"I still say it is highway robbery," Clayton said, impatient to get on with his evening. "I must say, after all I've"—he corrected himself—"after all *we've* been through, I do resent the delay."

"I do, too," Fred said. "But I think the man will do what he says."

"A good idea is to trust no one, but if you're confident . . . ," said Clay.

"Clay, I still have your check. He wouldn't take your money."

"Well done, Fred." Clay was showing real enthusiasm for the first time. "That gives me a pinch of extra muscle on the Heade."

"Right," Fred said.

"Tell me tomorrow how you made him see reason."

"Right."

"Telephone when you have the letter, in the morning. Telephone or come by. We need to plan our strategy for the main assault."

"Talk to you tomorrow," Fred said. "Bon appétit."

32

The lights were on over the field in Arlington, making a warm yellow pool in the just-beginning dusk. The children were scattered around the field, and Terry was pitching.

Fred found Molly and Sam sitting on the damp concrete bleachers, eating peanuts out of a bag. Fred put a kiss on Molly's cheek. He bopped Sam on the head. Sam, sitting on Molly's left, slid over to make a space for him.

"Stay where you are. Plenty of room," Fred said. He walked across Molly's feet, knees, and lap, sat down on her right, and put his left arm around her. He'd left Molly's flowers in the car for later, and Terry's chocolates, but he gave Sam his now.

"Yo," Molly said, flinching. "You're bringing your gun to a Little League game?"

Used to it already, he'd forgotten about the gun. He'd forgotten, for a moment, that he was dangerous.

"I can blow away the opposition for Terry if things get out of hand," Fred said.

"We're leading fifteen to three," Molly said as Terry slid an accidental curveball high and wide and the opposition batter chased it.

"That's good," Fred said. "I like to see her using that curve."

"Strike three," said Sam. "You know it's not on purpose. Fred, can I see your gun?" He leaned toward Fred across Molly.

Fred looked at Molly.

"Later," Molly said.

Terry's team was streaming off the field.

"Is the game finished already?" Fred asked.

"Top of the third inning," Molly muttered, shifting her backside on the concrete.

"Finished or starting?"

"Starting," Molly said. "And I always forget to bring a cushion."

Fred didn't want to bring the gun into the house with the fish and chips.

"I'll keep it in the car," he said.

"I'd rather have you tell the kids about it," Molly said. "Since it came up."

After they ate, Fred took the thing out, unloaded it, took it apart, showed them how it worked, let them handle it unloaded, and told them he was going to put it back in the car—unloaded— and he didn't want them to touch it again.

"What it does is kill people," he said.

"Has it killed people?" Terry asked.

"Did you kill someone with it?" Sam asked him.

"Other people had it before I did," Fred told him. Sam nodded, that answer enough for him.

"How did the Spanish go?" Fred asked, getting up from the table.

"I got better than half," Sam said tentatively.

"We'll have to work on that," Fred said. "Can you kids get

this fishy trash outside in the barrels while I put the gun in my car?"

He put it under the driver's seat. He'd have to hold on to it until he saw how things worked out tomorrow morning. Maybe he'd keep it through the afternoon, pull it out at Doolan's when the Heade came up, and see if anyone offered a stronger bid.

The kids were packed off to bed. Molly pretended to wash dishes, but they hadn't used any dishes, just forks and the glasses for Coke and beer.

"Why don't you sit down beside me and tell me your story?" Molly said. "We can go sit on the couch."

"That will be nice," said Fred. "When I have the energy. Right now I'm more inclined to go upstairs and stand under your shower and trickle warm water over my body and then get into bed and watch something on TV, hoping my friend Molly will come join me."

Molly said, "You're seeming pretty down for someone who's been wandering around the world saving folks."

"They're such stupid children!" Fred exclaimed.

Molly glared, looking as if she might hit him.

"God, Molly, not your kids. The ones I've been running around with the last three days. Old children. Sometimes I think about . . . ," said Fred. But he didn't want to think about what he thought sometimes, not now.

"You can talk about it when you want to," Molly said. "If I'm in the mood. Go take your shower."

"What you need," Fred said, "is a new water heater."

"What I need is a new water heater and a new bathroom and a slow boat to China," Molly said. "What you need is a shower. You told me yourself. Go to it."

Fred went up. He passed Terry in her room, listening to her radio. He gave her a wave before he stood under the shower in the little family bathroom.

He knew that what was disturbing him couldn't be fixed. It

had to do with Russell's feeding him to the sharks while he, at the same time, and even after, cared enough about Russell to take care of him. He'd wanted him not to be hurt. He cared even now that the kid, dangerous and worthless as he was, would go on hurting. Mangan, on the other hand, worthless and dangerous as he was, deserved whatever was coming to him—once he delivered the letter.

Sam knocked at the door. Was it a message? a phone call? No, he just wanted to use the can.

"Be right out," Fred said.

Wrapped in a towel, he went on into Molly's bedroom. That was four beds this week: Molly's, the hotel's, Teddy's, and the futon in those girls' front room, where he'd sat like the safe grandpa. Was that what he was down about? All that young animal flesh making him feel old?

He'd left his bag in the car. Traveling man. He would bring it in tomorrow. He turned on Molly's portable TV. What was keeping her? He liked Molly's room. It was good sleeping in this woman's bedroom. It had flowers on the walls and curtains, and stacks of books and magazines by the bed.

Molly had a big closet that she called a dressing room. When Fred first started staying over, she'd once mentioned that maybe it could be made into a study. She'd been very tentative, shy. She hadn't said "den," but that was what she meant: a room for the *man*, a place he could elect to call his if he needed a stronghold in which to defend his manhood from the women and children.

He climbed into Molly's bed. She'd changed the sheets. He slipped between them, dry enough, tired but not sleepy. Molly came in.

"You changed the sheets," Fred said. He'd be quick and get a point for noticing.

"What on earth are you watching?"

"I don't know," said Fred. "You want to watch it with me?"

"Fred, did you have to shoot anybody?"

"No," Fred said.

"And did anybody have to shoot you?"

"No." That was a good point.

"Then come off it. Cheer up." Molly took off her clothes and got in beside him.

"It looks like cowboys and Indians," she said. "Do we watch cowboys and Indians?"

"It's going to be our new thing."

"And you'll tell me your story tomorrow," Molly said.

People started shouting and howling on the TV.

"You sure this is what you want?" Molly asked.

Fred turned over and felt Molly's body next to his, her hand resting on the small of his back.

"Sounds good to me," he said.

33

Big fire. The same fire. Old friend.

Petals of ash falling.

Wind.

Petals of ash like cherry blossoms.

Smell, like rubber.

Old wounds.

Wake up and don't worry about it.

Big wind. Ash falling into the prairie, the clearing, open ground, whatever you would call it.

Wake up, don't worry.

Someone screaming, of course. The scream an old friend, like the scars.

Then wake up.

No edges to get hold of. Drown in fire. Drown in a dream of fire. Or wake up.

Fred, covered with sweat, opened his eyes.

At least he hadn't thrashed around this time and wakened Molly.

The room was black-dark. Molly's clock, beside her on the bedside table, showed almost three.

Molly was in a delicious sleep. He could wake her. She wouldn't mind. Probably she'd be grateful to be included in Fred's old friendship.

The subconscious was a slow animal, catching up now with events. The dream was the afterlife of Fred's concern from the night before: concern for Russell and the danger he was in, concern that he'd have to take a life or lose it, or be maimed in some way.

Well, that was over. Done. Fixed. If Clay's letter didn't turn up at all, it was no big deal. He had done all he could and had saved Clayton a lot of money in the process.

Fred was now awake. He'd flipped onto his back while he was dreaming, to face the wounds and fire again. Molly was curled on her side, sleeping soundly. She must have turned the TV off after he went to sleep and climbed back in beside him.

Fred stared into the dark room, his eyes growing able to distinguish objects, his ears alert, making the change from listening to the dream to listening to the dark house in the night of Arlington.

Was he listening for footsteps around the house?

No need. It was not that kind of house. Unless he was in it.

He heard a small snort from Molly, as if she were listening to him think.

Fred couldn't shake the feeling that there was something else he should be doing.

He had the Heade to deal with tomorrow. No, later today, this afternoon. But though the stakes were high, that would be relatively smooth sailing. He'd find out how high Clay wanted him to go, and go that high if need be, then stop. He would either attend in person, if Clay wanted him to be seen and wanted a report later on who else had been bidding, or bid on the telephone, if Clay wanted his role to be kept quiet. The auction house would not reveal the name of the purchaser any more than it would normally reveal the name of the original owner, the consignor.

The biggest potential problem was Finn, if he had stumbled onto the same clue Fred and Clayton had. There was no other way to explain his continued presence on the scene.

Unless . . .

Fred heard himself chuckle. Don't wake Molly, he told himself.

But why not consider and acknowledge the obvious—that Finn had finally met his match in the fair Ophelia?

O! what a noble mind is here o'erthrown. The observ'd of all observers quite, quite down. I have heard of your paintings too, well enough.

Fred started laughing. Molly stirred and protested.

It was not for nothing that Fred had played that small role in *Hamlet* during his brief, disastrous Harvard career.

He got up quietly and reached the door, about to wander naked through the house. That would not do. He pulled his pants on and went down to the kitchen, where he could laugh.

Ophelia, Ophelia. If thou wilt needs marry, marry a fool. God has given you one face, and you make yourself another. You jig, you amble, and you lisp, and make your wantonness your ignorance. If you marry a fool, let it be Finn.

Fred stood in front of Molly's fridge. Did he really want a beer? At three-thirty in the morning?

Well, then, coffee?

Molly had instant in the cabinet, and Fred put water on to boil. He took the screamer off so as not to wake the house.

He was so close to it, so occupied with his own business, so taken by Clayton's paranoia, that he'd forgotten about love. And he knew Ophelia so well that he'd never considered that anyone else in the world could take her seriously for a moment. He'd sold Ophelia short, the sister-in-law complex.

That woman at the Charles, Fran, at the reception desk—how full of starry admiration she had been for the way Ophelia's influence had changed her life!

Hadn't Ophelia been married three times, each time to a man of substance—at least until the divorce settlement?

And wasn't Ophelia Molly's sister?

The water boiling, Fred made his coffee and let it steam in front of him at the kitchen table.

Fires and wounds and dreams and floating ash, indeed. Finn was in love. Ophelia had bewitched him. Finn, like a puffed and reckless libertine, himself the primrose path of dalliance tread, and recked not Clayton Reed.

Ophelia was a past mistress of the judo twitch that lets your own weight fell you. Ophelia, who could sell anything to anybody, had sold Finn the image of himself as the darling of a TV series: the host, the pundit, the pander.

How nice that it should happen to Finn.

How pleased Clayton would be when he found out.

Taking his coat from the back of the chair, Fred put it on over his skin and strolled outside, carrying the end of the coffee. He stood in Molly's cold backyard to drink the rest of it. He pulled her back door closed. Let them be warm in there.

34

The dining room of the Charles was the best place in Cambridge to come upon the elegant and wealthy among the transient set. Fred walked in shortly before eight, not wanting to miss anything that might relate to the messenger he was expecting. He took a table next to the window overlooking the terraced brick courtyard between the hotel and the surrounding buildings, from which he could also see the entrance.

He ordered coffee and a bagel.

He looked at the international crowd approaching the issue of the American breakfast. A Japanese family sat in one corner, only the daddy speaking any English. Nigerians or some such were in their robes. A single man in a regular business suit, but with a turban, looked as if he were trying out for a part in *Kim*. He was shifty-eyed, eating bacon with furtive movements. There were women so simply elegant and fresh they must have come from Paris, and parents of Harvard students in from foreign parts like Mobile and Kansas City.

Fred had hoped that not having had a reply from him, Ophelia might conclude that her invitation to breakfast had lapsed. But it would take more than that to discourage her. At a quarter after, there she came, entering in a bright orange suit with a black shirt under it, high heels in black, and a different Hermès purse, in case you were tired of the first one.

Ophelia surveyed the room, spotted Fred, and made a beeline for him, flinging her arms out, crowing, letting the whole room know that the big, hard-looking guy by the window was waiting for her, a rough setting for a fragile jewel.

"They told me you'd checked out," Ophelia said. "But I could see through that." She winked. She ordered coffee and a half grapefruit and winked again.

"Who is she, Fred? Where is she? You can rely on me. I won't tell . . . anyone."

What? Fred had forgotten that Ophelia was operating on the fantasy that he was cheating on her sister.

"I'm here to see you, aren't I?" he said blandly.

"Yes?" Ophelia asked, her eyes delighted.

The waiter brought her coffee.

Fred paid as little attention to her as he could, looking out for the contact. He was watching for one of Mangan's runners from the South Shore.

"To tell you the truth, Ophelia, I'm working," he said. "There's no new girlfriend."

Ophelia nodded. She understood Fred's indiscretions. Her lips were sealed. His secret was safe with her.

Now down to business: "I want to talk with you about joining my project, Fred."

"The TV show?"

"Of course."

"Sorry, Ophelia. I don't have time. For whatever you want. I keep too busy."

Ophelia slowly revolved her grapefruit half, looking to select the winning section. Which would be the first through the pearly gates? Fred looked past her.

"Albert will want you, too," Ophelia continued, nodding in reassurance. "I haven't dared talk much to him about the project. He can't join us for breakfast, he's meeting an important client. He's so preoccupied. An important man. In his field."

She smiled at Fred. "A month ago I wouldn't have thought there could *be* an important man in your field. Is that all you're eating? Just the bagel? You know this is my treat."

Fred saw Finn at the entrance, wearing a brown suit. Ophelia always got her men into brown suits eventually. Fred thought it was her way of paying homage to her favorite American male, Ronald Reagan. Finn rolled in, portly and freshly groomed, his face glowing with rotund benevolence. Ophelia was oblivious.

"Sir Albert's here now," Fred said. "In the flesh."

Ophelia turned to look.

Finn, having bestowed the blessing of his gaze upon the assembled multitude, was moving toward the business-suited man with the turban. The man had successfully defeated his bacon and was at this very moment sipping at a large glass of fruit juice. Finn bent over him and whispered into his ear. The man's turban shook a negative. Finn whispered again, a question. The turban shrugged. Finn turned and left the room.

"A moving thing to see the great man at his work," Fred said.

"That was probably the servant," Ophelia said, "giving him a message."

"Of course," Fred said.

"Strange he didn't notice me," she said.

"You are very noticeable," Fred assured her. Ophelia selected another grapefruit section and chewed it vengefully.

Finn entered once again, this time preceded by a waiter, like a hunting pope using an acolyte as a beater. The waiter gently paged, "Mr. Arthurian? Mr. Arthur Arthurian?"

Fred grinned at Ophelia. He stood and gave Finn the heartiest of good-morning waves.

Ophelia looked helplessly around the room.

"Over here," Fred shouted.

"He doesn't want you," Ophelia whispered urgently. "You'll ruin everything. He's supposed to meet the recluse, Arthur Arthurian. He didn't tell me Mr. Arthurian was staying at the Charles. He's supposed to be at the Ritz."

Fred moved away from the table, went toward the waiter, tipped him a buck—which he was too surprised not to accept—and took Finn by the shoulder. Finn was disgruntled and bemused.

"You have a letter for me," Fred said. "William Merritt Chase to Conchita Hill."

Finn stared. "You?" he puffed.

Ophelia, rising now, took Finn by the arm. "Sit down, darling," she pleaded. "Don't let's make a scene."

Finn noticed her at last and shook her hand off his arm in its brown cloth. "You," he snorted, turning purpler.

"The letter," Fred said.

"Sit down, baby," Ophelia said.

Finn glanced around. He saw that he was becoming the star of a scene that he'd rather not play so publicly. He allowed Ophelia to lead him to the table, where he sat on the edge of a chair. A waiter bowed over him and asked, "Coffee?"

"Not coffee. Not anything," Finn said.

"I don't understand," Ophelia said, looking from one man to the other.

"Snake," Finn hissed at her. "You're in this, too."

Finn stared at Fred.

Fred's coffee was cold, but he took a sip anyway, savoring it.

"You're not Arthur Arthurian," Finn said finally, slowly.

"A nom de guerre," Fred said. Ophelia stared in incomprehension.

"It doesn't make sense," Finn said. "I have to make a telephone call." He made to get up again, but Fred put a big hand on his shoulder and let the fingers grasp it, denting the brown cloth, dragging the weight of his arm downward.

"We can ask to have a telephone brought to the table, Finn, but you're not leaving until I have that letter."

Finn sat.

"What about Mr. Arthurian?" Ophelia asked.

"Don't pretend," Finn said. "You and your pal here! Ha! You played me for a sucker, the two of you."

"The two of us?" Ophelia protested. "What, Fred and me?"

"I know Taylor is your relation," Finn said. "I thought you could rise above that."

Mud is thicker than water, as Molly's mother would say.

Ophelia, stunned, opened her handbag and began some displacement activity in there.

"Shall I call for a telephone?" Fred asked. "You may want to think about it first. Mangan's Providence connection sounded as if he was getting impatient with the whole thing."

Finn looked at Fred. He started to sag. Fred took his hand off the brown coat.

Ophelia, finding a tissue, looked as if her next move might be tears.

"Hold it, Ophelia," Fred said.

The waiter bowed over them all again.

"Nobody here wants anything," Fred told him. "Here's what I think," he said, turning to Finn. "Stop me anytime. A graduate student from the fine-arts department at Harvard—let's call him Russell Ennery—got in touch with you and told you about a painting he had found. Unsigned, but accompanied by a letter that gave it all the authority it needed. You got in touch with

Mangan to engineer a quick cash sale, and then you arranged, through Ennery, for the purchase."

"Correction," Finn objected, defending his professional skill. "Of course I examined the painting myself. Friday afternoon. In situ. Before I recommended purchase."

"Correction noted," said Fred. "What else did you examine there?"

Finn lost a good deal of color.

The waiter bowed over all of them once more. "The check, sir?"

"I'll take it," Fred offered. He continued, "Friday afternoon, unknown to you, there had already been a higher bidder. But you took the letter with you to examine while Smykal waited to see if the higher bid—ours—would materialize. Later that evening, Russ told you you'd been scooped. Meanwhile, Mangan was becoming impatient with your delay—"

"A delay," Finn exploded, "that's lasted a week now. I am supposed to be in Paris. I am *needed* there."

"You told Mangan, and Mangan said, 'I'll go back and take care of it,'" Fred said. "And in the meantime it seems to have become very complex. A small murder intervened."

Fred looked into Finn's eyes for a long time. At last he said, "About the phone call—how much do you want the Albert Finn saga to be publicly intertwined with Smykal's? Are you sure you want to make that call?"

Ophelia, licking her lips, looked across at Finn.

Finn took an envelope from the inside pocket of his suit jacket. It was a new white envelope, with an older one inside it. He put it on the table and made to stand.

"I'll just look it over first," Fred said.

He opened the outer envelope. The one inside was directed to Conchita Hill. It bore no address. Fred slid the letter out and read,

248

Conchita. Dearest. I leave you with this token. In tribute to the master who first brought us together, I shall think of this painting always under the title *Harmony in Flesh Color and Black.*

Will

Below that was a small pen sketch of the painting.

Russ, starting with nothing but the nickname Will, could have worked hard for six months before narrowing the possibilities down to Chase.

Fred nodded, dismissing Finn. Other parts of the story would be interesting to know, but they were not important now. He had the letter.

Finn rose. The breakfasters looked around in expectation. Maybe there would be a fistfight after all. Ophelia started rising as well, to follow her man.

"I'll come with you, Al?"

He looked down at her amazed, his face rich with disgust. "I shall be on the next shuttle to New York," he said. "An afternoon of work at the office. Sadly neglected. Then an evening flight to Paris. I have wasted a whole week."

Finn turned but held back, needing another exit line. "My commission on that transaction was to be fifteen thousand dollars. In my opinion, the commission is still owed. By Clayton Reed."

Ophelia was starting to cry now. Finn's crack about a week wasted had been pretty mean, considering.

"Why don't you send us a bill, Sir Albert?" Fred suggested.

Finn stormed out.

Fred accepted the check from the waiter.

Ophelia blew her nose into some very common Kleenex. "Al

was so hopeful about the Arthurian connection," she said, "and you just made him up!"

"You sure you don't want something else to eat?" Fred offered. "You can't get far on half a grapefruit."

She shook her head. "He was just another opportunist after all."

She held her hand out, keeping Fred at the table. She needed someone there while she put her face back together, which she now started to do, replacing the divots uprooted by her tears.

"He didn't look that good in the brown suit," Fred confided.

"He looked like a fool," Ophelia agreed. "You know, Fred, the reason he turned on me? All men are like that when they're disappointed. I heard him on the phone yesterday, really pulling strings and arguing to get this meeting, insisting on it.

"I told him what you'd said about Arthurian—confidentially, of course. But just to make sure I had his interest, I made up a lot of extra shit and threw that in too."

She started laughing.

Fred got up and took her arm.

"There's someone at the desk who wants to meet you," he said. "Fran, who says you changed her life."

35

Fred was at his desk at Clayton's by eleven. He couldn't stay long; he wanted to look at the Heade himself before the auction started, so he'd have to be at Doolan's by one o'clock. He wouldn't mind having the pressure lift after that, much as he enjoyed the feel of the sharp edges he'd been skating along and the skill of his own skating.

He pulled Conchita out again and gave her a long look. She was cool and smooth and filled with mischief: the artist out of uniform. He wondered, had the weight of the world she found afterward been such as to let her live the mischief into her painting? Her own paintings had still not been discovered, but maybe they would surface someday—unless she, like many another, had been distracted into the whirl of living like an artist, or a parent, and had lost her art.

So Whistler, according to the letter that Fred now placed on his desk, had introduced Conchita to Will Chase. Then what?

Fred couldn't wait to see the painting cleaned.

He glanced at the mail and called Clayton.

"How's Proust?"

"Proust led a life any man might envy," said Clayton, probably the first person in the history of the world to think so.

"I have the letter," Fred said.

"Good." No questions.

"And Albert Finn is on his way to Paris via New York."

There was a pause while Clayton took that in.

"Finn had the letter," Fred told him.

"Oh."

Another pause. A long one.

"Ah," Clay said. "You'll explain later, I imagine."

"Finn wants a commission."

"He wants a what?" Clay exclaimed.

"My thought exactly," Fred said.

"I shall come home, then," Clay continued, putting it together. "As long as Albert Finn is out of it."

"I won't be here long," Fred said. "I have things to do. There's Doolan's, you'll recall. Shall we talk about that?"

Seldom had Clayton left his final instructions until this late in the game. "With Finn gone," he explained, "we have no competition to be concerned about, unless Mangan drives up the price."

Fred thought. He waited. He said nothing about Mangan. Better not, on the whole. Not yet.

"I have been thinking," Clay said, "about testosterone."

There was nothing like Proust to get a man thinking about gonads.

"Conflict," Clay announced, "is the enemy of art."

Fred had a similar theory, which was that art was the fruit of conflict, but he was not inclined to argue, at the moment, against the combined forces of Clayton Reed and Proust.

"Also," Clay went on, "I believe I permitted the prospect of impending challenge to cloud my judgment. About the Heade."

Fred waited, looking at Conchita. She looked back at him, a young woman full of energy and skill and hopes and dopey ideas. Like Terry someday. Later a mother, a grand-mother, dead, the great-grandmother of a hideous, lost man, and so on.

"I think," Clay said, "we'll stop bidding at a hundred thirty-five thousand. That gives us a fair margin over the painting's value as a Heade and keeps us from making a naive gesture after fantasy. We have no hard evidence that the Vermeer is there, after all—nothing more than coincidence and hope."

Fred didn't often argue money with Clayton. That was Clay-ton's business. It was he who was going to be the owner. Fred didn't want to own anything. But he hated to see this one go without a fight.

"Give me some slack, Clay. Let me go to one seventy-five."

"No," Clay said. "I've been thinking it over as we've been talking. I let my animosity toward that man get the better of my judgment. He is no longer a threat. He is so filled with self-importance that he missed the obvious. A hundred thirty-five shall be my limit. That's hammer price."

"Of course," Fred said. The gallery would take a ten percent commission on top of the hammer price: $13,500 more for Clay to pay if Fred bid his top limit. "You're coming home, then? Do you want me to call after the Heade sells? Let you know if we got it?"

"If it's not too much trouble," Clay said. He sounded impa-tient, trying to get back to his Proust, his finger in the book. "Oh, and Fred?" he said.

"Yes?"

"I appreciate that—listen, Fred, please don't be insulted; I don't talk about such things easily. I want to make a gesture to acknowledge your exceedingly competent work, and even some awkwardness you encountered this past week."

"Thank you, Clay. I appreciate your saying so." Fred looked

around the office, itching to get out of here. It was a nice day outside, and he had a job to finish.

"You saved me a great deal of money," Clayton said.

That was true. It was interesting, too. Fred didn't save anything, not for himself. There was no place to put it. But he was happy to save Clay's money.

"I want you to have something," Clay said.

Conchita looked at Fred still in her knowing way. He'd have to get that girl upstairs. He wasn't exactly listening; he was wishing he could let down, get out of here, drive fast through the cold blossoms.

"Please keep the check I made out to you yesterday as a token of my respectful admiration," said Clay.

Fred thanked him, too surprised almost to do that much. "I'll call after the sale, then," he promised.

"If we are successful in our bid," Clay went on, "find someplace safe to keep the painting, will you, over the weekend? And bring it in Monday when you come."

Fred locked up, took the car out of its spot on Mountjoy Street, and headed back across the river. It was a bright day, and sailboats skidded on the water. He went west, out Route 2 and so on, dodging Concord. The willows furred the edges of the roads and hills with their defiant color, yellow tempting green. Apple orchards were beginning their bloom. Doolan's was twenty miles out of town, surrounded by orchards and overgrown farms, in an area ripe and yearning for mall culture if only the economy would change.

Fred had a totally unexpected, amazing, unbudgeted check for twenty-five thousand bucks in his pocket. It was like suddenly owning a giraffe. Ridiculous. He wasn't like that.

There was a good crowd at Doolan's and twenty minutes left of the preview, Fred having been held up by a flaming accident about five miles out. He had to look fast before they locked everyone out of the showroom in order to line things up for the sale.

You couldn't tell what was going to happen by who was present, since the wild cards might operate over the phone or by means of surrogates. Still, he took note of who was there. Mangan was prominently absent; in fact, Fred mused, his absence stuck out like a sore ham . . . a hem . . . what was that thing Oona had been trying to put into her *mot juste?*

A knot of folks stood in front of the Heade, a mixture of players from the art biz and others hoping to beat the dealers by finding something they wanted and buying it at only a bid beyond the dealer price, which they couldn't guess at but relied on the dealers to show them through their competition. Because it was Saturday afternoon, it felt like a barbecue or a sporting event.

If Richard Coeur de Lion could sing from his prison window and be recognized, shouldn't Fred be able to hear Vermeer singing to him from within the hay? How could a thing with such passionate reality as a Vermeer be hidden anywhere?

A stout fellow wearing white loafers was handling the Heade under the watchful gaze of Betty Feely, the person at Doolan's charged with knowing her onions in the art area. The sale consisted mainly of rugs and Chinese crockery from the Apthorp estate, so Betty didn't have much to do but stand by the Heade and assist potential buyers in feeling positive about it.

The stout man examined it front and back. He looked naked, as if he needed a cigar. The picture was blessedly dirty except for a patch in the sky that Doolan's had tested so everyone could see how much better the thing would look once it was cleaned. When the cleaning was actually done, however, you would lose not only the contrast but the spice of hope. And it was hope—their own—that most people paid for.

"So what do you think it'll go for?" the man asked. Fred had seen him before. He bought to impress a wife who had learned the names of some desirable painters.

Betty Feely simpered and dimpled and looked professional and confidential all at the same time. Fred watched the man turn the picture around and glance at the back. Canvas of considerable age, no question; primed with glue. Nice old Dutch stretcher, Fred thought—unless he was selling Clayton's hope to himself now.

"There are aggressive left bids on it already, of course," Betty Feely said confidentially, hanging the picture on the wall again so it could bathe in the full gaze of the spotlight. "And telephone bids lined up as well, as you'd expect with a piece of this quality."

The man had heard it all before and was turning away to talk to his eager wife. "To me it looks like haystacks, honey," he was saying, whether to Betty Feely or to his wife or, making use of the editorial or imperial *honey*, to the world at large.

Fred stared hard at the cleared patch of sky. It told him nothing, only that Heade had used a white pigment that would cover reasonably well. On the whole, the painting seemed uncharacteristically sketchy, the sketchiness making a scrim that was hard to penetrate.

With all this money in my pocket, Fred thought, I should look at the pots, maybe see if there's one I can take to Molly as a present. But he knew that this thinking was just the money trying to find a hole in his pocket—or, no, the hole in his pocket trying to find the money.

The crowd was thrown out, and Fred got himself a bidding number and drank coffee with some of the rug and crockery people. He noted a rumbling buzz of interest in Mangan's absence. Nobody could figure out why the man was not in attendance. Fred didn't much like being visible, because anyone who knew him would understand that he had to be here for the Heade. He should have been on the phone, but this was what

Clay wanted, even if advertising his interest drove the price up. A couple of other painting people in the crowd might or might not have any interest in the cannon fodder; some of them were capable of fronting for big money.

But nobody who knew his stuff could think the Heade was much of a picture.

Fred found a seat in the house from which he could watch the stout man and his wife and be seen from the podium without making such a commotion as to attract attention from the rear.

The auctioneer, Bill Goodfellow, in a loud white-and-brown checked sport coat and no necktie, had a sleepy style, like a crocodile letting the lazy water lap, tempting the thirsty audience to move out deeper and deeper to drink until he struck at the fattest. Fred watched and admired his style, fighting off sleep himself while Goodfellow sold the first seventy-five lots of pots and rugs. The paintings started then, with the Heade reserved until the end, lot 100.

Fred saw the stout fellow's posture become ever more indifferent the closer they moved to the century, and noted his eager wife's simultaneous and contradictory body language, her buttocks tensing until Fred thought they'd pop when the Heade came up.

Goodfellow had to make a romance of it, telling the story, going on about how the honest auctioneers, called into the house to evaluate the residue of the estate for the hospital (note, folks, the charitable cause we are involved in), had discovered the Heade, this treasure, in the attic.

"Are the telephones ready?" Goodfellow asked, doing his imitation of Ed McMahon bringing on Johnny Carson in the old days for those not able to sleep otherwise. The eager wife whispered into her man's ear while he leaned back with still greater indifference.

The telephones stopped at ninety grand. It had been the stout man's bid against the phones up to seventy-five thousand,

and then the stout man against one phone to ninety; and then Fred slipped in, the bid now rising in increments of five thousand. Goodfellow looked wildly into the audience for Mangan. There seemed to be nothing pushing from behind him, and Fred watched the eager wife cajole her inamorata up to one-fifteen before he shook her off, saying loudly, "It's a couple haystacks, for God's sake," as he signaled Goodfellow that he was through.

Fred had it at one-twenty. Goodfellow pushed and milked and squealed but couldn't get it higher. Fred had it. No: Clay had it. Or, one could say, Goodfellow had Clay. The remainder of the herd applauded.

Fred delivered Clay's check and took his picture, feeling the chemistry in him starting to work now. It had been a hard few days. Then he had to stand and let the eager wife, who had followed him out of the auction room, admire his prize, and listen to her tell him how lucky he was.

The air was wet and cold, but it wasn't raining as he took Clay's picture to the car. He wrapped it in a blanket and laid it in the trunk. It didn't feel like anything but what it said it was: a slightly expensive Heade of about average quality. From here on it would be Clay's puzzle, and Clay's problem.

Fred's problem was the sudden wealth in his wallet: Clay's check, a bonus now and, by golly, well earned. He'd finished everything else he'd had to do, and the damned check was starting to worry him.

He drove fitfully, wanting to be out from under it.

And then he thought, I'll buy Molly that new bathroom.

He'd show her he was serious. He could buy her the bathroom and still have some left over.

36

Fred picked up some cold champagne and had it with him when he got in. Molly wasn't home. He stuck the Heade, give or take a Vermeer, in Molly's bedroom closet. He called Clay and reported their success, wincing at the graceful way Clayton accepted the inevitable.

"You see," Clay told him, "it is as I thought. We budgeted sufficient money for the project."

"I'll bring it in now if you want," Fred offered. "I imagine you're anxious to have it in hand."

Clayton said, "True, Fred, but I am gaining something from my period of enforced contemplation. With Proust's assistance I have learned to relish anticipation. There is no hurry, Fred. No hurry at all."

"I thought you'd want to test our theory," Fred said.

"There will be time enough," Clay replied.

Fred knew what the trouble was: Clayton had got cold feet.

He'd hover on the edge of his great discovery (or disappointment) until Fred found a way to tip him in.

Fred had the kitchen clean when Molly appeared at the back door, carrying groceries and a bottle of champagne.

"Ha," said Fred in greeting. "I beat you. Where are the children?"

"Ophelia called. She had a sudden attack of the aunts and wondered if she could take them out for supper, and to a Godzilla triple feature, and keep them overnight, and I said yes."

They talked while Molly made Fred show her the Heade and then keep his promise to tell her everything. They opened her champagne first, and he poured, explaining his night with Smykal's film.

"Poor boy," Molly said. "Having to spend all night with naked female models. Are you going to show me the tape?"

"Come on," Fred said, shocked and surprised. It wasn't Molly's kind of thing at all.

"Come on yourself," Molly said. "I've seen people in their birthday suits before."

They went back and forth on it until Molly said that if Fred didn't stop protecting her, she was going to poke him with something sharp.

"I'm fooling, Fred," she said. "I'll take your word for it, okay? There's nothing I'd rather spend my time not seeing. You are a Puritan at heart. Come sit beside me."

She was on the couch. Fred went over.

They'd finished one bottle of champagne and started the second. Molly had thrown supper together while they were talking and got it set up in the living room.

"I feel bad for Russ, in a way," Fred said, "even though he's an awful kid, because he actually found the painting first. Smykal met him at Video King, told him he needed some advice getting started making videos, had him come over, and got him involved in the art photo scam. Russ saw the picture, figured out eventually what it was, and put the whole thing together, going through Finn, who was pimping, unwisely, for Mangan.

"In fact," Fred went on, "Finn really had bought the painting. It was just his bad luck that Clay turned up when he did and Smykal started playing games."

He stretched and yawned. He was tired. He hadn't slept much.

"Now," Fred said, "since we have the evening free, and since the kids won't be home until morning, is there anything you'd like to do? I'll give you a hint. I'm sleepy."

"Go on to bed, then," Molly said. "And don't come looking to me for sex after all the dirty stories you've been telling me. I've had enough sex for one day."

Fred started up the stairs. He could afford to be tired.

"Oh, honey?" he called.

"Yes?" Molly was in her kitchen cleaning up after their supper, like one of the Valkyries after a big feast.

"Clay gave me a bonus. I thought I'd put a bathroom in, with a good shower, in that room you call your dressing room, if you want. What do you think?"

"Sounds great," Molly said. "Let's talk about it later. I was thinking a study, but maybe a bathroom is better. It's a lot of mess, but it's a good idea. And a sweet idea, Fred. Thank you."

She came out of the kitchen drying her hands and gave him a kiss. "That's not sex," she said. "Just a kind of hello."

Fred went up, took off his shoes, and lay down on Molly's bed.

Twenty-five thousand would buy a lot more than a bathroom—if you kept the bathroom simple. He could get a pool table for the guys in Charlestown.

Or, if Molly agreed, they could do the slow boat to China. No, he'd take them down the Nile at Christmas, Molly and the kids, on one of those excursion boats with the dancing girls. That would open the kids' eyes.